TWO NECKLACES

A Novel by
Paulette Mahurin

Black Rose Writing | Texas

ISBN: 978-1-68513-513-3
PUBLISHED BY BLACK ROSE WRITING
www.blackrosewriting.com

Printed in the United States of America
Suggested Retail Price (SRP) $21.95

Two Necklaces is printed in Tradition Arabic

*As a planet-friendly publisher, Black Rose Writing does its best to eliminate unnecessary waste to reduce paper usage and energy costs, while never compromising the reading experience. As a result, the final word count vs. page count may not meet common expectations.

PRAISE FOR
TWO NECKLACES

"While showing us the increasingly aggressive actions of the German fascist government in the 1930s, Mahurin laces into the tale a beautiful romance between two young people whose joining became verboten under the new order."
–Terry Tallent, author of *Making the Reata*

"Paulette Mahurin once again shares her keen sense of human strength and frailty to capture a poignant love story in the midst of the devastating hardship and losses of WWII."
–Kat Drennan, author of *The Cloisonne Brooch*

"*Two Necklaces* is a beautiful, compelling story of young love set during the rise of Nazism in Germany that you won't want to put down."
–Geneviève Montcombroux, author of *Racing North*

"*Two Necklaces* is a brilliantly written, deeply horrifying story of a young woman's courage in the face of fear to save her beloved no matter the cost to herself. A novel the reader will not, and should not, forget."
–Marina Osipova, award–winning and best–selling author of *How Dare the Birds Sing*

"Heartbreaking, romantic and utterly inspiring. A tumultuous journey through one of humanity's darkest eras."
–Johanna Craven, author of *Firelight Rising*

"It is a brilliant piece of historical fiction that immerses the reader in the terror and struggles of living under the Nazi flag."
–Gary Gerlacher, acclaimed author of *Last Patient of the Night*

"A deeply emotional and thought-provoking story that resonates with current world events."
–Regina Buttner, author of *The Revenge Paradox*

"The story is touching, heart-breaking, and filled with bravery. You can't go wrong with any book from this author. One of my favorites!"

–Ronesa Aveela, **author of** *A Study of Household Spirits*

"Writing with a keen eye for detail and a sense of compassion, *Two Necklaces* will keep you immersed in the story long after the final page. Don't miss this book!"

–Travis Tougaw, **author of** *Last Call*

"While this beautifully written story offers important insights into what good people become forced to do and believe to survive, " *Two Necklaces*" is, at its core, a profound tale of love that eclipses time, place, and politics, and is an unapologetic ode to female empowerment."

–Susan Groves, **author of** *You'll See: A Story of Narcissistic Abuse, Survival, and My Journey to Understand*

TWO NECKLACES

"Being deeply loved by someone gives you strength, while loving someone deeply gives you courage."
–Lao Tzu

CHAPTER ONE

1933, Ravensburg, Germany

Rain clouds were filling the sky as I entered the hallway leading to the auditorium abuzz with excitement. Hundreds of girls filed past female guards, their uniforms adorned with swastika armbands. In my dark blue skirt, brown jacket, black neckerchief and a white blouse, I stepped before a stiff, tall blond guard who gave me the once-over. "Clean, but…" she pulled on my blouse to straighten a small wrinkle, "tuck that in."

I felt small before her towering gaze and quickly complied.

"You need to better tend to your appearance." Once satisfied my uniform was up to code, her attention shifted to my face. Satisfied I wasn't wearing makeup or any cosmetic modification, she gave me an acceptable nod and with a firm hand to my back moved me along.

Unfortunately, the girl behind me didn't meet the dress code. I felt for her when the guard raised her voice. "What is this?"

I glanced back to see the guard with a short, underfed looking girl who I didn't recognize as one of the girls in my group, one of many divisions of the *Bund Deutscher Mädel* (BDM). The guard grabbed hold of the front of the girl's blouse. "Pink! You are not in proper dress!"

"I'm sorry." The girl cowered, trying to explain she had accidentally laundered her only white uniform blouse with a red garment that bled into the wash. Too poor to replace it, she told the guard she wore what she had.

"That is unacceptable. You may not enter, and you must wear the correct attire before being allowed back into your group."

"Please. Can I just attend this meeting?"

The girl's pleading fell on deaf ears. With a no-tolerance tone the guard escorted her to the door, getting the name of the girl's BDM group and leader, threatening to report her.

I swallowed hard, glad I wasn't in that girl's shoes. Glad my family had the capability to dress me appropriately. While Germany was in an economic recession, a mess from the Great War, my stately father was well connected. Although food and other items were scarce, we fared better than most.

I continued into the auditorium, where my friends had saved me a seat. The large space was filled with titters and whispered gossip.

"He's so handsome." My friend Gertrude was boy crazy, talking frantically whenever she saw a cute boy about how she was going to marry someone like that and have tons of beautiful blue-eyed, blond-haired Reich babies for Germany. But the person she was yapping about was no boy; he was today's speaker, Baldur von Schirach, the Nazi Party national youth leader. She sat there gawking at him like he was a movie star.

I'd heard about him, but this was the first time I had seen him. There he was up on the stage, all decked out in a stiffly starched uniform, sitting next to a couple of other men in uniform and several women who led BDM groups. I didn't understand what all the fuss was about, especially since my brother Jürgen had mentioned some unkind things about him. Things I'd been forbidden to share. Perhaps if I hadn't been tainted by my brother, whom I adored, I'd be squealing like Gertrude and Brigitte next to me on my right. Making up the fourth girl in our clique, sitting to my left and looking forward, was turquoise-eyed, wavy flaxen-haired Vera, who had a crush on my brother.

I was glad this was a meeting for girls only, glad Jürgen and the rowdy boys weren't joining us. My brother didn't have the warlike militaristic passion most of his friends had, and in private conversations with me he was empathetic about those deemed inferior. He shared things he didn't dare share with his friends in school or the *Hitlerjugend,* the ones bent on ensuring the future of Nazi Germany by what my brother said were nasty means of spying on church groups and breaking them up, disrupting anyone not in complete agreement with the government. I became uncomfortable when he began facetiously referring to Hitler as the mighty ruler who wanted to remove all distinctions between classes. While I was ill at ease over some of those conversations, I admired my brother for speaking his mind, for being fair in seeing all sides, like my Oma, my mother's mother who lived with us. My discomfort with my brother abated when he'd let me have my say about the good I felt Hitler was doing for Germany. Then, he countered, while I was entitled to my opinion he was entitled to his, ending our conversation with an amicable disagreement.

A hush fell over the auditorium when a woman rose from her chair on the stage and stood behind the podium with a microphone. A screeching, distorted sound bounded, giving rise to a scramble of commotion on stage. The microphone and speakers were rearranged. A few tests and the woman, now with a flushed embarrassed look, introduced the prestigious speaker who was traveling throughout Germany to speak to the future women of Nazism.

Chests swelled. All eyes were forward. The space emptied of all noise except for von Schirach's booted footsteps as he approached the podium and looked out over a sea of girls. He stood tall and proud as he calmly mentioned how pleased he was with the turnout, not just the hundreds here for the present turnout but numbering in tens of thousands throughout all the meetings he'd been to. "The future of Germany rests in your hands. You are the hope to expand our ideal race." He wasted no time getting right to the main purpose of what the BDM had been established for. To create dedicated wives and give birth to superior Aryan children. "You and you alone possess the power to further the Third Reich for generations to come. I am here today to thank you for your allegiance to Nazi ideals."

The place broke out in raucous applause lasting over five minutes. Prideful jubilation washed over the room, smiles from ear to ear adorned faces. The energy was breathtaking.

A tap on the podium and von Schirach continued. "Your enthusiasm is admirable."

That pumped us up even more. Riding on the fervor of the massive group agreement, I listened to the powerful official tell us to maintain good health, stay active with exercise, and when the time was right we needed to choose an appropriate partner with whom to start a family.

More boisterous cheers broke out to which he raised his hands with more to say. I was swept up in the exhilaration until I heard him mention that to guarantee our future we must inform authorities if our neighbors or parents were not acting in a manner conforming with the regime.

Snitch on my family? Never! It was then I lost focus, the excitation draining from my pumped up body. All I could think about was my brother, how freely he voiced disagreements. Benign to my ears for he liked the good Hitler was doing and never ceased to bring that into our conversations along with the but this or that.

The speaker went on for several more minutes, and while everyone around me had heads full of glorified superiority, my head was in a spinning jumble. I wanted to leave the room, clear my head. Breathe. A few breaths and I replaced my objection to tattling on my family, specifically my brother, with a sense things would be all right. By the time the meeting ended, I had persuaded myself I was right and I felt better.

As time moved along, by the beginning of December when my fifteenth birthday was approaching, I felt assured any hint of disagreement with the new regime expressed in the walls of my house stayed there, and our home would remain a sanctuary. A safe place at this time of year for Jürgen to continue to sing the Christmas carols he loved instead of the ones the Nazis advocated. It was his way of protesting Hitler's attempts to create a national church and change religious celebrations, Christmas traditions, into Nazi ones. While I didn't care that attempts to change the national church weren't successful, my brother gloated. Nothing was going to stop him from celebrating and attending church like we always had, like most of German citizens continued to do. It made me feel good that Jürgen felt safe, that our home was safe.

CHAPTER TWO

The aroma of apples baking in the oven hit me the minute I entered the front door. Wet from the rainy weather I had walked home in from my girls' meeting, I looked in the ornate mirror in the entrance hall. It didn't paint a pretty picture. My light-brown hair lay plastered against my forehead; my face was pale. I pinched my faded cheeks to get rosiness into them, neatened my appearance and made my way to the kitchen. To my Oma, who was collecting apple peels from a cutting board. Apples were like gold, a rare commodity my father somehow obtained through a friend. While I welcomed them I wondered who this friend was who favored my father, supplying him with gifts very few of my friends had.

"*Apfelkuchen?*"

Hard of hearing and not aware of my approaching, my Oma jumped. "Christa!" She turned around with a dry arthritic hand to her chest.

"*Apfelkuchen?*" I asked again, envisioning apple cake, my favorite.

"Yes. Yes." She winced, lowering her hand. "For tomorrow. Now I need to finish cleaning up."

I offered to help as I saw her massaging her left hand.

"I need to use my hands." She continued rubbing the palm of her left hand as she turned around and got back to cleaning.

Tomorrow's my birthday, I thought, standing there watching Oma. She made the best apple cake in all of Ravensburg. She showed love through baking, which is why she was making the cake and not our maid, Liddy. Although I appreciated her matter-of-fact manner, it didn't always meet my emotional needs when I was feeling vulnerable and in need of a hug. No, my Oma and my mother were not the hugging type. They had a lot in common, but where they differed was Oma was more circumspect than my mother. The difference between the two of them had become more apparent in the last year when my mother became more emotionally driven while Oma maintained prudence, her ability to consider all aspects and not just information fed to her. Data fed like in my BDM meetings. It was my Oma who helped me hold onto my ability to think for myself. It didn't mean I openly expressed my thoughts like Jürgen, but I didn't have to believe everything I'd heard at face value. To balance my mother and Oma's lack of physical affection, I had my father and brother.

I breathed in the warm air escaping the oven, remembering earlier birthdays when I had Gertrude, Brigitte and Vera over to share in the festivities. It was discouraging I wasn't allowed to have them come to the house in the last several months, since April when Germans were advised to boycott Jewish shops and businesses. My mother feared my brother wouldn't hold his tongue and we'd end up in trouble with those in power riding the wave of anti-Semitism. She couldn't control what came out of my brother's mouth nor who he remained friends with. When all his other friends dropped Arthur, a mutual friend, because he was Jewish, Jürgen refused to obey my mother's wanting him to cut ties. Jürgen remained loyal.

My father wasn't happy about it but he let it be, telling us if things got worse we would have to comply with demands placed on us. Demands? Comply? At that time he didn't want to clarify what that meant and trusting him, I dropped it.

Earlier, having seen Jürgen challenge my mother, I asked her why I couldn't have friends over for my birthday.

"It's better that way."

7

"Better for who?" My brother interjected himself into our conversation.

In the silence that ensued, what was unspoken chilled the room. It was the same chill that ran through Germany since Hitler was appointed chancellor in January. With all the promises of change and the hope it instilled, that chill still entered our lives when in April Dachau was opened. I heard the rumors about that camp at my BDM meetings. When I went home and told my mother I'd heard about the abandoned munitions factory being used to intern Hitler's political opponents, she shook her head. The disgusted expression in her brown eyes reappeared whenever we fell into that cold silence.

I refocused my attention off earlier conversations to my Oma, now rinsing the cutting board, a few gray hairs cascading across her brow. She removed her apron and shook out the flour on it over the sink. "For you, I make and clean this mess." She looked toward the door leading from the kitchen, a smile spreading across her lips smoothed her wrinkled face.

My eyes followed Oma's to the doorway, where Liddy was finishing her house cleaning before leaving for the day. "Your baking is better than Liddy's. Better than the bakery in town." What I didn't say was the one owned by the mean man who wouldn't sell to Jews.

Oma placed a finger to her curved lips to stop my saying anything else Liddy might overhear. That finger to her lips, another way silence entered our home, was annoying. I didn't like all the new rules. The do this and don't do that, the harsh rules enforced by the Gestapo. I didn't understand all the excitement when my friends at school and in the BDM squealed about how powerful they were. Powerful yes, but to what means I often wondered, especially when that power was exerted in May at the book burning in universities. Nazi minister Goebbels' efforts to bring German arts and culture in alignment with Nazi goals seemed to go overboard when the American author Ernest Hemmingway's books were included. I failed to see the harm fictional literature could pose. It didn't matter what I thought, both my parents warned I had to go along. Had I discussed it with Oma, it's my bet she would have agreed with me.

When Oma removed her finger from her lips and a scowl formed on her face, I knew we shared feelings. Just then Liddy banged through the doorway, mop in one hand, water bucket in the other. "Hello, Christa." She welcomed me home as she emptied the bucket in the sink and put it and the mop away in the cleaning closet.

"All done?" I asked.

Oma turned away and continued cleaning.

"Yes. I'll be on my way home now. You have yourself a happy day tomorrow." We'd long given up on the tradition of not mentioning a birthday before the special day. Being a rather unconventional, more liberal, household, it was considered a silly German custom.

Rules! Law! What sense were they if they ostracized people? My thoughts came and I couldn't stop them. I wish I could. I wish I could just blindly go along, but my head's conflicting ideas wouldn't allow rest when things got stirred up. I could no longer wholeheartedly agree with something that didn't sit right with me than I could stop water from running through a sieve.

In the past, my father had encouraged us to be free thinkers, which now put us at odds with new laws. What good was maintaining a righteous viewpoint when laws came out barring Jewish people from holding civil service, university, and state positions? Laws that made no logical sense to me since several of Germany's most noted professors were Jewish. Due to the paucity of available jobs and the changing political climate, Arthur's father, an economist and university lecturer, fearful of Hitler's plans for Germany had arranged to move his family to France. That really put a burr in Jürgen's side.

"Thank you, Liddy. We'll save you a piece of my apple cake." Liddy's usual day off was Sunday, but I knew she was taking the next morning off to tend to a family matter. Mother agreed with Oma that since we weren't having company over there was no need to ask Liddy to come to work in the afternoon.

My mother arrived home from work at her box factory as Liddy was leaving. My mother owned and managed the factory near our house where boxes of all sizes for various uses in manufacturing, including

Maybach in Friedrichshafen, were made. My father worked as an engineering consultant at Maybach, a factory that manufactured heavy-duty diesel engines for marine and rail purposes. He helped negotiate a contract for my mother's box factory to provide boxes to ship parts for engines. The contract was beneficial for my mother's factory and kept the family comfortable.

Without so much as a hello, she asked where my brother was.

It gave me a bad feeling. My mother's upright posture was stiff, more than usual. How she appeared when holding something back. A strong-willed, opinionated woman, she didn't make it a habit to hold back, not unless she felt it too risky to speak or remained mute to protect those she cared about. More and more, she muted her strength, her words, but whatever wasn't spoken showed on her body. Her rigid shoulders. Her sharp eyes. Her narrowed lips.

"He isn't in his room?" I asked, assuming Jürgen arrived home before me and was studying in his room. Without waiting for Oma to respond, I made my way down the hall and upstairs. His room was empty.

When I told my mother he wasn't home, she turned around and leaving my communication mid-sentence, she rushed back out, got in her car, and sped off. I furrowed my puzzled brow, assuming she went to the meeting he'd attended to see if he needed a ride.

A half hour later, she returned home alone. "Your brother will be late tonight. He has taken it upon himself to say goodbye to Arthur."

"Goodbye to Arthur?"

Oma turned away from us, wiped down the counter and quietly went to the oven to check on the cake, while I waited for my mother to respond.

"Your brother is going to be the death of us."

"Mother!"

"Arthur's family is leaving. Tonight."

"Why so soon?" For some reason, the news, their haste, startled me.

"That we won't discuss."

Oma broke her silence. "You might as well tell Christa."

Not taking kindly to Oma interjecting herself, my mother clicked her tongue and gave her a look that said mind your business. "She doesn't need to know."

"Tell me!" I stamped my foot to get their attention.

My mother jerked back.

Oma had enough. "Inge. Tell her or I will."

My mother let out the breath she must have been holding. "Jews are leaving."

"Tell her the rest." Oma prodded.

My mother sat and looked out in space. For a brief while she disappeared to what I imagined was some dark unknown where legal repression and physical violence were looming on the horizon. When she regained focus, she revealed my father had information he'd shared with her and Oma. "Things he'd heard and encountered working at Maybach. Things will get worse for the Jews and anyone sympathizing with them. The news has leaked and rumors are spreading to German citizens, including Jews."

The changes the regime imposed were driving Jews away, not just from university jobs but also from their homes. I wondered to what extent they would go to rid Germany of Jewish people. Germany and everywhere else their machines would take them. Machines built with engines my father helped design. What was happening to Arthur's family didn't frighten me as much as wondering what would happen to mine.

Oma took the baked cake out of the oven.

With a pulsing ache taking residence in my head, I went up to my room. My birthday seemed a hundred years away.

CHAPTER THREE

That night I tossed and turned, listening to my mother pace the downstairs hallway, schlepping her feet like a lame dog. Where were my brother and father? Neither had arrived home. I pivoted the Hermle clock on my nightstand to get a better look, it was just after three. It felt like I'd been in bed twenty hours. Several loud crashes like ceramic vases hitting the wood floor resounded. I shot out of bed and went to where the sound came from.

My mother was by the ajar front door, down on her hands and knees picking up pieces of broken KPM porcelain figurines. Her left hand was spurting blood. "It was an accident." When her sad eyes met mine, I knew she was lying. Those costly pieces of precious art looked like they had been angrily thrown to the floor, one after the other, what looked like four in all. One antique bowl remained on the decorative antique table in the entrance hall. All were gifts to her from my father.

"Let me help you." I got down on my knees and took hold of her hand to see how deep the cut was. Blood spurt onto my nightgown, and I feared she might have cut an artery. I knew the difference between veins and arteries from biology classes in school. Using the skirt from my nightgown, I applied pressure holding firm for what must have been five minutes. Once I let go the small seepage was a relief. "That should do it. I'll get something to dress it."

My mother said nothing through all that, and although she was trying to remain stoic, she looked ready to burst into tears. Nothing about what happened that night, from my brother not coming home, my father's absence, to my mother's uncharacteristic tantrum, was understandable. I hated not knowing. Hated the void it created. Hated what I was filling the void with. Nothing with a good outcome.

I cleaned and bandaged her hand, closed the still ajar front door, and began cleaning up the shattered figurines. Just then the phone rang. I stopped what I was doing to eavesdrop on my mother answering the phone in my father's study. As I stood close to the open door, I heard her raised voice sound alarmed. "What!"

What? The way she said that word could only mean one thing. Bad news. I moved closer to the doorway, my heart jumping.

"Is he alive?" Her words came out in a rush. Then hearing what must have been the answer, she heaved a sigh. "I'll get dressed and be right there." Before she hung up, out came another, "What!" and a long panting silence on her end followed by the handset banging down.

Was my father hurt? My brother? A fist of worry grabbed my chest making it hard to breathe as I went to her. "What happened?"

She was a frightened sight, standing by the phone, frozen, her complexion pale. "Christa." Her eyes were filled with oceans of pain.

"Tell me what happened."

"That was your father."

"Is he all right?"

"Yes, he is." The emphasis on he and right away I knew.

"Jürgen."

"Yes. A boy from the *Hitlerjugend* followed him to Arthur's." She stopped herself like she does when unspeakable topics come up, the keep-quiet topics, when in the past she'd say the walls-have-ears and saying something can get you in trouble–big trouble.

I had to know. To calm my disquiet, I had to find out what she held back. "What aren't you saying?"

She was well aware I would not drop it, that I'd nudge her until she told me. After closing the study door and taking a seat, she motioned for me to sit down. There beside her by my father's desk, I listened to her moan about my brother being in the hospital. The boy who followed him to Arthur's accused my brother of being a Jew lover, said he was going to report him, and got into his face. Arthur struck him with his fist, but the boy picked up a heavy gardening tool and smashed it against Jürgen's head. "Arthur's father contacted your father. He's at the hospital with Jürgen."

"We need to go to him."

"No!"

My mother's response came out so fast and hard I jolted back in my seat. "We need to be with him."

"Don't you think I know that!"

What's with the attitude? The shift from sullen to anger? What else isn't she telling me? I would not back down. "Mother, please help me understand. Tell me what father said."

She lowered her head to her right hand, elbow resting on her thigh. Murmured words came out about my father finding the boy who did that to Jürgen and handling the situation with him, something about threatening him with jail time for attacking the son of a well-known engineer who works closely with the Reich higher-ups. When the boy protested Jürgen was a Jew lover and he would report him to defend his actions, father simply pointed out who do you think they'd believe. "Apparently, your father helped the boy gain an understanding that if he kept it between them the matter would be closed."

Worried sick about my brother and unable to find a suitable response, I sat there fuming. I needed to know what this had to do with our going to the hospital. "Why can't we go there?"

"Your father clearly forbid us to go. He is handling it."

"I thought you said he already handled it."

"Not known is how many other boys knew your brother went to Arthur's. There may be a situation."

"What kind of situation?"

"This whole mess could endanger your father's position. The box factory contracts. Our livelihood."

All I could think to say was, "It could go that far?" I couldn't bring myself to spit out the rest dangling on the edge of my tongue, like a boulder ready to fall from a cliff. I would not say it was despicable you could no longer chose who you wanted to be friends with.

"Yes, Christa, it could go that far. What we do now is play by the rules."

The rules! The ones we don't make! The ones that incited violence against my poor brother. "How long will Jürgen be in the hospital?"

"They'll watch him tonight to be sure there's no brain swelling. He should be able to come home tomorrow."

Just like my father went to clean up the mess at the hospital, feeling as broken as the shattered figurines yet on the floor, I went to finish cleaning them up.

CHAPTER FOUR

My birthday had begun on the unhappy note that my father was at the hospital watching over my brother and handling any political ramifications. My mind was too active for any sleep. Worry about my brother and that the situation might not be confined to one boy's attack whirled in my head like a spinning top going round and round.

My father returned when the sun was creeping above the cloudy horizon. As fast as my arms and legs could move, I grabbed my housecoat and ran downstairs, two steps at a time, to find him in the living room with my mother. Both with doglike–droopy bloodshot eyes and wrinkled clothing looked as if they hadn't slept in days. Sitting upon the couch, she looked out through the window as if to distract herself from what my father was saying, what she didn't want to hear. What I heard upon entering set the hair on the back of my neck on edge.

"And he'll be transferred this morning. To Rügen."

Rügen, an island in the northern part of Germany, but to me it might as well have been in another country across the Atlantic Ocean. Why Rügen? You can't even get to it without a ferry. My feet felt heavy as I barged in asking what was happening to Jürgen.

My father turned around and stood to greet me. "Christa." The smile on his lips did not rise to his weary eyes. Eyes that had seen things I was sure he'd never share with me. The ever-protective, loving father.

"Come, darling, sit with us." He reached an arm around my back and guided me like an invalid to a chair facing the couch where my mother sat, still glancing out the window. The north-facing window—in the direction of Rügen.

"Sit. Sit." He repeated that while he took his place back next to my mother, extending a hand to her thigh. He gave it a little affectionate shake as if to calm what he'd already told her, what she was silently brewing over.

As I descended on the plush rose cushion, I asked him again what happened to my brother.

He looked sideways to my mother. "I was telling your mother that Jürgen will be transferred where he will be better cared for."

"That's not right! I thought he was going to be coming home. He'd be better off here with us."

"I'm afraid not, Christa. He's seriously injured and needs special care. Sophisticated care that we can't give him."

I may have been young and inexperienced, not savvy like my father, but I wasn't stupid. None of what he was saying made sense. Rügen was not the best place in Germany for medical treatment. As I was about to open my mouth to ask about the diagnosis and plead with him to tell me what was really happening, Oma walked in. "What is this?" She had slept through the events of last night.

My mother pivoted to look at Oma.

"Inge, you look like someone died. And your bandaged hand!" Then to my father, she said, "Harald, I expect to be informed of whatever is going on." Her stern tone and puffed-out lips meant she wouldn't tolerate less.

"Sit, please." He got up for Oma to sit next to my mother and took the chair opposite mine. Once he had everyone's attention he repeated what he'd told my mother from the hospital on the phone last night.

"And?" Oma's jaw muscle twitched. She had the patience of a hungry lynx, and the bad habit of curtly nudging.

"He's being transferred to Rügen."

"That's ridiculous." Oma defiantly stood with both hands on her hips. "What exactly is the diagnosis?"

"Head injury. The brain swelling has caused injury and he needs good care."

"Well he won't get it in Rügen, that postage stamp place. He needs to be in a major city, in a modern hospital near us."

Oma's insistence broke the dam of what my father wasn't saying and out poured the real issue. "If this gets out it places my job in jeopardy." His speech slowed, and when he saw my Oma open her mouth to protest again, he coughed out the rest. "Anyone associating with Jews will be imprisoned."

"That's not legal," Oma said.

"I'm afraid that is a moot point. I've been privy to conversations from higher up. Things are changing at a pace we need to heed."

"So you lose your job. You'll get another."

"Helga." My father looked at Oma with an aggravated pucker on his face. "My job is the least of the concerns. Associating with Jews could label us sympathizers. Sympathizers are being viewed as dissidents violating the law. Sympathizers are being imprisoned." He hesitated and mumbled a few inaudible words, of which one was clear. "Worse."

"Worse?" Again, Oma pushed.

"Death."

My mother moaned. Whatever she had to say, she'd already said to my father before I joined them. Subdued, she looked worn out.

When she seemed to understand Jürgen's connection to Arthur endangered all of us, Oma fell back on the couch. Out came a meek reply. "That's why Arthur's family is leaving? It's not just about his father's job?"

"Yes."

"Did Jürgen know this?"

"Yes. I warned him about the consequences of his friendship with Arthur, but he refused to heed my warning."

"That's why he's being sent to Rügen?"

"Yes."

Oma sat there shaking her head. My mother was beyond consolation and needed time to get used to the all the changes. Not just within our family but the entire country. What was deemed as a government for the betterment of the German people did not in reality include all Germans. Only desirable Germans aligned with Hitler's definition. Undesirables were to be weeded out. They were not to benefit from the government's promise to fix the economy, to put people back to work, and return Germany to the status of great world power. What my father told us concurred with what I'd learned about the designs to unite all Germans along racial and ethnic lines. It reminded me of what I'd heard about Jews being blamed for our losing the Great War.

On my fifteenth birthday, sick at heart, I had a greater understanding about the importance of attending the BDM meetings and hiding behind a mask of compliance. Not just to the agenda of the girls' wing of the Nazi Party but to the entire regime.

My father pointed out it wasn't all bad, like what we had just encountered with Jürgen's association with Arthur. No, he told us, there was much good happening with efforts to improve the economy and get people back to work.

Once it was clear Jürgen was to be shipped off to a far corner of Germany and we wouldn't be visiting him, we all got up and left quietly. My mother was the last one out, trudging as if to a dirge. She was a resilient woman and I trusted that in short order she'd snap back.

The day progressed with my normal activities. I was glad for the distraction school and the BDM offered, particularly when taking part in physical fitness. I ran faster to lessen my grief and threw a ball harder to relieve my nerves, hiding the loss I felt over my brother, the sorrowful void relegated to the deep recesses in my mind for things too painful to think about.

I avoided any conversations about my family with Gertrude, Brigitte and Vera. I knew soon I'd have to mention something, but right then I didn't want to bring it up.

When I arrived home my mother was in the kitchen with Oma readying the birthday meal. Oma did wonders with the provisions she

had, and in concert with the Nazi sanctioned *Eintopfsonntag* campaign–
a push to make German families eat one-pot meals–she came up with
delicious meals for special occasions like tonight. In addition to the
Apfelkuchen, Oma was making *Käsespätzle,* one of my favorite dishes.
My mouth watered as I envisioned the alternately layered hot spaetzle
and grated hard cheese topped with crisp fried onions. The special
occasion meals were the only ones Oma cooked so as not to step on
Liddy's toes. Mother had threatened Oma if Liddy left, housecleaning
would be delegated to her. That's when Oma's persnicketiness
miraculously vanished.

My mother was grating cheese. It was a good distraction for her, and
the rest of us, for although it didn't dissolve the dullness that had settled
into her eyes, it kept her focused on something in the environment here
and now and not the events over the last twenty-four hours. Oma was
smart to give her something to do. To keep her busy. Production boosts
morale, my father often professed, and by the looks of it my mother
would agree.

Our stoic family sat at the table making light social conversation
about the intermittent rain and how fortunate the farmers were to look
forward to fields of crops come spring. Spring, my favorite time of the
year when beautiful Ravensburg came alive with blankets of vibrant
colors spreading across the land. My father had told us we were lucky we
lived in such a beautiful relatively peaceful place, with emphasis on
peaceful meaning it didn't harbor an arms industry like nearby
Friedrichshafen where he worked. There was no further mention of
peace, or the regime, at the table that night.

"Driving home by the Schussen River, I almost detoured to the
Guelf's ancestral castle but decided against it. I didn't want to be late for
my Kätzchen's birthday." My father looked at my mother to see if she
was paying attention, not sinking into herself. When she made eye
contact with him he continued talking about his drive home, about how
much he loved Ravensburg.

Kätzchen. My father's voice echoed in my head easing the hole in
my heart. Kätzchen, he nicknamed me that because when I was

younger, smaller, I liked to hide in boxes–like kittens do–in mother's box factory. My father was doing his best to lighten the ambience, and to acknowledge his worthy effort, I smiled.

My father's clever conversational hook latched on to my mother. "Guelf's ancestral castle?"

"Of all places." He stopped himself, as if thinking better about continuing to mention anything about rulers, until in good form Oma nodded for him to continue. "Henry the III's birthplace."

"The Lion," mother said, and off they went on a history chat.

Oma and I looked at each other, sharing a moment of relief my mother had seemingly enjoyed the conversation. "I'll clean up." She pushed her chair back but my father stopped her.

"A minute, Helga. We haven't begun with the gifts."

My father's expression changed when he said gifts. He seemed a little toned-down, speaking softer. My interest was piqued as he reached into his jacket pocket and pulled out a small unwrapped box. It wasn't one of my mother's boxes but rather something that looked like it was from a jewelry store. As he handed me the gift, he gave Oma and mother a sheepish look that made me a little nervous.

"Here, my Kätzchen. This is from Jürgen."

I gasped.

The levity on my mother's countenance lessened, her face lost a shade of pink.

Oma wrinkled her brow and tilted her head.

In that little white box was a beautiful heart-shaped gold pendant on a gold chain. I lifted it out and fingered the heart's smooth rounded surface. I was about to ask how he could afford such a lovely gift when it occurred to me my father must have purchased it to bring my brother back to us, albeit it emotionally. The thought was more moving than the gift. "I will treasure this always."

Oma looked at my mother as if cluing her to do something.

My mother held out a hand for the necklace. "I'll do the honors." She stood behind me for a minute, resting her other hand on my shoulder. Before she clasped the hook, I reached my hand to hers and gave it a gentle I love you pat. "There you are." She shifted to my front, her lips slightly risen, her face appearing lighter. "It looks lovely on you. Perfect length."

I moved my hand over the golden heart, feeling the pain I'd been holding on to loosen, and allow in what was greater than all the disagreements and dislikes over what was happening in Germany. In flowed love and appreciation. For my parents. My Oma. But right now mostly for my brave brother. Loyal and decent to the marrow.

The pendant wasn't the only gift, for in my father's pocket was an envelope with several Reichsmarks in a card. A birthday card from him, mother, and Oma. Funny how my mother and Oma looked just as surprised as I was when I opened the card and thanked them.

CHAPTER FIVE

While gathered together that evening, my father, mother and Oma did their best to make it a nice birthday meal for me. Even though we all felt Jürgen's absence, I accepted the fact he was alive and would be well cared for despite it being a long distance away. That he'd get better and come home. I figured that's what the rest of my family felt as well, but later that night in my room readying for bed, I heard differently.

My mother's angry voice sounded loudly from the study. I sprang out of the room and went halfway down the stairs to make out what she was screaming about.

"I want to bring him home!"

When my father gave an inaudible reply, I moved further down the stairs and hung over the railing to hear better. I strained to hear but was only able to make out a couple of words before my mother raised her voice again, repeating something my father must have said.

"Weeded out!"

Weeded out? What are they talking about? The answer came with my father sounding irritated. "I am simply relaying what I've been told. I don't make the rules, nor can I change them. Disabled citizens are being weeded out. How many times do I need to repeat that?"

"But he's not Jewish. Can't your friends in high places help!"

"They already have. He's in Rügen… not jail."

23

"Harald." Her voice trailed off.

Hard as I tried, sure I'd worked an indentation into my abdomen, that's all I was able to make out before the sound of the door slamming shut and footsteps moving away from the study scared me I'd be found out like another time that didn't turn out well. I rushed back to my room and got in bed, willing myself to sleep. It was no use for my mother's words played like a never-ending refrain keeping me awake. A chorus of *weeded out* repeated. What the heck does that mean? No answers came. The only reprieve from the monowheel rotating in my head was the ticking of my Hermle clock shifting my attention. As the words *weeded out* drifted from my consciousness, exhaustion got the best of me and I fell into a dreamless sleep.

Morning came and with it Liddy arrived in good form, humming *Die Fahne Hoch,* the Nazi Party anthem. She marched up the wooden stairs sparing nothing as she knocked on Jürgen's bedroom door. Another knock and she opened the door, "Wake up." The joviality in her voice died when she must have seen his empty made bed.

Tired and cold, I waited for her. That was our morning routine. She knocked, the doorknob turned and the door creaked open. What had my parents told her? Certainly she wouldn't have gone to wake my brother had she known. I sat up as she approached, anxious about what to say. My worry over what to tell her was unfounded for she went about her business in a discreet unquestioning manner.

"Time to get up, Christa." She attempted a tight smile, but her squinting suspicious eyes betrayed her. Liddy was a good German woman who'd been with us since I was a baby, a single mother whose husband died from battle wounds incurred in the Great War. He made it out but shortly after succumbed to infection from lack of proper nutrition and medical attention. Liddy had a baby with another on the way when he died. For several years she'd bring them with her when tending to my brother and me. Once she had saved enough money, she sent for her mother to live with her and help raise her girls. I liked Liddy, who had a family to support and knew better than to stick her nose where it didn't belong.

As Liddy stepped out to wake Oma, I quickly washed, put on my uniform and rushed downstairs. My mother and father were at the dining room table, he reading a newspaper and sipping a cup of tea, she spreading jam on a piece of toast.

I immediately asked, "What are we going to tell Liddy about Jürgen?"

"We'll tell her what happened," my father said.

"What happened?" I needed clarification because I was confused. I thought we would not mention anything about Arthur or the fight with the other boy.

"Yes, Kätzchen." My father became distracted by my mother's moving the piece of toast around her plate. "Are you going to eat that?"

She moved her hand to her lap, her cheeks turning a deep rosy color.

The tension between them was uncomfortable. On a daily basis they had a good rapport, communicated well, and displayed mutual respect. Although my father showed more bodily affection than my mother, from the way she supported and cared for him I knew she loved him. In one day that changed. One day there's an accident and my brother is gone. Next day my parents are in disharmony. Is this thing with my brother going to tear us apart?

Left hanging, I asked him what exactly did he mean.

"We tell the truth. He injured himself and is in a hospital with a head injury."

"That's it? That's the story we—"

"Kätzchen!"

The way he said my name stopped me cold. An affectionate term was being used to rebuke me and I didn't like it. "I'm just asking." I spoke sotto voce, intending no harsh reaction or to make anyone wrong. "I need to understand."

My tormented mother let out a breath and jumped in. "What we tell people is just that."

"But." I caught myself from blurting out that was a lie and I didn't want to get caught in a lie. I wasn't a liar and didn't want to start now.

"We say anything else and risk trouble." My father responded in a calmer manner. "You just have to trust me on this. Everything we say… everything we do is to protect our family. Keep it intact. Things are going to change and we may have to alter facts."

"I don't like to lie."

"Neither does your father." In her weakened, vulnerable state, my mother came to my father's defense and that really got through to me. "None of us want to—"

Liddy's footsteps moved down the stairs truncating the conversation. It may have been cut short but my mother's last comment, along with her uncharacteristic softness made the point. That was when I learned at times lying serves a higher purpose. That was when I decided it wasn't a sign of immoral character but simply a necessary way to survive. If telling a fib, or even an out and out huge fabrication, kept my family together–secure and alive, then so be it.

When Liddy came into the dining room my father asked her to have a seat. He told her that Jürgen had an accident and hurt his head.

"I'm sorry to hear that, Herr Becker."

"Thank you, Liddy. He'll be in the hospital until he's well. We don't know how long that will be."

"Yes, sir. I understand."

When my father pushed his chair back, Liddy took the hint and stood to get back to work.

"One more thing, Liddy."

She pivoted back, arms to her side waiting for what he had to say.

"If you hear anything untoward, I expect you to let me know."

"Yes, sir. I understand."

"We won't tolerate rumors and falsehoods about our family, our good name."

"Yes, sir." She waited a minute. "Will that be all, Herr Becker?" She then looked to my mother. "Frau Becker?"

Yes, my father said, while my mother inclined her head.

I hoped when I got to the girls' group it'd be this easy to tell my friends, in particular Vera who had it bad for Jürgen.

CHAPTER SIX

The hall where we had our BDM meetings had been prepared for the day's lesson, which was nursing skills so we'd be able to tend to our husbands and children. Long tables were lined with gauze, tape, salves, scissors and various other items useful for first aid, including makeshift cardboard splints. Vera and Gertrude were at a station waiting for class to begin in twelve minutes. Brigitte hadn't arrived yet.

Vera, in animated conversation with some girl next to her, set my mind at rest for clearly she was in good spirits, and hadn't heard about my brother. I'd wait until later to tell her. Why upset her just before the lesson was to begin?

I rehearsed what I would say, repeating what my father told Liddy. My nerves were tingling. I had to grow into being comfortable lying. It was a new coat I had yet to try on and didn't know if it would fit. While I was worrying about what might be, one of the younger girls rushed in through the door screaming. "Frau Schmidt!" The lanky girl looked to the right and left for the group's leader then ran to the back of the room toward her office. Before she got halfway, Frau Schmidt stuck her head out of the office door, not looking pleased with the commotion from the girl frantically making her way to the office.

Brigitte came in the door as the girl was screeching something about her brother. Something about not joining a group. Brigitte tiptoed to the seat we'd saved for her and sat. "What's that about?"

"Shh!"

Frau Schmidt, an intimidating, large-framed woman, carefully listened and questioned. All eyes were on them, all ears finely tuned to their conversation. "Are you sure?"

"Yes." The girl coughed out a scenario about her brother ripping his *Hitlerjugend's* uniform, saying he refused to continue in the group.

"What exactly did you hear him say?"

"He said he was tired of being told what to do. What to read. Something else about he'd never join the military."

Frau Schmidt straightened her broad shoulders and sounding affronted asked, "You sure?"

"Yes. I heard him." The lanky girl smirked like she had just done something praiseworthy.

"You did good. Now go to your seat while I tend to this new information." Frau Schmidt turned on her heel, returned to her office and slammed the door shut. A few minutes later, she came back out to state the class would have a late start as the matter brought to her attention demanded immediate action.

Immediate action, I thought, my stomach turning flips. What action? An image of Jürgen, his face bashed in and bloodied, clouded my view of Frau Schmidt. I shivered it off as I regained a clear sight of our leader's searing elocution, what she deemed vitally important to drill into us about our expected behavior because any deviations on our part were on her head. Anyone connected with what was objectionable behavior would remain unscathed if they reported it.

"If you see something and do not report it…" Her neck veins looked like a well-fed viper as she paused a minute to clear the tightness from her throat before continuing her venomous attack. "Any action not conforming to acceptable behavior will not be tolerated."

She enumerated what had been drilled into our heads about the Enabling Act of 1933, the law to remedy the distress of the people and the Reich. Translated to my simple understanding, it meant Hitler and his cabinet had unilateral power to make and enforce laws. Up until that day new laws and regulations were something out there, something to follow, and as long as you obeyed them your life would improve. What happened with my brother, with the girl in my group, changed my perspective, and now they were no longer just something out there to comply with, what had happened in the last day brought it home.

As I listened to her tell us straight-out we were to report all suspicious activities in school, church, and with our family, in my peripheral vision I caught sight of a girl closing her eyes, nodding off. The girl next to her kicked her foot to wake her, unfortunately not fast enough for Frau Schmidt had noticed and was on them like a speeding train. She grabbed hold of the collars of both girls, lifted them out of their seats and dragged them to the door. "You dare to fall asleep!" She looked at the whimpering sleepy girl then to the other. "You do not disrupt class nor do you cover up negligent behavior!" Her fiery words hissed through the room as a car pulled up outside.

Two uniformed Gestapo entered.

"These girls think our laws are a joke. One fell asleep and the other interrupted the entire class to wake her. I suspect they don't have their hearts in the right place." Frau Schmidt then mentioned the other matter she had phoned about.

The shorter of the two men looked to where Frau Schmidt had pointed to the lanky girl who'd reported on her brother. "Come here."

The Gestapo escorted out the two unfortunate girls along with the lanky one, I assumed to be questioned about her brother.

Once the example was made, Frau Schmidt began the nursing skills class.

To avoid Vera who had a tendency to ask me questions about Jürgen, I paired with Gertrude. Vera paired with Brigitte. Halfway through practicing bandaging, Gertrude complained I wasn't tying a dressing tight enough. "That'll never stop the bleeding." She pulled the slack tourniquet on her arm back up to where it should have been wrapped much tighter.

"What?" My attention wasn't on practicing what Frau Schmidt had just shown us about applying a tourniquet to wounds to stop the bleeding but rather eight hundred kilometers away, in Rügen.

Gertrude dug a nail into my arm. "Pay attention." She spoke under her breath, her eyes disapproving.

"Sorry." I whispered I didn't sleep well, all the birthday excitement. That lie slipped out of me with ease, paving the way for more to follow. I fingered the pendant around my neck as if it were an amulet to protect me from my lying sins.

The next time I tied the tourniquet, Gertrude whimpered it was too tight.

"Good!" I smiled.

For the rest of the session we practiced applying compression dressings to lessen swelling and using material easily found to make splints, like cardboard boxes. I could splint an army with what my mother had in her factory. I kept my focus on what I was doing, which helped me not think of Jürgen. It taught me once again I can pull myself out of a down emotional situation by keeping busy and maintaining my focus on what's happening now. I welcomed the reminder.

***

My father came home late, after dinner as I was readying for bed. I wanted to talk to him alone to tell him what had happened at my girls' group, away from my mother's skittish reactions about my brother, which was causing all of us to tread lightly around her.

In his study with the door shut, I told him about the lanky girl who had turned in her brother. I mentioned I purposely avoided bringing it up with my mother and Oma as I did not know how they would respond. Nor did I know how it would affect me. Too much uncertainty had been etched in my brain from what I had experienced, hammered in with a resounding bang I doubted I would ever forget.

After mentioning something about my mother's appetite slipping, my father responded, "She's a strong woman and will be fine. What happened with your brother was a shock to her. Give it a little time."

It was a shock to me as well. Not just what happened with Jürgen but what I saw that day. My rock solid innards, my strong sense of self, had been reduced to feeling like jiggling jelly. I needed a little time also, but I also needed to vent to my father who I trusted could handle whatever I had to say.

When I finished what I wanted to say, I rose and gave him a hug. I soaked in the warmth of his embrace, the strength of his body, the comfort of his love, and I breathed a little easier. Easier but not relaxed. I was still bothered. I needed more from my father. More than his listening and love, I needed to understand.

I pulled back from his arms and told him I wanted to ask him something, that I needed answers.

"I don't know I will be able to oblige you, Kätzchen. There's much I am not at liberty to share."

"Why can't you trust me?"

"Kätzchen, my darling, it's not a matter of trust. You have the best of intentions but under pressure you… no one can know what they will say, and that could cause great harm."

I curled a loose strand of hair around my index finger, feeling antsy. "Great harm? What are you saying?"

He drew in his lips, lowered his eyebrows, appearing like he was trying to think of how to say what he wanted to diplomatically. "Let me put it this way. You know what you saw today?"

I knew what I saw, and I also knew he wasn't really asking me a question. I nodded.

"Do I need to spell out for you what will happen to that young lady's brother?"

He made his point, and I didn't like it. Not one bit. A mountain of pressure sat on my shoulders for in that moment I really wasn't sure if

Jürgen was even in Rügen or if he'd disappeared like other sympathizers. For now, it was probably better I didn't know. It was easier to entertain he was all right, being tended to by medical people on an island off the northeast coast of Germany.

CHAPTER SEVEN

The next day I told Vera about Jürgen.

"What happened?"

"I told you what I know."

"Tell me again."

"He injured himself. Hit his head and…" I tried to remember exactly what my father told me to say. "Injured himself."

"You just said that."

"I meant to say he injured his head." My fumbling wasn't making me sound credible. I moved an index finger over my gold pendant.

"I don't understand. Why does he have to be so far away?"

"I don't know."

"How could you not know!"

"Vera, calm down. I'm upset too. I told you all I know."

"He can't be gone." Tears pooled in her moon-shaped eyes.

For several days, she moped around and kept asking me if I'd had any news to which I repeatedly told her I'd let her know the minute I knew anything. It didn't take too long for her to accept the sorrowful fact that head injuries take time to heal and those injured could remain in a coma for a long time.

That was months ago and since then we both fell into the groove of life, like the excitement in June when Germany advanced in the semifinals in the World Cup against Czechoslovakia. I thought of how excited my brother would have been, for he loved to play football. He would have also been as disappointed as we all were Germany lost. Long after that loss my father complained Czechoslovakia shouldn't have won, echoing loyal German citizens asserting Germany was superior well into lively times at the German Grand Prix.

There was no questioning this proud superiority except on the rare occasion when people let their guard down in the sacred confines of their home in rooms behind closed doors. I took advantage of not being seen on the other side of those doors when my father was in his study on the phone or when my parents were engaged in conversations. Such was the case later in July.

"Who is this Himmler?"

"Who is Himmler?" My father repeated my mother's question, sounding like he was angrily insulting her.

I didn't understand his being demeaning. Apparently my mother didn't either when she snapped back. "Don't use that tone with me, Harald. I'm not one of your flunkies."

It took a long time for him to calm down from whatever caused him to lash out at my mother. The sound of shuffling feet must have been my father, for the next sentence out of his mouth came from a different position in the room. "This whole affair has me concerned."

"I can see that, Harald. Perhaps you are taking on too much and need to delegate a little?"

Her trying to soothe my father was useless and what he said next, what he needed to say, explained not just his earlier tone but his vacillating reactions. "I'll tell you who Himmler is." Pausing for a few seconds he didn't sound like he was ready to open up.

"Go on."

"He's responsible for the Röhm purge."

"I see."

What did she see? What purge?

"To reward Himmler for murdering Röhm and his top commanders, Hitler made the SS an independent arm of the Nazi Party, directly subordinate to him."

"I don't understand. Why no legal action and I thought everything was already under Hitler."

"The SS was formerly under the SA, now it directly reports to Hitler. As to why no legal action, Hitler asked parliament to declare the killings legal. After the fact, based on a false accusation that Röhm and his men were planning a coup."

"This is what has you so on edge?"

"This in and of itself, no Inge. That's not what's bothering me. I hesitate to say more because—"

"Say what you have to. Rest assured nothing goes further."

"It's not that simple." He groaned a distressed throaty sigh.

"You're going to give yourself an ulcer!" My mother's dainty feet moved and her voice grew faint.

I moved closer to the door to get a better listen but all I heard were fractured sentences. I tried to change my position to hear better. It was a bad idea. When I moved I foolishly had my attention on trying to make out what they were saying and lost my footing, falling to the floor.

"What's that?" My mother's staccato abruption stabbed my gut.

My father rushed out before I could get up. One look at what I was sure was my red face, and appearing like a scared rabbit sensing a fox, his worried countenance disappeared. "You were listening?"

I stood, afraid to confess I had been eavesdropping and overheard my father venture into forbidden communication with my mother. The last thing he would have wanted was for me to hear what he'd been protecting me from for fear I would accidentally let something slip to my friends. The way his fists were clamped tightly by his side, the tight-lipped frustration smeared over his face, and his quick turn toward the study calling for my mother gave me a frightful feeling.

My mother approached, panting.

"She overheard, Inge."

My mother gave me a questioning look, a narrow-eyed did-you-violate-our-privacy-again look. Again because I had been forewarned not to when caught doing it earlier outside the study door. I was aggravated I got caught. I twirled a loose hair around my index finger and couldn't stop, and just like I couldn't stop that bad habit, I couldn't stop eavesdropping. I tried to wiggle my way out of my misdeed. "I… you sounded so upset." I lowered my eyes from mother's.

"Don't even think of trying to justify your behavior, young lady!" My mother was eyebrows-raised furious.

The whole situation stank, from what I'd overheard to how they looked like they were in a seriously compromised position. I didn't fully comprehend what it all meant. "I heard little and—"

"Christa, you have been warned about this."

"Quiet! Both of you." The angry tone I heard from my father earlier with my mother had returned. It demanded we listen and as he put it, listen good. "There will be no further talk of anything with a hint of disagreement with the regime in my home. Nothing but their positive actions and all the superb improvements being made will be tolerated." He went on about how things were improving from the horrible circumstances Germany was in after the war and drove home the point we had Hitler to thank for that.

My God, he sounded like von Schirach, Frau Schmidt, and many other leaders instructing us on what to read, what to think, how to act, who we could be friends with. I didn't understand my father's sudden shift, what sounded and looked like a closed subject. I didn't like the way my mother hung her head like she'd done something wrong to question him, to want to understand what the regime was doing. No, I didn't like it one bit. Apparently that didn't matter for I had no choice but to go along.

***

As time moved along, that night was relegated to the compartment in my mind where other painful, best-be-forgotten memories were stuffed.

On a walk home with Vera from a BDM meeting, we stopped at a kiosk selling sundries and newspapers. The owner, Herr Meier, was an agreeable man with a pumpkin-shaped midsection who loved children. His big round jovial face and puffed-out cheeks looking like they were full of cotton made me smile. He reached into a big jar of chocolate-covered caramel candies.

"Herr Meier." Vera skipped to Herr Meier, who held out two pieces of candy.

"For you two lovely young ladies." His eyes lit up like a Christmas tree as he handed us each a piece of candy, the chocolate melting on his fingers. He licked his fingers, wiped his hand on a handkerchief, and said, "It's a grand day," as his eyes moved over one of the newspapers on his stand dated August 19, 1934. The headline read, *Hitler abolishes the office of the President to become the Führer of the German Reich and People.*

Whether it was the chocolate melting in my mouth or the news, I felt his enthusiasm as I followed his eyes to the article to read that Hitler was the absolute ruler with no legal or constitutional limits to his power. More was said in the article I didn't fully understand, but because I truly liked Herr Meier and felt him to be a good man I joined his smiling cheer. Vera, too busy devouring her candy, gave us no notice.

CHAPTER EIGHT

When my birthday in December, 1934 drew near, Himmler, the man my father mentioned to my mother in their bedroom months earlier, had become well-known, not just as the head of the SS but for consolidating control of the German state political police into the Gestapo office in Berlin under his deputy Reinhard Heydrich. He also created the Inspectorate of Concentration Camps under the leadership of SS General Theodor Eicke.

Their names regularly made headlines in the newspapers I saw at Herr Meier's kiosk. Headlines I shared with Oma. Other than with Oma, I'd given up on trying to bring up political news at home for whenever I tried I was hushed by my mother or coldly told to change the subject by my father. Oma was the only person I could safely confide in when I needed to gain an understanding or help to feel better.

On a drizzling, hazy day in the middle of March, 1935, I arrived home early to find Oma glued to the radio in the living room.

"Oma—"

"Listen." She motioned to the radio.

The snappy voice booming out of the brown wood radio stated, the Führer announced today his intentions to rebuild the German air force, reinstate conscription and to arm the nation. The commentator said that in Hitler's speech to the Reichstag, he said, "The principal effect of every war is to destroy the flower of the nation. Germany needs peace and desires peace. The German government is ready to agree to any limitation which leads to the abolition of the heaviest arms suited for aggression, such as the heaviest artillery and the heaviest tanks. Whoever lights the torch of war in Europe can wish for nothing but chaos."

Oma looked up from the radio while further commentary praised Hitler's actions. "I'll be darned… conscription to serve peace. I had my doubts, but he really seems to want peace."

I didn't understand how rebuilding armed forces was an action destined towards peace, but what Oma said sounded encouraging. It lifted my mood that had been down from the constant enforcement to follow rules. My spirits didn't stay up for too long, for a few days later while out with Brigitte, Vera and Gertrude we ran into a Jewish woman wheeling her baby in a perambulator. On her neck was a tiny star of David necklace she quickly tried to cover by pulling her sweater up over it. She wasn't fast enough for Gertrude's eyes. "Look!"

That was the day we had studied passages from *Mein Kampf,* specifically parts about extermination of Hebrew corrupters. *Sacrifice of millions* ping-ponged in my head giving me a headache. I simply couldn't imagine killing anyone, let alone millions!

That unfortunate mother was in the wrong place at the wrong time.

"Pig," Gertrude spat at the woman's face.

That shocked me, and when Brigitte joined in and told the woman, "You don't belong here," I felt nauseous.

"Please." The woman tried to protect her baby, covering it with a blanket. "Please leave us be."

Her pleading was to no avail but rather incensed Gertrude. "You want to be left alone!" Loud smart-mouthed Gertrude couldn't stop there. "Vera. Did you hear that? What do you have to say to that pathetic piece of feces!"

Vera looked at me like she didn't know what to do. Like me she acted reluctant to join in until Brigitte threatened to report her for sympathizing with a Jew. Now considered a crime. I broke out in a sweat when Vera kicked the woman and ran off leaving me next in the gauntlet.

I moved a step back. I didn't know Gertrude and Brigitte could be so violent. Was this the same anger that brought the vicious attack to my brother? Their hateful actions opened my eyes to a frightening new perspective of them. The trust I felt for them had been tainted.

"Christa." Gertrude got in my face, tapping a finger on my chest. "Let's see how you feel about this Jew bitch."

The Jewish mother cowered and tried to leave but Brigitte and Gertrude blocked her.

"We're waiting, Christa." Brigitte got impatient with me for standing there and not joining in. I didn't want to hurt that woman. I didn't want any part of what was happening. It was wrong, but if I did nothing and they reported me as a sympathizer I feared what would happen to me. One more shout of my name and I slapped the woman's face. Under my breath, I said, "I'm sorry but I had to," before I backed off.

The baby in the carriage began wailing. A shadow hung over the woman's face as she reached a hand to soothe the crying child.

A store owner within earshot, witnessing what was going on, rushed over yelling for us to leave her alone.

Gertrude tapped a hand on Brigitte's shoulder. "Let's go." She looked at me but I stayed still for a minute wanting to apologize for my bad behavior, wanting to explain I had no choice, not if I wanted to make it home unscathed.

"Be on your way," the man said, stepping between the subdued woman and me.

The rest of the way home I was too ashamed to make eye contact with anyone. Ashamed of what Gertrude and Brigitte willingly did. Ashamed that I went along. I was so disappointed in them, in myself. I went to my room and cried. I stayed in my room through dinner and refused contact with anyone until Liddy knocked at the door with a dinner plate.

"Christa. I brought you some food."

"I'm not hungry." I wiped my eyes and sniffed to clear my stuffed nose.

"You've been crying?" She put the plate down on a nightstand. "What's the matter?"

Liddy was a kind woman, a good mother, but she was a steadfast Hitler loyalist. I couldn't trust she wouldn't turn any of us in if it came to that. I knew Liddy loved me, and my family, but how sturdy would that be if she ever had to make a choice. I looked at her sweet face, tired from end-of-the-work-day wear and tear, and felt sad I didn't trust what she'd do under pressure. After all, look what I'd just done to an innocent mother. Guilty of nothing. Forced to go along, I hated what I was becoming.

"It's nothing, Liddy."

"All that sorrow written over your face? That's nothing?"

I wanted to tell her, to talk like we used to, like family. I wanted to fall into her arms and weep my eyes out like I did as a child when I scraped my knee. My hand reached for my knee, the scar yet there, rough and uneven like my frayed nerves. "Really, I'm fine, Liddy."

She knew not to push further. "The soup's nice and hot. That should help whatever is ailing you."

"Yes, I'm sure it will." I lied.

That night as the soup sat cold and untouched on my nightstand, I lay in bed until around three in the morning when I must have dozed off. Later, fully clothed, I jumped awake when the neighbor's Rottweiler barked. Max, my stocky, wide-chested friend with a perpetually wagging stub of a tail, had managed in the past to sneak through a loose board on the fence in his yard to come visit me for treats.

His barking turned to growling.

"What is it, Max? You see a rat?" I got up and went to open the window, to stick my head out into the cold starless night. The moon was a sliver and it was hard to see anything but a moving shadow of Max's thick legs running back and forth to find whatever it was he smelled. That dog had a nose like a bloodhound. We never got very far when I dog sat him and we went for walks. Two steps forward, five minutes nose to the ground.

Being with Max, even thinking of him, made me happy. He made my heart feel good, for with him I could be myself, drop my barriers and say whatever I wanted to. The only other living being I could do that with was Oma, but while she at times tried to control what came out of my mouth Max didn't care.

Max let out another guttural rumble before running to Herr Weber's calling him back in from his pee excursion. I knew his patterns, the old boy—now getting up in years—had some bladder problems and needed to be let out several times a day. It made me sad to think of him aging. Not being around anymore. A breeze picked up sending a shiver down my back.

A friend once asked me if I had a favorite teacher. I thought about it and my honest answer was Max.

"A dog?" The way she said it was too sarcastic to be a question, and I got defensive when she laughed.

"Why not a dog? He's intelligent, protective, loyal, doesn't try to change me." Merely thinking about running my hand over his long back and short, coarse black and tan coat, I didn't care what her response would be. I loved my friend Max.

As I pulled back in from the window, the sweater I had on caught on the latch. I tugged it free and went back to bed thinking of Max, feeling better.

CHAPTER NINE

The next morning as I was washing and looked in the mirror, I was surprised at how tired I looked, older than my sixteen years. My pink-tinged eyes and colorless complexion were more than just signs of a night of fitful sleep. Even when I got enough rest, when alone and I dropped my cheerful smile and took a good look at myself, I still felt I looked exhausted. Constantly being on guard, presenting my best behavior, and all too often trying to find the right thing to say, frequently a lie, was wearing me down. What happened yesterday with my so-called friends didn't help.

I ran cold water over my face and neck. I felt my neck again and looked in the mirror. My gold pendant and chain were gone. Seeing they weren't in the sink or on the countertop, I rushed back to my bed and ran a hand over my counterpane. Nothing. I pulled the cover from the bed and inspected the sheets, bent down and looked under the bed, and crawled on my hands and knees across the carpet and wooden floor. Still nothing.

When did I last have it on?

Liddy stuck her head in the door to tell me breakfast was ready. She looked at me down on the floor. "What's wrong?"

"Liddy, I lost my necklace." Then it came to me. The window. Sure enough the chain was there but the pendant was gone, both must have come off when my sweater caught on the latch. I swept the chain into my hand, telling Liddy I'd be down for breakfast in a few minutes. I rushed downstairs and outside. There it was, under the window, by a few scattered leaves. The relief I felt was short-lived, for the clasp was ripped clean off, my necklace unwearable.

I fingered the hollow space on my neck where my gold heart should be hanging. When I wore it, I felt close to Jürgen. It offered me a sense of security. I had to get it fixed and back around my neck.

***

On my way to the BDM meeting, Vera caught up to me, panting. "I'm not going to the meeting." Vera's forehead scrunched together, something was bothering her. "I wanted to let you know." Trying to catch her breath, she leaned in close as if wanting to confide something.

"What?"

Tears welled in her eyes.

"Tell me."

"This is so difficult." She spoke into my ear. "My father wants to leave."

"What?" First she said she wasn't going to the meeting. Then this. After all our years together that's the last thing I expected Vera to say. Her father, a dentist with a thriving practice, always seemed content with his life here, and with his wife and Vera, an only child. "Germany?" I whispered, not sure if that's what she meant for maybe he wanted to move from Ravensburg to a larger city in Germany. It made little sense, not with what I knew about Vera and how she spoke of her parents.

"Yes."

Stunned, my pulse beat in my throat. "Why?"

"I don't know." Tears dripped off her chin. "I mean… I know what he told me but my mother told me something else. Oh Christa, I don't want to move. What am I going to do?"

A black Mercedes sedan sped by truncating our conversation on the sidewalk, and Vera said she had to get home.

"Wait. Can't you tell me what they told you?"

She looked at the sedan speeding down the street. "I have to go. My parents don't know I left to tell you."

I watched her move away from me, wondering what was going on.

Once home after the meeting, I asked Oma if she knew anything about Vera's father wanting to leave.

"Leave? No, that can't be right." Oma was as surprised as I was. Vera's father was our longtime family dentist and as far as she knew no announcement had been made from the office. Surely she would have heard from her close friend Irmgard, Vera's paternal grandmother, about her son.

"That's what Vera told me."

"She must be mistaken." Oma went to the phone and dialed Irmgard's number.

Other than a few shocked-sounding outbursts interspersed with softly spoken words, I couldn't make out what was said. When she dropped the handset in the cradle, looking like she was at funeral, my chest felt like a tornado hit it.

"It's true." She told me Vera's father had his license revoked.

"She told you that?" I couldn't believe my ears. A dentist in excellent standing, loved by the community, who serviced the poor–gratis–losing his license to practice made no sense.

"I'm afraid so." A heaviness moved over her as she went elsewhere, into dark memories. After my Opa's death she sulked around for days, refusing to come out of her room and not wanting to eat. Watching her day after day looking so defeated was hard to take. I was sure she was trying to join Opa and had lost her will to live. Not that long ago, only six years, it took me a long time to pull her out of the depressed state she had sunk into. It was my tending to her, forcing her to eat, sitting with her at night, and pestering her that finally brought her out of her depression. Here, now, after seeing how she reacted to the news she received, I was worried she'd sink back into that swamp of pain.

"Oma." I said her name to distract her from whatever she was reminded of. To bring her back to me. I needed her. I needed to know what was happening with Vera's family. "Why did that happen?" I pulled a string from the collar of my blouse unraveling a small area of material while waiting to hear what she had to say.

Her attention went to my fidgeting. "Stop that."

"Why, Oma?" I repeated, continuing to play with the top of my blouse.

"Stop fidgeting. You'll tear your uniform blouse."

"Oma!"

"There's nothing more to say. It's the way it is."

It made me mad she was holding back. I had a right to know why my closest friend was moving. To know what her father did to deserve having his job ripped from him. "Oma. I know there's more. Tell me." I continued to nag her until she told me to be quiet and the conversation was over.

I raised my voice, disrespecting Oma, when I told her it wasn't over for me. "I want to know. Why can't you tell me?"

"Because she is your friend. That's why. A good friend and what I know is best left unsaid. It's for your own good."

I refused to accept her closed off attitude. "I have to know."

"She's dangerous to you. There, I said it. Now leave me alone."

Oma's upset wasn't from my pestering her. It was from whatever she heard on the phone call and it frightened me. No way was Vera dangerous. On the contrary, she had a kind nature. I saw it in her actions, like when she tried to resist Gertrude and Brigitte pushing her to be mean to that Jewish mother. I told Oma about that incident to drive home the point I didn't agree with what she'd just said.

"What? What did you just say? You were socializing with a Jewish mother?"

"No, Oma. We weren't socializing." I told her what had happened and how upset I was about it, how upset Vera was as she protested and once forced to do something against her will she left in a huff. "Please tell me what you heard on the phone call."

Oma looked pensive, like she was rethinking what to do. What to say. She then went to the door to ensure it was closed and listened for a minute to be sure Liddy wasn't in earshot. When we sat, her voice cracked as told me what she'd heard from her friend.

I felt like I was drowning in her sympathetic words, and it took a minute for me to grasp what she meant by Vera being dangerous to me. My hand went to my neck, to the ball of thread on my blouse. I couldn't believe what she'd told me, that Irmgard was Jewish and that's why they decided to leave. Oma had been friends with her for years, surely she must have known. I couldn't help wondering how much else had been withheld from me. The anguish in her eyes told me not to ask.

I thought of Vera mentioning nothing about it, but what did it matter, it didn't change my affection for her. Vera was a good person, a good friend, and whatever religion was in her family line I refused to accept it would change how I felt about her. Like my brother remained loyal to Arthur, I would not violate my bond with Vera, stay or go. Loyalty ran in my family. Not just to Germany but to our German friends, all of them no matter their ethnic or religious affiliations. That presented a whole new set of problems I would have to learn to navigate.

"Stop that." Oma moved my fidgeting hand from my blouse. "Where's your necklace?"

"It's broken. I have the parts in my bedroom." I pulled my hand from her grasp to feel where it should have been.

"I know someone who fixes things. Was a jeweler."

Was? My thoughts flamed to raging fire. Was a jeweler. Was a dentist. Too upset over Vera leaving with her family, Oma's comment didn't take hold.

CHAPTER TEN

My broken necklace sat in a small ceramic container on my dresser as 1935 moved along without Jürgen. Without Vera. They weren't the only people disappearing and by September vacant shops and houses spread across Ravensburg. Particularly disturbing were the rumors I heard why people left.

Gertrude was an endless well of gossip and what she passed along was unquestionable. Kurt Hess, cousin to Rudolf Hess, was her father. Unknown to him, her source of information was his unlocked briefcase he left in his study when he had a nightly drink, most likely causing him to be careless. She'd giggle telling us how her father said he would give his life for Hitler but not his drink.

"The Führer doesn't drink or smoke but my father told my mother all the men under him including cousin Rudolf do, consequently he sees no harm in it."

Even though Frau Schmidt frowned upon those habits, they didn't make me uncomfortable. What made me uncomfortable was listening to Gertrude tell me and Brigitte how she meddled in her father's affairs peeking through unsealed papers. There was no point in my removing myself from the conversations for she'd find me later only to enforce her gossip on me. That was Gertrude and I just had to put up with it.

"When I hear him go for the bottle—" Distracted by someone approaching where we were huddled together before our meeting, she paused waiting for the girl to pass. Gertrude leaned in closer, and told us about new laws soon to come out. "Nuremberg Laws." Those laws, she paraphrased, meant Jews were no longer German citizens.

"No." That slipped out before I could catch myself. Oddly, it wasn't a surprise, but yet to hear Gertrude say it was jolting.

"That's not all." There was a crazed ardor in her voice, and she appeared pleased she could tell us Jews could no longer marry Aryans or fly the German flag.

Frau Schmidt walked out of her office to the head of the class, ending the conversation. To a few giggles, she tapped on the desk before her and introduced the lesson for the day. "Service." She glanced over the room, and when her eyes met mine, my back muscles stiffened. "Some of you will be approaching advance studies or entering occupations but before you do, you will do a year of land service."

The longer she talked the tighter my back became and it was hard for me to stay put. I didn't want to hear about working on a farm or any other approved form of service. I didn't want to listen to her talk about the importance of young people from cities learning to work the land.

"Another way to be of service is to do domestic work in homes of families with many children."

That didn't appeal to me either. I wanted to be of service, I wanted to help, but I wanted to do something appealing. Gertrude told us earlier her father would arrange for her to do something interesting, not menial were her words. If she could arrange that, why not me? Determined to see what other options I might have I made a mental note to talk with my father once we were both home.

The hour passed with Frau Schmidt dominating the space with more talk of the importance of self-sacrifice for Germany. As I looked around at all the nodding heads, I felt ill at ease. I hadn't started my adventure with the BDM feeling disaffected and out of sorts so why now? Why did I now cringe at the idea of obedience to the Führer, his officers and the Nazi regime? I felt pretty certain it wasn't simply stemming from my own losses and the harsh treatment I'd heard about concerning Jewish people. No, it went deeper than that, but my yet maturing brain couldn't make sense out of it. I couldn't join the pieces of the puzzle to give me the clarity and I needed to understand why my gut was roiling.

Something happened on my way home that added another disturbing piece to my uncertainty. I saw Herr Meier alone at his news kiosk hunched over a stack of newspapers, his bent arms wobbling, his hands flat against the papers trying to steady himself.

"Herr Meier." I moved closer, close enough to feel the heat his body was giving off, to see his moisture-soaked shirt. "Are you feeling all right?"

"Christa." He straightened his bent frame and pulled back from me. "You should be on your way."

This was not the friendly gesture this kind man displayed on a daily basis, his inviting affable chitchat and offering candy to children. What had put him in such a state?

He looked over his shoulder, down the street toward a men's clothing store, to painting on the window. *Jude.* Next to it was a hexagram. He shook his head, and said tautly, "You better go."

I followed his glance down the street, nodded I understood and moved on toward the store that had the hexagram on it, the paint still wet, dripping like teardrops. Inside, the owner was picking up clothing scattered over the floor. The man's expression was shamefully pained, his eyes clouded over.

What did he do to deserve that terrible treatment? You did nothing to deserve this, I thought, placing my palm against the window and smearing a glob of wet pain on the e. I was about to move my hand across the rest of the word to wipe it away when a black sedan turned the corner. I drew my sticky hand back, regretting not smearing the rest of *Jude* to make it unreadable. The sedan grew closer, slowed and came to a stop with a uniformed man rolling down the passenger window. "What are you doing?"

I ran off in hopes they wouldn't pursue me. The image of the poor shop owner, his sunken eyes looking like death warmed over, lingered.

I kept running until I turned a corner and looked back, catching my breath. My heart banged against my ribcage, for I feared if they caught me I would be labeled a Jew lover. I breathed out a sigh of relief they hadn't followed me. My pounding heart didn't slow as I made my way past a carpenter's storefront where two Nazis in brown uniform with swastika arm bands were painting the window. They couldn't have been much older than me. I slid my paint-stained hand in a pocket on my skirt, turned my lips up and kept going feeling like I was going to throw up.

My parents and Oma were at the dining room table when I arrived home later than usual. The floorboard squeaked giving me away so I wasn't able to sneak past them to wash my hand before going to them.

"Christa," my mother called to me.

Liddy stepped into the hallway on her way out, coat on and purse in hand. She said a quick goodnight, see you tomorrow, and she was out the door.

All eyes were on me when I entered the dining room. I kept my painted hand in my pocket. "I'll wash up and be right back."

Soap and water didn't work. Neither did scrubbing so I used a small piece of pumice Liddy kept in the bathroom to clean the sink and toilet. It was old and rough with something stuck on it I didn't notice until it abraded my skin making it bleed. I didn't want to fib to my parents and I didn't know what to do. Didn't matter for Oma was now at the door and saw my hand.

"What's all this?" She motioned to the bloody pumice on the counter.

"Oma. I did something—"

"What's taking you so long." My mother was coming down the hall. At the bathroom door her aggravated look turned to creased-brow concern. "Your hand."

"Just a little mishap. Nothing serious." At least that wasn't an out and out lie.

Oma didn't open her mouth

"Mishap?"

51

"Mother, let's just eat and I'll tell you later."

"You'll tell me now or you can go to your room without dinner!"

Better to shut up and go to my room than suffer whatever explosions would ensue if I told them what I'd been up to. I'd gotten myself into this situation and I'd have to find a way out short of lying to my parents and Oma.

Luckily, the phone rang and my mother went to answer it. She didn't return to the bathroom while I bandaged my hand, nor did she go to my room later to ask me what happened. Something must have taken her attention off it.

CHAPTER ELEVEN

Oma came to me with a plate of food. My parents were asleep in their room.

"I brought you some stew. I added a little extra sauerkraut and a piece of bacon." She winked, for bacon was scarce and she knew how much I liked it.

Even though I wasn't hungry, I ate to please her.

"So…" She watched me finish the last spoonful. "Do you want to talk about what happened?"

"Oma." I said her name and out poured the tearful words about the Jewish man with the clothing store, and what had by now also happened to the carpenter's place of business.

"Shame on them."

"Them?" I didn't know if she was referring to the Jewish store owners or the German perpetrators.

"Our men, our strong German stock. That's who." After making a few more cynical comments about the inhumane treatment being dished out, she solemnly spoke. "Make no bones about it, this will only get worse. What you did was foolish. From your heart, Christa, but foolish. You mustn't overtly show your sympathies. Look what happened to your brother."

"I know, Oma, but it's hard for me to do nothing. I'm told what to read, what to study, how to act, who to marry, and now…" I fumed remembering Frau Schmidt's lecture that day. "I don't want to work the land. Be someone's babysitter. I don't want to be told I have to do something that will make me miserable."

"Stop pouting!" Her stern words snapped me out of my complaining about what's being done to me. "Take control if you don't like it."

"How? I have no control. That's the problem."

"That's where you're wrong. You always have the ability to control your situation."

"Up against the military? Me?"

"Don't get histrionic. I'm not talking about directly going up against the establishment. Find ways to exist that makes you feel better and if you can't find a way then change your attitude. No one can control what you think. Never forget that."

That hit me right between the eyes, moving deep into my brain. It made sense. It helped me feel better. It didn't, however, address the actual problem I had over not wanting to do the work Frau Schmidt brought up. How to get out of that, to be able to spend my time doing something I liked, was on the forefront of my mind.

"Is there anything I can do to get out of the designated work?"

"Perhaps." Oma's attention went somewhere else. "Hmm, let's see. Yes." Her face brightened, the edge left her voice. "Your father might be able to help."

"At Maybach?"

"Why not. Not all women are being slated for staying home, looking after the family and producing children. Many are still needed in the jobs they have especially with men joining the military."

"Like what?"

"Teachers, nurses, secretaries to name a few."

I liked what she was saying but it smacked against what I'd been learning about the push to marry and have children. The laws I'd read about, and how girls were getting pregnant by SS men to produce babies for the Reich, made me uneasy. Would it be possible for me to work at

Maybach? Could my father pull this off? Would he even want to risk his position to do this for me? Doubt floated around in my head.

"I'll have a word with your father when you are at your meeting tomorrow. It's late, now go to bed." She picked up the dirty plate, bowl and spoon, gave me a goodnight kiss on my forehead and left.

***

My father's response came as a surprise. "I could arrange to have you placed at Maybach, a secretarial role, but I don't want to risk it."

"Father, please."

"No, Christa. That's the end of this conversation!" He paced the study, lost in thought.

I didn't want to yield without understanding why he responded so adamantly. "Gertrude told me her father would arrange a job for her, so I thought you could do the same. Can you at least tell me why you won't help me?"

He stopped moving to look at me. "You need to drop it."

"No."

His closed lips turned into a crescent moon and he let out a guttural laugh. "Stubborn like your Oma."

"Yes." I waited.

He continued pacing.

I continued waiting.

"Christa. Let's have a seat."

Settled in next to each other on the back side of his desk, he began. "It's not the best place for a pretty young girl to work. There are too many officers coming and going from other parts of Germany without their wives. I don't want you around that."

"I can handle myself."

"No, you can't."

"Father, please, I don't want to do an assigned job. Gertrude's father is—"

"Enough with Gertrude's father. I don't have the same connections and privileges as Herr Hess that offer Gertrude protection."

"That's not fair!"

Oma heard my raised voice and came into the study interrupting my outburst. "Not going well?" She looked from me to my father. "Harald, can't you do anything to help her?"

"You were listening?"

Oma admitted she had been outside the door and overheard the conversation.

As my father ran a hand through his hair, strands of gray curls encircled his fingers, more than I remember seeing from the last time I looked. It pained me to see my father aging and I felt guilty I was adding to his stress. It didn't help my guilty feeling when he made a comment about not liking everyone in the house always listening in on others' conversations despite his admonitions against it.

Oma ignored his comment and asked again if he could help.

"Helga, it's not easy to place girls outside assigned locations. She's not even eighteen, the age when her BDM service ends and she'd be assigned a job. While she's underage, there are rules I can't circumvent. Herr Hess may be able to but I can't."

Eighteen, my mood sank like a flushed toilet. With my seventeenth birthday two months away waiting until I was of age would be fourteen months. Fourteen months felt like forever. Envisioning what those months would look like, I tuned out until I heard Oma ask, "When she turns eighteen can you arrange for her to work at Maybach to avoid an assignment elsewhere?"

"I don't want her working at Maybach."

"I heard that, Harald. I see no harm if other women are working on the assembly line there."

"Not my daughter!" He smacked his hand on the chair, shaking his head looking like he wouldn't hear of it and that was that.

Determined, Oma continued to push. "If not there, what about the box factory?"

The building, pressure-cooker energy let off steam and his torso relaxed. "That would be all right. I'll have a talk with your mother."

The next day my mother told me she'd spoken with my father and arrangements would be made for me to do secretarial work for her box company.

Although I would have to wait until my eighteenth birthday, I was relieved I didn't have to expect being assigned to farm or domestic work.

CHAPTER TWELVE

My seventeenth birthday came and went, yet well into 1936 I still hadn't fixed my necklace. My life was busy. Monday to Friday I attended school and the BDM, which comprised domestic training, instruction in German culture and history, and worldview training with emphasis on the Nazi Party's racial ideas. Frau Schmidt hounded us that to better serve Germans and Germany, Saturdays were to be spent promoting good health through physical education by taking track and field sports, gymnastics, route marching and swimming.

I used to enjoy physical fitness classes, but sadly now they reminded me of Jürgen. How he always challenged me to run, swim and climb trees to catch up to him. Thanks to him, I was very fit, unlike Gertrude who didn't like physical education classes and had trouble keeping up. In the past, I had offered her encouragement like my brother had done with me. Although she improved little, it had strengthened our friendship. As I thought about both of them, I felt sad. I missed how things used to be.

My necklace. When did I have time to take my broken necklace to a jeweler?

Sunday, Oma said, more times than I want to remember, but she was right and I should have used the time after church to tend to my good luck piece.

On a temperate morning in early May, Liddy was at the hospital tending to one of her girls who had an emergency appendix operation so Oma came to wake me. As she opened the door to my bedroom, she found me standing at my dresser, my broken necklace in the palm of my right hand.

Once again, she reminded me to get it fixed. "The cold and snowy weather has passed. This current warm spell is a perfect time to take the train to Friedrichshafen."

Oma told me about the jeweler she knew there, an accommodating man who worked out of the garage in his home. He owed her a favor and would fix it at no cost.

"It's a beautiful train ride." Oma drifted off to another time, her breathing slowed and she spoke as if in a trance. "The lush green hillsides, the winding rippling Schussen River, towering majestic spruce trees and sheep grazing heather." She sounded like she was floating on a cloud.

I didn't want to interrupt her dreamy reminiscence for she was clearly in a better place than the daily grind we had to put up with, but when my hand twitched and the pendant clanked against the chain in my hand, Oma's spell was broken.

"A pleasant memory." She looked refreshed like after a good night's sleep. She gazed at the broken necklace in my hand telling me a little more about the jeweler and where his house was. "Nahum will take good care of you."

Nahum, I thought, wondering why she referred to him by his first name. So informal. Come to think of it, the silvery way she cooed like a dove about the jeweler named Nahum was unlike her matter-of-fact manner. The only other time I'd heard Oma cooing like that was with Opa. She was devastated after his death and it took everything in me to help her, to make her want to live. I remembered her off-and-on depression and then something changed.

"Oma." I had to step lightly for what I was about to ask was for my own curiosity and none of my business, but if Oma was sending me off to meet someone she'd been, well... close to, I had a right to know.

"Yes."

"When did you meet the jeweler?" I felt uncomfortable calling a grown man by his first name so I simply referred to him as the jeweler.

"1932. June." A small smile moved over her face, lighting her eyes. "On a trip to Friedrichshafen with your father. He went to work and I went to do some shopping."

She remembered the exact month and year. I have trouble remembering dates a few months ago and she just recalled a time four years ago. Fascinated, my curiosity was bubbling over. "Oma, did you and—"

Oma laughed. "You want to know if I knew him as a man?"

Not expecting her to answer what I blurted out, I felt embarrassed. I knew she was straightforward, said what was on her mind when she wanted to, but this stretched the boundary of what I imagined she would want to talk about. She opened the door so why not go through it? "Yes, if you care to share."

"You know what I went through with Opa. I got back to living, doing things, but my insides felt hollow, my heart an empty shell. That day when I went with your father, I wandered into the most wonderful jewelry shop. There behind the counter was a man with the waviest thick dark-brown hair flowing over his forehead. He was looking through an eyepiece working on a tiny stone, no bigger than a sesame seed. I watched him, intent on his work, fix that tiny gem into a ring. When finished setting the stone, he put down his silver tweezers, removed the eyepiece and looked up at me." She told me how nice he was, how he took a long time showing her various pieces of jewelry he had made. "He told me his family had been in the jewelry business for three generations."

Oma softened as she told me she'd been back to see Nahum several times through the years but stopped in 1935 when things heated up. When she mentioned that year, she lost her glow. Her lips partially opened and she hesitated, then sounding poignant said, "Next Sunday on your day off would be a good time. I'll take care of telling your parents and give you the rail fare."

***

My parents insisted I not go alone and since they already had plans next Sunday, Oma agreed to accompany me. We boarded the train and found seats in the back of the first car next to a window. A woman with a baby entered followed by two men in business suits, all paying no attention to us, but then two Nazi officers entered and sat across from us. My stomach rose to my throat.

As the train started to move and pick up speed, its steadily increasing chugging sounded while Oma, ever the diplomat, mentioned something to them about it being a good day for travel.

The officer on the left ignored her while the one on the right said yes, it was.

"My granddaughter has done so well in her studies, I'm rewarding her with this ride and walk around Friedrichshafen."

The officer on the right smiled back but said nothing while the other officer stared out the window.

"She's also excelled in her sports activities. She's a good gymnast but excels at track, a fast runner with strong legs."

Feeling self-conscious, I bent my long thin legs under the seat.

"If she had trained when she was younger she'd be preparing for the upcoming Olympics."

She was driving me to distraction, but apparently she connected with the officer who'd been listening to her, for he responded he had a nephew running in the Olympics. "Will you be attending?"

"Wish we were." Oma smiled at me then continued her conversation with the officer. "We'll listen on the radio while we cheer Germany on."

"Germany will win." His statement was firm, sounding as if practiced and there was no room for disagreement. He made a few more comments about the superiority of Germany's athletes before the train slowed.

The whistle sounded like a forlorn dog howling in the night. The brakes hissed and screeched. "This is where we get off." Once the train came to a complete stop, Oma rose and told the officers to have a safe journey. Only seventeen kilometers that ride felt like hundreds.

A couple of streets from the train station, Oma facetiously said, "That was painless enough."

"I don't know where you get your gumption from, Oma."

She laughed.

It felt good to hear her laugh.

We walked a few flat streets before making our way up a windy hillside that overlooked Lake Constance in all its fascinatingly beautiful expanse. The last time I saw the lake it was replete with reveling visitors sailing and enjoying water sports. Replaced by a few lonely fishing boats, gone were the throngs of sailboats and waterskiing enthusiasts.

Oma looked out over the calm freshwater lake. "I used to love to visit and walk along the shore of the lake, enjoying the vivid views of its exquisite gardens and old castles."

I tried to imagine what life looked like through her eyes back then. Were they filled with love, empty of painful experiences? Were they seeking escape from the loss in Ravensburg?

"Let's have a seat over there." She motioned to a bench in a small triangular park on a hilly corner, a street from where Nahum lived. We sat and she grew silent, kicking around a few pebbles.

I felt the envelope in my skirt pocket, holding the broken parts of my necklace, and wondered if we were sharing the same nostalgia for times past when our family was whole.

Oma broke the stillness. "I haven't seen him in what seems like a long time." She reached for my hand as if needing support, comforting physical touch.

I wanted to ask why but my insides told me to stay put and let her have her say.

"There are different kinds of love, Christa. What I had with your Opa was sustaining and for a lifetime. I still miss him." She gave my hand a reassuring pat. "But the heart has capacity for many loves. Nahum taught me that. My friend Nahum is a good man."

When I heard her use the word friend, I wondered what she had with him. I loved Vera and missed her, is that what Oma is referring to? But then I never lit up about my friendship with Vera or spoke with a wistful longing like Oma talked about Nahum. A long few minutes passed and I wanted to know more. "Was he just a friend?" The minute that was out of my mouth I was sorry I said it, sorry I had trespassed into an uncomfortable area, at least uncomfortable for me.

"No."

I was sure she could hear my loud thoughts begging for more but when she didn't elaborate I asked something else, something more appropriate for Oma to discuss with me. "When was the last time you saw him?" What I really wanted to ask was did he even know we were coming?

"Over a year ago." She took her hand from mine and wiped her eyes. "He wanted to stop seeing me."

"I'm sorry."

"Nothing to be sorry about, Christa. He was protecting me. That's the kind of man he is. Refused to allow me to visit and phone him."

"Why?"

With a hair's breadth between us she said, "He's Jewish."

CHAPTER THIRTEEN

Jewish, I couldn't stop thinking about what Oma had said as we rose and made our way to his place. A lot of things I had wondered about Oma became clear to me. Why she defended Jürgen's friendship with Arthur, saying it wasn't breaking any laws. How upset she was about Vera's family leaving and losing her friend, Vera's grandmother. How she let me vent without making me feel I was talking out of turn.

While my parents were closemouthed, Oma, albeit judiciously, expressed her opinion. Perhaps that was why her friend Nahum stopped seeing and talking to her. If she felt about him as she apparently did, he must have known how she'd react when the heat was turned up against Jews.

Standing before the walkway to his front door, she finally told me he didn't know we were coming. "I wanted to see him... before things get..."

She didn't finish her sentence. I took it to mean she didn't want to jinx him.

Aside from a couple of cars parked along the curb, a man walking a dog and two boys playing ball on a front lawn, the street was quiet. Modest by the standards I grew up with, his two story home looked to be only one-hundred-forty square meters, and except for the slight differences in the half-timbering and design of the gables the houses on the street looked alike. A few geranium plants in ceramic pots sat on the covered porch, flowering rainbows of pink, red and white which told me they were well kept and actively tended to. It was an inviting touch to the quaint entrance.

Oma knocked on the door, leaving her palm upon it as we waited. A barking mongrel dog came around the corner by the driveway, followed by a tall man with dark-brown messy hair, appearing to be in his early twenties.

"Bengle come here."

When he approached, taking hold of the dog's collar, I saw his rheumy, red-rimmed eyes make contact with Oma.

"Frau Koch. Is that really you?"

He knew my Oma, her full name. Who was this handsome, unhappy man?

"Paul!" She looked from his head to his feet. "When did you get so tall? So handsome? Like your father."

Paul looked down, away from Oma's affectionate expression, her lips and eyes soft.

"Paul. What is it? Where's your father?"

Unable to speak, words failing him, he mournfully shook his head.

"Paul. No, he can't be." Oma's softened countenance ran off her face like melted butter.

Paul took a deep slow breath and asked us to follow him away from the street out back to the shop in the garage. He let the dog loose in a fenced yard, and brought us in to have a seat on a couple of benches before a worktable filled with jewelry tools and equipment. There he offered a drink of water and told us after his father set up his new shop in the garage, probably a couple of months after the last time he saw Oma, he had a massive heart attack.

"He hung on for a few weeks after that but was weak, unable to work. I came home from university to take care of him and handle the few customers we had left."

Oma slumped over, head in hands. "I should have never listened to him." She mumbled about not wanting to listen to Nahum when he insisted they stop relating.

I felt out of place listening to them like I was intruding on a sacred space when I hadn't even been introduced to the devastated son of Oma's friend. I edged forward and gently said, "I'll wait outside."

Oma straightened. "You stay right here. Paul, this is my granddaughter, Christa."

Paul wiped his dirty hands on his work apron and extended a hand to shake mine. "I apologize for my rude—"

"Please don't apologize. I understand." I lived through a very hard loss with Opa's passing and Oma's reaction to it. I thought I had a good idea of what Paul was feeling. I certainly felt for him, for what must have been a tragic thing for a son to experience. His father's loss of his jewelry shop because he was Jewish. His losing a woman friend for the same reason. His broken heart couldn't take it and gave out.

"Thank you." As he looked at me, a translucent light shone through the pall in his eyes. His attention then shifted back to Oma. "Tell me what brings you back here?"

"We came to ask your father to fix a broken necklace."

Wise to what Oma had done, a tight smile moved across Paul's face. "No jewelers in Ravensburg?"

"None like your father."

Paul's smile widened.

My heart expanded.

"Perhaps I may be able to help. Growing up and on summer breaks I learned the trade to be able to assist him when his load got too heavy. I still remember what he taught me."

"Show him your necklace."

I handed Paul the envelope with the chain and pendant. He took a quick look at what I gave him then dug through a metal container with small drawers holding jewelry pieces. A couple of minutes later, he put down his soldering iron and held out my necklace. "Here you are. Allow me to put it on you."

Paul clasped the necklace and removed his hand, lightly stroking my neck. The touch of his fingers against my skin sent a tingling down my spine. It was a strange new and inviting sensation, warming my cheeks.

Oma must have seen what was happening for when it was time to leave, she told Paul to not be a stranger and he should come visit us.

"I don't think that's a good idea."

I felt disappointed until Oma refused to let him bow out.

"It's not illegal, Paul. You are welcome in my home."

I couldn't allow myself to fully experience the excitement I felt over the possibility of seeing him again. How could that happen in my home, when I knew my parents were skittish about our associating with Jews? How in the world would Oma handle that if Paul took her up on it? I couldn't imagine how she'd get away with it, but wished with everything in me he would come.

He gave Oma a cheerless nod that showed no promise we'd see him again.

His reaction dashed my hopes.

Oma hugged Paul goodbye.

Nahum's death hit Oma hard. On the walk to the train station she shut down like a broken motor, but there was no hiding her feelings behind a stoic mask for I knew my Oma's heart. I was the one to help it heal after Opa's death. Was she thinking of him? Did the news of Nahum's death open that wound?

Not much was said between us as we boarded the train and it picked up speed. As the evenly paced alternating clicks and clacks of the wheels moving over the tracks chorused through the train car, my thoughts moved from feeling bad for Oma to Paul. A man with one name. I was drawn to him. To his tall slim physique. To the way his hands adroitly moved when he fixed my necklace. How his big masculine hands maneuvered the tiny objects. My neck tingled, exactly the same way it had when he touched me closing the clasp on my necklace, and that feeling spread through me like a sponge absorbing liquid. Something had awakened in me and I was lost in the intoxication of what it would be like to be with him.

While I was daydreaming, the train's rattling vibrations slowed and squealed as we turned a corner heading into the Ravensburg station.

CHAPTER FOURTEEN

Oma remained quiet and mostly kept to herself as May moved into June. All eyes were on preparations for the summer Olympics being held in August in Berlin, some seven hundred kilometers from Ravensburg. The Führer saw the Games as a way to promote Germany as a strong and united country, while hiding the regime's treatment of Jews and its growing military aggression. Germans had been put on alert that the country was to be ready for the onslaught of tourists.

During dinner one night in the middle of June, the phone rang. Moments later Liddy announced, "Telephone for Herr Becker from—"

My mother, annoyed with my father's recent late nights at work and not showing for the evening meal, slammed her fork down on a china plate. "Not while we're eating! Take a message." Her brusque reply was becoming as commonplace as my father's absence and Oma's withdrawal.

My father ignored my mother's reaction. "Who's phoning?"

Liddy looked from my mother to my father, remaining still.

"Liddy. You will answer me right this minute."

My mother lowered her head.

Oma kept eating while I watched the tense interchange.

"Herr Pfundtner's secretary."

My father ripped his napkin from his lap, threw it on the table and rushed to the phone.

Mother pushed her chair back and went to her room.

"What could he want with your father?"

Oma's question went over my head. "Who is he?"

"A very senior civil servant."

"How do you know him?"

Oma let out a small laugh. "Read the papers, my girl. Hans Pfundtner is the State Secretary of the Reich Ministry of the Interior and has been overseeing the construction of the Reich Sports Field." She told me about an article she had read that mentioned him then seemed to drift off for a minute before continuing. "I remember reading another article about the day Hitler first visited the site. It was nothing but a field of tatty grass and sandy earth. And now, many structures are being constructed for the Games. How he's paying for it beats me."

Oma went back to eating her meal while I pushed food around on my plate wanting to know why that man's secretary phoned my father. I'd have to wait, for when my father came back and didn't see my mother at the table, he went to find her. In a short while, they both returned. My mother appearing calmer. My father had a big smile on his face.

"Herr Pfundtner asked me to go to Berlin to help with some glitches in the construction of the Reich Sports Field. This is an immense honor."

"Berlin?" Oma raised an eyebrow. "As if you're not gone enough."

"Helga, you all can come visit."

Upon hearing Liddy bring the garbage outside, Oma let loose. "My daughter can't leave her box factory. How is she to visit?" Whatever had been bottled up inside of Oma since our visit to Nahum's came out directed at my father. "What kind of life is this? Do this. Do that. Go here. Go there." Her voice grew louder with each blast at my father, yet he stood there taking it, his smile only growing wider.

When Oma's criticism ebbed, he asked, "Are you finished?"

"I'll be finished when Germany rightfully returns to its people." Oma snorted.

That wiped the smile off my father's face but it was my mother who scolded Oma. "We will not tolerate that talk." Then as surprisingly as my father remained standing patiently waiting to say what he came back to say my mother reached for Oma's hand. "There is some good news, mother."

The kitchen door opened and shut and we heard Liddy going about her chores putting us on alert to watch our words.

My father said, "I told Herr Pfundtner I would be honored to help but that I needed my wife to be able to spend time with me there. In order for that to happen someone needs to assist in managing the box factory during her absences." A little smile returned when he looked at me and continued. "A door has opened for you, Christa. We don't need to wait for your eighteenth birthday for you to be placed in the factory. Herr Pfundtner told me to consider it done."

I sprang out of my seat to hug him, knocking my chair to the floor. No more Frau Schmidt. No more boring demonstrations and lessons. I felt like a baby taking my first full breath. I felt freer than I had in years.

Oma nodded.

"Thank you." I repeated that until my throat became raspy.

My mother straightened my chair and motioned to my plate. "Finish your meal."

Oma's plate was empty, but instead of getting up and going to her room as she had been doing since our visit to Paul she snapped out of the funk she'd been in and chatted up a social storm with mother. "I have a stack of sewing that has piled up that needs attention. Plus there's gardening I want to do."

The rest of the meal felt like old times, before topics were verboten, when we spoke our minds and enjoyed our food. When mundane everyday happenings brought us joy. That phone call brought something back into our lives we'd lost and that night when I went to my room I prayed for it to continue.

For a while it did. Even the stormy anti-Semitic air around Ravensburg thinned out and morale lifted when groups of soldiers and citizen volunteers cleaned persecutory graffiti from store windows. My hopelessness was replaced with optimism and nighttime sleep came easier. A special bonus to beginning work at my mother's factory was I had my evenings free. To draw. To dabble in the kitchen with Liddy. To offer to take Max for walks.

Max always brought out the best in me, especially laughter. I burst into giggles when his tail got going, whipping from side to side at my approach. I loved that dog, his prickly short black and tan hair that shed on my clothes. The clothes I no longer had to worry about keeping spotless. Max, tirelessly eager to please, listened to me with a side-tilting unquestioning presence. It was with Max I shared my innermost feelings, things I didn't feel totally comfortable talking about with Oma. The most recent, Paul.

"I can't stop thinking about him." I looked down from the backyard bench I sat upon to Max by my feet.

Max lifted his head, torquing his neck to look back at me.

"Thank you, Max."

He plopped his head down between his front paws and let out a sigh.

"I want to see him again. I feel something… I don't know how to explain it." Lost in fanciful images, I thought about Paul's touch and how his fingers brushed over the nape of my neck arousing me.

Max twitched and let out a whine that distracted me from my vision. I looked down at my sleeping friend watching his snout relax then let out little yelping cries.

"What are you dreaming?" Sounded on the wave of a bare mutter, he heard me and raised his sleepy head. He cast his big brown eyes my way, to ensure I was all right. With him, I was.

More walks and talks with Max and I decided I had to return to Friedrichshafen, but how? I didn't want to go with Oma and my father was in Berlin. My mother wouldn't approve so what was I to do? Did I dare use my saved up allowance and sneak off? I worked myself into a headache trying to come up with a way to go, a plan that wouldn't get me in trouble.

That night I had a dream, so vivid when I awoke I was disoriented. In it Paul called to me. Over and over, his sensual voice magnetically rang in my ear, "Come to me." Sitting up in my bed in my soaked nightgown, I made my decision. On the Sunday, several days after my mother would leave to meet my father in Berlin, I would visit Paul.

***

The following week in the box factory, I diligently went about my chores learning new tasks I would perform when my mother wasn't there, such as helping with bookkeeping, taking calls for orders, and assisting the foreman, Herr König. To make a good impression, I spent several late nights helping Herr König ship out orders. That went over well with him. My mother was particularly pleased and made it a point to mention it while packing a suitcase for Berlin.

"You're doing splendidly, Christa. Ulrich König is very satisfied with your work and happy to have you help him while I'm away."

I worked hard for that compliment, hoping to pave the way for what I planned to do when mother left and I took my day off. Everything was working according to plan.

Early the next morning a black limousine pulled up before our house and a uniformed chauffeur got out. At the front door, he said he was here to transport my mother.

"She'll be right here," Oma said, looking back over her shoulders to the stairs. Mother was rushing around upstairs finishing the final last-minute packing.

Dressed for work in a skirt and sweater, I stood next to Oma waiting to say goodbye to my mother. She looked beautiful in her dark-blue suit, a hint of makeup on her cheeks and her hair in a chignon, coming down the stairs banging a large suitcase behind her. The taciturn chauffeur went to help her and waited while she gave us hugs. Once they were out the door and the car pulled away, I could taste my newfound autonomy.

CHAPTER FIFTEEN

The days up to Sunday, when I planned to visit Paul, moved at a snail's pace. Mother was away and wouldn't return until the following Wednesday, Sunday was Liddy's day off, and Oma concurred it was a good idea for me to take time for myself. To have a spontaneous day of exploration and extroversion. I was sure she could use some alone time and have the house to herself as well.

She didn't pry into where I was going, incorrectly assuming Max would be a part of my day. "Give Max a pat for me."

Oma shared my love of animals but her arthritis and fear of falling and fracturing a limb kept her at a distance. She'd often smiled when I told her about my time with Max. It was a vicarious thrill for her to listen to me talk about his playful and mischievous antics, his chasing squirrels and erupting into fits of howling when he heard a siren. She chuckled when I told her about his rolling in mud on a rainy day.

I dressed in a soft cotton beige blouse and maroon below-the-knee skirt, combed my hair that had grown to the middle of my back into a single stylish braid, and slipped into comfortable flats. It was the understated look I wanted. I had one last thing to do at my mother's vanity. I gazed at my work in the mirror, a tiny pinch of lipstick smeared over my cheeks and lips, and was ready to go.

I donned a cardigan and with my handbag over my arm, and the allowance I'd been saving in my change purse, I hugged Oma and was out the door walking at a leisurely pace. My heart was racing, and as much as I wanted to race along with it, I kept to a slow pace to avoid attention. Things had calmed down somewhat with anti-Semitic posters coming down but there was still a strong military presence on the streets.

Arriving at the train station, I immediately saw a group of uniformed soldiers walking toward the platform in loud conversation. One pointed a finger at a man with frizzy hair and I heard him say something to the effect that things would return to… after the Games. Although I missed a few words, their message left a bad taste.

My legs felt heavy and I didn't want to move. It hadn't been that long since my meetings with the girls listening to Frau Schmidt, her strong, commanding voice. Men in uniform were a stark reminder of officials carting girls off from the meetings, and seeing those men in uniform laughing and boisterously commenting with a superior air made me nervous.

The anticipation of going to see Paul, the excitement that kept me awake at night and counting minutes during the day, was taken over by resentment. I wanted to walk up to the loud-mouthed brute who was laughing at the man with the frizzy hair, stick my finger in his chest and tell him to stop! I stood there, biting my lower lip, frustrated I had no voice.

"You going in?" The man behind me shifted my attention to where I was, blocking the entrance to the waiting room where tickets were purchased. Lost in my ill will I hadn't realized I had moved to the doorway.

I turned my head to see the man. "Yes, my apologies." It was dangerous for me to slip away like that, to get so lost up in bitterness I didn't even know I was moving in a crowd. I needed to get a firm grip on my emotions.

We shared a few words while standing in the lengthy ticket line. He was returning to Frankfurt from a visit to help his son and daughter-in-law move.

"Not easy with three young ones. Thank God we've the means to move."

There were ugly stories written on the wrinkled grooves of his face and for some reason he wanted to talk. His son and family were moving, where and why he didn't explain, but I understood when he indicated with things calming down it's easier. Everything he said in a melancholy way spoke to me, he was Jewish. I wanted to assure him things were getting better, but how could I when I had just overheard *things would return.*

Paul was on my mind as the man's voice moved in and out like the soundtrack on a movie. Paul's brown eyes beat down on me as the man mentioned he'd be moving as well. From Frankfurt where things had changed since the mayor was removed. The conversation stopped when we reached the ticket window.

The nameless man caught up with me as I neared the train and said something but immediately stopped when one of the uniformed soldiers by the train gave me the once over, his eyes remaining on my chest. "What have we here?" He lisped, sending frothy spittle to his pudgy chin. A mist of stale booze hung around him, the same smell I'd inhaled on Herr Hess when visiting Gertrude's. He moved in on me. "How about we make a beautiful Aryan baby for Germany? Make the Führer happy."

Refusing to let me pass, the pudgy soldier moved before me, the man from Frankfurt still at my side.

As he reached for my shoulder grabbing hold of my sweater, I stepped back tugging my sweater out of his hand and tried to move around him.

The man from Frankfurt came between us. The soldier shoved him away, causing the man to lose his balance and fall to the dirty ground. Looking down at the man, the soldier reprimanded him. "You don't want to get in my way."

I'd had about all I could take from him, his repulsive nearness, his groping eyes and disrespectful actions, and his assault on the man from Frankfurt. "How dare you!" My eyebrows lowered and pulled together as I looked the soldier in his eyes. "I'll have you know my father is an important man who has the authority to send you to the camps."

Despite his alcohol-fogged brain, the soldier hesitated then spat out, "Who is your—"

"Felix." Another soldier approached taking the pudgy soldier's arm before he could finish his sentence. "Come on, let's go."

As they moved away, the pudgy one stumbling, I helped the man from Frankfurt get up from the ground. He avoided eye contact, looking more humiliated than mad.

"Thank you. Please, go get aboard." He wiped the grime off his neatly pressed wool suit.

I didn't know where that man sat but thoughts about him and his family's plight lingered through the ride. How was it possible my eyes set on the gorgeous view outside the window saw nothing but two faces, Paul's and the man from Frankfurt. Their shadowy faces rested over a blur of green backdrop, verdant hilly areas surrounding the sparkling blue lake, all smeared into one messy stroke. Like the smear I left on the Jewish man's store window. I looked down at my clammy hand, all traces of paint washed away. What else had been washed away?

The train rounded the curved, azure bay on the north shore of Lake Constance bringing into view the majestic stone lighthouse towering high above the cityscape of historic monuments clustered around the shoreline. A few minutes of slowing clickety-clacks, moving parallel to the lakeside promenade, the twin towers of the castle church smiled a welcoming hello.

My concentration kept shifting back and forth, in and out of the present moment, until I saw a man walking his German shepherd along a row of houses with patches of flowers. The dog was a big boy, like Max, strongly built with a long body. I wanted to reach through the window and pet his dense coat, feel his straight hair move through my fingers. With a black, pale gray, and brown coat, he was a handsome boy. I knew he was a boy the minute he stopped sniffing and lifted his hind leg to do his business.

No longer was the man from Frankfurt's situation plaguing me, for seeing the man walking his dog reminded me of Max and brought me back. I felt like I'd swallowed a feel-good pill as I disembarked.

I was happy to be out of the train and able to stretch my legs, to move away from the group of soldiers remaining aboard. I took in the surroundings of normal people going about their daily lives like the man walking the shepherd, excited I was on my way to see Paul.

CHAPTER SIXTEEN

I looked down the driveway and seeing the garage door closed I went to the front door. Aside from the sounds of children playing football and a boy riding a bicycle clicking loose gravel on the road, the neighborhood was quiet. I knocked expecting to hear Bengle bark. Nothing, no dog barking. Was Paul home?

My chest grew tight as I waited. A minute passed before I knocked again, this time louder. This time wondering if I had made a mistake by coming. What if he saw me and didn't want to open the door? The increasing tightness in my chest felt like a corset being closed.

I knocked a third time with a hard fist.

Lumbering footsteps approached the door.

My heart was thumping, my breaths labored.

"Who is..." Paul's mouth fell open when he opened the door. "Christa?" His head angled stressing the charcoal shadows under his eyes and the hair on the left side of his head was plastered against his scalp as if he'd been asleep. At midmorning? Something was wrong.

"Hello, Paul." I cast a glance past him to a dark unkempt living room with a dirty dish on an end table and clothes thrown on the floor and over a chair.

"What are you doing here?"

I waited a couple of seconds for him to invite me in. When he didn't I said, "I've been thinking of you, and I have time off today so I figured why not visit. Of course to thank you again." My hand went to the pendant's smooth curved surface.

"I was happy to help."

I wished he looked happy. His reticent manner gave me pause.

He must have seen how awkward I felt looking away, shifting my feet when he said, "I'd ask you to come in but the place is a mess."

I felt unwelcome and silly I came. This was a mistake. Why did I think I could just show up? I was about to thank him again and turn to leave but he looked so out of sorts I wanted to help him. I didn't want to leave without finding out what was going on. "I don't care what your house looks like, Paul."

He ran a hand through his matted hair and pushed the door open stepping aside for me to enter. "Have a seat."

I sat on an overstuffed faded floral armchair with thinning areas in the fabric as he moved about picking up clothes from the carpet and another similarly worn chair. The room smelled musty and could use an open window to air it out.

"Can I get you a drink? All I have is water." A weak smile moved over his lips but his eyes looked lifeless.

I didn't want him to feel bad for having nothing more to offer so I graciously accepted. "Yes, thank you."

No I'm glad to see you. No how was the trip. Nothing asked about Oma. This was a man not interested in engaging in conversation, not like the last time I was here. Then he was communicative, eager to help. It didn't feel right to ask him why the solemn non-communicativeness, instead, as I received a glass of water and Paul sat opposite me, I babbled about being happy he fixed my necklace. One lame comment after another poured out of me, about how it was my lucky charm, about how I felt lost without it when it broke, and then I mentioned it was a present from my brother. "He's ill."

Paul's slouched posture straightened a little. "Ill?" There was interest in his voice, like a commiserate nerve had been hit.

"He's in Rügen." How much do I tell him? Do I share my brother was accosted and injured because he defended a Jew? I didn't want to lie to Paul, there was something about not being honest with him that felt wrong.

Paul waited, his dull eyes now attentive on what I had to say.

I began with Jürgen's friendship with Arthur and continued right up to the night of my birthday dinner and the gift.

"Your brother was hurt… because…" He shook his head, unable to finish his sentence. There was a faraway look in his eyes.

He didn't need to finish his sentence for I realized how he must have felt, clear as polished crystal. Suddenly the room grew quiet. Too quiet. Where was Bengle?

Not wanting to dwell on the situation with my brother, I thought bringing up Bengle might cheer him up. "Paul."

He came back from wherever he had drifted off to. "Yes, sorry."

"Where's Bengle?"

That was the wrong thing to ask. It created the exact opposite of what I wanted for his eyes pooled and when he spoke his voice was brittle. "He's gone."

Jürgen's gone. Vera's gone. Paul's father is gone. My chest tightened. Not Paul's dog, please, not the dog. "Gone?" Maybe he was with a neighbor.

Paul swiped a finger across his eyes and wiped it on his pant leg. "He's dead."

That hit my chest like a bullet. I grabbed hold of my cardigan, jolting back. "No, Paul. Was he ill?"

"No!" An angry pomegranate red spread over his face, his nostrils flared.

The penetrating way he said no, harsh and cold, stunned me. "What happened?"

Paul looked through a crack in the closed front window curtains and blew out a long breath. "Someone poisoned him. Some bastard did to my dog what they wanted to do to me!" Angry, he opened up and told me he had found Bengle lying on his side in the yard frothing at the mouth, seizing. There were pieces of grayish tainted bread by his snout. "Earlier I caught a couple of boys in the neighborhood taunting him. I was in the garage working when I heard Bengle yelp and ran them off. At night trying to sleep, I could still hear their profanities. The cussing didn't bother me, but their trying to hurt him, throwing stones through the fence, calling him a Jew's dog..." Paul stopped and seemed to go elsewhere, to a place that held pain for he looked like he was about to cry a moment before he rubbed his eyes.

I sat still, not wanting to move or distract him from what was troubling him.

After several more minutes, still into himself, he said, "I know who's responsible."

I remained quiet, waiting for what I hoped he would share.

"When I was much younger, I had two close friends. The three of us were inseparable. One is dead. The other embraced the Nazi ideology and became an SS member. But long ago, we were close, until..." He sniffed in, and as if he swallowed something down the wrong way, he started coughing, his face growing dark. He cleared his throat and continued. "Dieter, the one who joined up with the SS, was jealous of me and grew to hate me. He came after me for revenge, stupid jealous revenge." He cleared his throat again and looked back out the window. "I saw him here after what happened to Bengle. Smiling." His hands clutched his thighs.

Halfway through whatever was on his mind, encased in a well of pain, he had stopped himself again. Half-opened, half-closed, I wanted him to let it out, to fully release what was deeply bothering him. "Why was he so jealous of you?"

When he looked over to me, he must have seen I meant it, that I wanted to help him free himself of whatever demons were inhabiting him. "I was always better than him at sports and academics which made him jealous, but it really got bad when I had a friendship with a girl he liked who rejected him. He wouldn't listen when I told him there was nothing between us and broke off our friendship, separating himself from me and our other friend."

I nearly cried when Paul told me that Dieter was around after Bengle was poisoned. But when he told me his neighbor was in Nahum's shop one day and witnessed Dieter threaten him I was alarmed.

"That was right before my father had his heart attack."

Feeling at a loss for words, I simply said, "I'm so sorry."

"So am I. It kept getting worse. Not only was Dieter harassing us but his father came to his defense when I threatened to harm him if he ever came near my father again. If I ever raised a hand to his son, he said he'd take care of me."

Two bad seeds, I thought, and continued listening to him telling me Dieter's father worked at the ferry station.

"He was distasteful to my neighbor when she needed to take the ferry. Would send her home with nasty messages to give to her neighbors, *the dirty jews.* She thought they were both menaces."

I continued to listen and my heart felt like it was going to implode.

As if coming out of a nightmare, he shook his head and looked around to get his bearing. He mumbled Bengle's name, his hands turning to fists. "How can anyone hurt a dog!" He looked killing mad, clenching his jaw, and muttering a few more angry words. When he seemed drained, he turned to me. "That's what happened."

"That's awful. All of it." That sounded so insufficient coming out of my mouth, but what else could I say? What else could I do? I simply steered cleared of putting his attention back on the awful Dieter and his father. "I can only imagine how you feel. I love dogs." As natural as flowers blooming from seed, I told him about Max and how devastated I'd be were anything to happen to him.

"A Rottweiler." This time his thin smile weakly moved to his eyes.

The facts I had shared about what happened to my brother allowed Paul to open, perhaps to trust me a little, then when I told him about Max, he softened. Paul's grief had tripped a deep caring in me, something that went beyond religion and race.

The conversation moved from loss and sorrow to normal boy and girl things. Where did you grow up? Where did you go to school? Did you like sports? For the next hour as we shared things about our lives, and I learned Paul had gone to university in Munich until he cut his studies short to help his ailing father. Studying biology, he wanted to become a doctor to help people. Taking it in stride, he told me he found other ways to help.

He adapted, made the best of unfortunate situations, but sadly his survival rubber band had stretched too far by the time his father died and then with what happened to Bengle it snapped. It felt like I had given him back some of his resilient elasticity, at least that's what I wanted to feel when he told me he was glad I came. Told me it made him feel better.

"Then let's meet again."

"How?"

In a flight of imagination I told him I wanted him to come visit Ravensburg. "It'd be good for you to get away from here for a day." I knew it made me feel rejuvenated when I took the trip with Oma, but then a lot of that was from meeting Paul. I was drawn to him, and wanted to see him again but he drew me back down to earth when he said he couldn't come.

When I asked why he clammed up. That didn't stop me so I made my case, said what I'd thought about before coming. "We can plan it for a Sunday when both my parents will be in Berlin and Liddy's not working."

"Liddy?"

Not wanting to emphasize our family position, I didn't want to say our maid. "She helps with cleaning our house. Paul, please, Oma would love to see you. We could—"

"I can't go to Ravensburg."

"Why not?" I hoped my mentioning Liddy wasn't off-putting.

"We've been pretty straightforward with each other."

"Yes."

"Here's another dose of honesty. I'm not all that comfortable saying this but you deserve the truth. I can't afford it."

That's all? Thankfully, that was an easy problem to solve. "I'll take care of the ticket. I have an allowance and—"

"No, Christa. I'm not taking your money."

"Then I'll come back to you."

"It's not safe for you here."

I looked out through the window where the sun was moving past midday. Soon I'd have to leave. A quick glance at my wristwatch confirmed I had only fifteen minutes left. "I have to catch my train but please don't let me leave without knowing I'll see you again." I'd never been that forward with a boy before but time was running out and I had to see him again.

He got up and came to me, extending his arms to help me up. Standing in his arms, he hugged me. "I want to see you again as well. I'll pay you back. I'll find a way to make money and pay you back."

In the warmth of his embrace, with his body against mine, the world of gun-toting Germans evicting Jews disappeared.

CHAPTER SEVENTEEN

Something had changed in me during that visit. It was the first time in my life I had entered into such an intimate conversation with the opposite sex. In a strange way and despite being so upset about what Paul told me about the cruelty Dieter had subjected him and his father to, it felt comfortable like a well-fitting glove. I hadn't told Oma where I was going, but after what Paul shared with me about Bengle, I wanted her to know and I needed to unburden how I felt about seeing him. I needed my Oma's support. Assuming she would have mentioned something to me, I doubted she knew anything about the Dieter incidents. I didn't want to mention them to her. Why chance her becoming riled about my visit, the danger Paul had been subjected to, which could create problems when I wanted to see him again.

"You went to the Landmann's place?"

"Landmann's?" She had never mentioned their last name before so it took me by surprise she referred to my visit with Paul that way, so formal.

"That's their name." She wiped a bead of perspiration bubbling on her chin. "A Jewish name."

I could have done without her passive warning there was danger in associating with Jews. I wanted to say it was all right for her to go, but that would have put Oma on the defensive. I didn't want to do that, not when I needed her support.

"Oma. Be nice."

"Be nice, she says!" Oma looked into space as if talking to a ghost, as if I weren't in the room. "There's no being nice when it comes to wearing a flashing neon sign that says you're associating with Jews. You can't do that."

The ferocity in her tone rained down on me like a hailstorm and I lost it. Any composure I had was gone. "You did. You did and you were the one who took me there." I indignantly snapped back at her half surprised she didn't stop me. "There are jewelers in Ravensburg but *you* wanted me to go with you an hour away to fix my necklace. I didn't do that. I didn't plan on meeting someone I'd like, like you probably hadn't planned what you had with—"

"That's enough, young lady!"

She was struggling with her frustration as much as I was. The untenable situation whirled around us in a tempest of vacillating emotions. She'd been decent enough to allow me to have my reaction and I regretted lashing out at her. I slumped down, sure she could tell I was sorry, but said nothing.

She paced in circles, smoothing a few new gray hairs back onto her hairline. "Christa." A few more steps and her taut stance loosened. "It's dangerous."

There it was. The issue wasn't with Paul, a Landmann as she referred to him, it was the protective armor she shielded me with. How could I be mad at her when she had acted out of love?

"Things are getting better." Despite what I'd heard the soldier say at the train station, I wanted to believe that. I'd seen improvements with my own eyes, but then Paul had experienced something to indicate I was wrong and Oma was right. There was no getting around Bengle's death and everything he had shared with me. Was it more than a jealous act of revenge? Was Paul naively incorrect about why Dieter and his father treated Paul and Nahum the way they had? A sick feeling moved into my throat when I remembered what Paul told me about Dieter's father calling Paul and Nahum *dirty Jews*. I didn't want to entertain Dieter's actions were not just a childhood vendetta, but there was no getting around the anti-Semitic roots digging deep into the mud.

I had just about convinced myself things would continue to get better until I saw the way Oma looked at me, the same way she looked when she found out about Jürgen. That look ended the debate I was having with myself. It was then the fog I'd been in lifted and I saw Paul must have been in denial wanting to believe it was jealousy that turned Dieter and his father against him. No, it wasn't just jealously, it was the same sickness spreading through Germany.

"Christa. Christa. Christa." She sounded my name like an incantation, a song of verboten love. "You like Paul?" She stopped pacing and stood looking at me with an accepting stillness in her posture.

"I do."

"Impossible relationships." Nostalgia threaded her words together.

She wasn't just referring to my visit with Paul but what she had with Nahum, of that I was certain. I moved closer to her. "You'll help me?" I beseeched her, placing a hand on one of her elbows.

"With the Landmann boy? Yes."

"Yes?" Did I hear her right?

As I watched her nodding confirmation, Landmann echoed in my head, flipping a light on. Why did it sound familiar? "Why do you keep saying their last name?"

"To remember." The last half of the word remember trailed off as she moved back to a tumultuous time explaining what she meant, bringing back to me why that name sounded familiar. She had mentioned it a few years earlier at the beginning of 1933 when she must have been seeing Nahum.

As she spoke she ignited memories of what she'd told me directly and what I'd overheard her telling my parents. Her friend, the jeweler in Friedrichshafen, had a brother who had lived in Frankfurt, Ludwig Landmann, a liberal politician of the Weimar Republic, who became the first Jewish mayor of Frankfurt in the mid-twenties. After the Nazi election victory in 1933, he was exposed to anti-Semitic harassment and expelled. "He left Frankfurt and Nahum lost contact with him after that."

Frankfurt. Anti-Semitism. The man at the train station. With the memory of mayor Landmann lurking in my subconscious, it made sense I sympathized with that man. It also made sense Oma would want to remember that turning point, when the molten-rock anti-Semitic volcano began spewing gaseous warnings heralding a separation between German and Jew was imminent.

Saddled with that memory, Oma must have known the expulsion of mayor Landmann was the beginning of the schism between her and the only man in her life beside Opa she ever loved. Just like Nahum wanted to protect Oma, she wanted to protect me. Only I didn't want to live a life under a claustrophobic protective umbrella not being able to be with someone I yearned to be with. It was a godsend Oma agreed to help.

***

When I last saw Paul, we ended on the agreement he'd come visit. I left him with train ticket money and an open invitation to come any Sunday before the Olympic Games ended. He said he would come but as the days moved beyond the first weekend after my visit to him, I worried it would not happen.

The following Sunday Max's barking and running along the fence line in the neighbor's backyard alerted me to a visitor. Paul? It must be Paul. I rushed to the bathroom mirror, releasing the knotted ribbon holding my hair back. A shake of my head and my wavy hair fell naturally to my shoulders. "Good. I like that look."

Max stopped barking. A knock came from the front door.

I pinched my cheeks to give them more color. Paul, I sang his name to myself. Paul... I nearly fell over when I opened the door and it was Gertrude.

"Surprise."

My disappointment must have drained the color from my cheeks.

"Aren't you going to invite me in?" She pushed forward into the entrance hall and arrogantly made her way to our kitchen. "Come on, what do you have to drink?"

"Gertrude." It took a minute for me to find my voice. "What are you doing here?"

As if not hearing my question she said, "Brigitte is busy making babies."

"What!" I stepped back watching Gertrude look in our refrigerator making a racket trying to find something to drink.

She pulled out a bottle of cold water. "This all you have?"

Gertrude dominated the conversation, not letting me get a word in edgewise.

She put the water back and closed the refrigerator door. "Where's the liquor?"

She was off to our dining room in search of the liquor cabinet, when I raised my voice. "Gertrude!"

"Don't yell at me." She testily smacked back.

To calm the mood she was in I slowed my speech. "Stop and talk to me."

"I need a drink."

"No, Gertrude. We're not drinking liquor." What happened with the no drinking and smoking rules that had been jammed into us? What happened to Gertrude? I wasn't about to challenge her, not with the state of mind she was in. I took hold of her arm and we sat at the dining room table. "Now tell me what's going on? What do you mean Brigitte's making babies?"

Her sentences came out in machine–gun delivery. "Brigitte's out being wooed by a handsome officer. My father forbids me to get involved with anyone he doesn't approve of. Said he'd find me the right man." Gertrude's lips puckered like she'd sucked on a lemon. "I want to find my own… he's too old–fashioned. I should turn him in and get my own guy."

"Turn him in? What are you talking about? Your father is a loyal Gestapo."

"I know… but he drinks and smokes and …"

"And what?"

"Leaves his briefcase unlocked."

I found that an odd thing to say since she relished snooping and gossiping about what she'd seen, acting all high-and-mighty she had important information. I bit down on my lip, holding my tongue, for something had her worked up and I doubted it was Brigitte making babies. Whatever it was, I wasn't sure I wanted to hear about it. I wished Oma wasn't out visiting a friend. When she's around Gertrude behaves.

When Gertrude started rambling on about what she'd seen in the briefcase, she confirmed it was something I should not be privy to. The earful she dished out was making me squeamish. It reinforced what I overheard the soldier say at the train station. Her ramblings used his exact words, "things would return to," but she filled in the rest.

I tuned in and out, thinking of Paul, fearful for him. Fearful for Jewish people, others deemed undesirable and those not in accord with the Führer. Anti-Semitic posters, windows with stars and slurs, and defacing Jewish property had all stopped but only until the Olympic Games were over. What I thought was the case but prayed I was wrong about turned out to be true. Gertrude had seen the directions in writing about the return to the overt policy to remove Jews from Germany.

Turns out her bad mood was over her father finding out she was snooping. Failing to mention his reaction, she told me his briefcase was now locked.

CHAPTER EIGHTEEN

"Oma, I have to go to him."

"You will do no such thing." She waved a finger in my face to make her point. "I can't agree to that."

"I have to warn him."

"Stop with the dramatics! Gertrude is up to no good. Stop listening to the rubbish she spreads around. Better yet stay away from her."

As if I had a choice. Gertrude has always been arrogant, pushing where she's not welcome and not caring. When we were younger and first became friends, I thought it gutsy. I even admired her gumption, saying and doing things I hadn't the nerve to do. That's no longer how I felt, not since the political climate changed and she changed with it for the worse. She was spoiled rotten and thought because her father's cousin was a bigwig and her father was in the Gestapo she could do whatever she wants.

"Oma." I plopped down on the living room couch next to her. "I have to do something."

"No you don't, Christa." She patted my hand. "No you don't."

"It's not fair."

"You're right, it's not. Nothing we can do about that."

I didn't like feeling helpless and after what I had heard, I desperately wanted to alert Paul. I picked at a pimple on my right temple drawing blood, not knowing what to do about Paul, refusing to let it go.

"Stop picking at your skin." She reached into her dress pocket and brought out a hankie. "Here." She motioned to my temple. As I wiped it with the cotton cloth she asked, "It's bothering you that much?"

Oma knew what it was to care about someone, not to sit by when help was needed. It went against her nature. She was struggling with my situation, fighting to do what was right but in a battle of two opposing wrong forces there is no right. No winner. If I went to him and Gertrude saw me that would raise a red flag. If I stayed put and he showed up with her stopping by again... I didn't want to think about that. I wished Gertrude would disappear.

Gertrude wasn't the only problem. She was a part of the whole dirty mess about to resurface when the disguises of friendly men in suits change back to military uniforms. Thinking about militaristic revenge directed at innocent citizens, the cogwheels in my brain were churning.

"Yes, Oma. It really is."

"He doesn't look Jewish. And Paul is a common Christian name."

That was unexpected. "I don't see what—"

"If he comes here, you tell him what happened with Gertrude. Tell him we will only say his first name and won't mention his last name or anything about him being Jewish. That he doesn't look Jewish is in his favor."

I thought about what she'd said. He did have wavy hair but then so did I. So does my brother. He also has a straight narrow nose. Just thinking about him coming lifted my doldrums, but... Why is there always a but? "What if she asks him questions?"

"You answer. Paul's a smart man, he'll catch on."

We had navigated our way through another skirmish. Oma was smart to bring up the supposition of him coming. Smart also with her answers. It gave me something to hold on to.

Days moved along and weekends came and went. Oma's constant reassurance to continue to give it time and not lose hope kept me going.

***

July brought warm days and nights that cooled. Playgrounds were filled with mothers and their young children while teenagers anticipating the Olympics were busy running, swimming, and involving themselves in other sports activities. Birds flitted from tree to tree, squirrels scavenged for food, and Germany was abuzz with preparations. My mother continued her visits to Berlin to be with my father.

Once home from working at the box factory, I listened for outside footsteps, for Max to bark, for a knock on the door or the doorbell to ring. Oma monitored me like a mother swan tending to her cygnets. I had gone off on my own to see Paul, telling her after-the-fact, which didn't go over well and she didn't trust me not to do it again. It hurt my feelings but it was my own fault. In meeting Paul and spending time with him, I knew I wanted more. I couldn't help how drawn I was to him. What would I do to achieve being with him and what were the consequences? Naively I didn't think they could be all that horrible therefore I decided if he didn't visit the next Sunday, I would go to him. With the Olympics being close, weekends with my parents gone would come to an end. I needed to act.

The next Sunday Paul didn't show up. Frustrated, I was resolute that the following Sunday I would make the trip back to him. That never came to pass for when my mother returned looking like a walking corpse accompanied by a nurse in a dark blue dress and white pinafore my world came tumbling down.

Oma met them at the door and escorted my mother and the nurse to my parents' bedroom shutting the door behind them. I ignored her effort to shut me out and barged in. "Mother."

She was non-responsive to my presence. Didn't so much as turn her head to look at me.

Oma inserted herself between us before I reached the bed. "You need to wait outside."

"No. She's my mother!" I looked around the side of Oma, who was trying to block the view of my mother staring into space, breathing shallowly, looking like the blood had drained from her face.

Oma clamped down on my arms and led me out while the nurse positioned a pillow behind my mother's head.

"Oma, what happened."

In the hallway, Oma said, "Wait here."

"Please, Oma. Is she dying?"

"No. Your mother is not dying. She's heavily sedated. I need to get back in there." Behind the closed door, metal on metal sounded. She had locked the door.

Up against the door, it was hard for me to make out what the nurse was telling Oma but what I was able to hear was something about my mother taking the ferry to Rügen then the words faded.

Rügen. Mother went to see Jürgen.

The nurse said a few words I couldn't make out before there was audible talk of medications for my mother. "She will be groggy while she's on the drugs but in three days I will wean her off." There were more instructions and indiscernible words, feet moving around the room.

What happened to Jürgen? Thinking the worst, my heart cracked like a tree struck by lightning. I tried the door knob but it was still locked. Oma must have heard the clicking sound for she was at the door a few seconds later. "Come in."

"What—"

Oma's weird look eyeing the nurse, signaling be careful with what you say, interrupted me. "Christa." She stopped to look at the uninviting square-shouldered nurse. "Frau Vogt will explain to you what you need to know. Do not ask questions."

Oma sounded like Frau Schmidt giving orders. That was so unlike her. My stomach twisted like a wrung dishrag when she told me to sit down and listen. I sat on the chair by my mother's vanity like a dog obeying commands.

"Frau Koch, we could use some tea in here." The nurse waited for Oma to leave then very matter-of-factly began. "I am Frau Vogt on loan from the Lebensborn Program to assist your mother. My orders come from high command and must be followed. You are most fortunate your father is a valued man or my visit here would be alone, without your mother. As for your father, Herr Pfundtner has ordered him to stay in Berlin through the Games. He cannot be disturbed or relieved of his function. Every effort must be made for the Reich to be successful."

Alone, without my mother? I thought of those words, feeling like someone had strangled the air out of my windpipe. And what exactly was my father's reaction? I was suffocating with questions, not understanding what had happened. Distracting me from my thoughts, Frau Vogt continued. "What I will tell you, I have already told your grandmother. You are both being informed in confidence and are not to repeat anything said here. Do you understand?"

Left with no option, I inclined my head.

"Good." The nurse then mentioned Oma would let the maid have time off while she was with us tending to my mother. She didn't want anyone other than my family present while she was here.

I stood there, mouth shut, trying to get air in through my nose.

She walked back and forth before me like a soldier marching. There was no preparation, no preamble to lessen the bomb she was about drop. "Your brother is dead."

I swallowed hard to speak, to be sure I heard her right. Nothing came out.

"I am against informing you of what I am about to say but I have been instructed to tell you. He has been euthanized. His earlier head injury deemed him mentally handicapped. Of no use to the Reich."

Stop talking! Stop your lies! My mind was active but nothing left my stone lips. I glanced over at my catatonic mother at last understanding her state. Her son had been murdered like an animal put down. I knew from my mother's unresponsiveness that what this creature before me said was true. My brother was dead. Whatever else she had to say was lost on me. There was no room left in my spinning head for more horror. No space in my cracked heart to embrace any more of her venin.

I wanted to strangle the life out of her, to do to her what was done to my brother, but I sat motionless not speaking a word, closing myself to her drone, until she mentioned my mother. "Your mother is fortunate to be alive. She had a very poor reaction to your brother's death and carried on contrary to what is expected of a German woman's proper behavior. As a favor to your father, she is here with you and has not been sent to a camp." She said something else to the effect that if there are any further protests against the regime by my mother there would be consequences. That also went for Oma and me, she said.

I bit down, swallowing the bile in my throat, pushing down the hatred rising. The news was bad enough but her commanding tone turned my shocked grief into unmitigated anger, anger I had to suppress.

"I will be here for a few days to ensure your mother is stable and comes out of her drug-induced state and behaves properly."

What she didn't say sent a chill through the room. There must have been an *or else* in that foul mouth of hers she didn't verbalize, for if my mother didn't behave, same for Oma and me, we would meet with extremely unpleasant circumstances. Of that I was sure.

Oma must have been at the door listening for she was ready with the tea minutes after the one-way conversation ended. Tea we could choke on as far as Frau Vogt was concerned.

The next few days felt like breathing molasses as I went to work and Oma stayed behind tending to Frau Vogt who hovered over mother like a hornet. On the fourth day, my mother woke out of her state but I would hardly say she woke up for she barely spoke and hardly made eye contact. The only emotion I saw in her was a stream of tears running down her cheeks the first time she seemed to take notice of my presence.

CHAPTER NINETEEN

Three days later on Thursday evening Frau Vogt left, leaving behind a residue of cruel words and devastated souls. The heartless woman had followed her orders. Orders! What good were they when they caused so much pain? I found no sensible logic that justified the harm infiltrating Germany, swarming around us like deadly bacteria.

Oma was fit to be tied, boiling over with frustration for being deprived of time and space to grieve what befell Jürgen. It shoved her into an angry, rebellious state. When Frau Vogt stepped through the front door and marched off, Oma's pressure valve burst open. Her lips curved into a snarled ball of resentment as she slammed the front door and turned to see me standing down the hall. "Come, Christa."

From the sound of her gruff, commanding voice, I feared Oma had taken Frau Vogt's follow-orders stand and was going to enforce it on me. Nothing could have been further from reality for when she went to sit on the brocade couch in the living room, she opened her arms for me to come to her. In her embrace, she softly told me we'd get through this. She also said, "I will not take this mess lying down."

I pulled back to look at her, sorrow mixed with hostility welled inside of me. "Oma." I froze and words couldn't break through the hardened cave I had crawled into.

"I know. I know." She kept repeating the words that acted like a torch to ice, beginning to crack me open. "Let it out, Christa. Then we'll talk."

I melted into my Oma's arms and cried my heart out.

She held me firm, not speaking. Allowing my tormented breaths to spasm against her. When I was emptied and my breathing slowed, she released her hold and moved back a trifle.

"What are we going to do, Oma?"

"Do?" Her lips raised ever so slightly, her eyes held a mischievous glint. The air was thick with revengeful energy as I listened to her tell me that on a shopping trip while Frau Vogt was here, she contacted a friend. A friend of hers, not a friend of the regime was how she put it.

Out of habit I looked to the door but Liddy wouldn't be returning until Monday. Oma, mother and I were the only ones home. My attention back on Oma, I listened as she told me about this friend, who had known Nahum. "He shall remain nameless but trust me when I tell you he's a reliable source of information on what is really going on behind the friendly propaganda."

What she had just said oddly perked me up but it was out of the ordinary for Oma to confide in me like she was doing. "Oma, why are you sharing this with me now?" Prior she'd been protective, close-lipped about her private dealings that young ears shouldn't know about.

"You need to know what's going on so you can protect yourself and not be lulled into something that will lead you astray."

Not being sure exactly what she meant I asked, "Like what?"

"Your talk of going to Paul for instance."

The mention of his name felt like a hand squeezing my heart.

Oma said it wasn't safe for me to go to him. "Frau Vogt's visit wasn't just about your mother."

The more she talked, the more the hand around my heart increased its grip, but I remained quiet listening to her tell me why I shouldn't go to Paul. Apparently my mother's trip to Rügen had placed her and our entire family under the microscope of suspicion. She had been in direct violation of high up orders when she got on the ferry to go to see Jürgen.

"Once the stone of doubt has been cast there's no undoing it. The nurse mentioned it was a favor to your father your mother wasn't sent to a camp."

I didn't know where she was heading with this conversation or what it had to do with Paul. Not until she told me we were probably under surveillance and if I was seen visiting a Jewish man in Friedrichshafen we'd all be sent to a camp.

"Your father doesn't have limitless favors. No one does and there are a few lines in the sand not to cross – where there is no redemption, where there are camps and death."

Death! That hit me like a ton of concrete. "What are you saying?" After the last week of bad news and even worse treatment to hear now I couldn't connect with Paul was too much. The room felt smaller, devoid of oxygen.

"You can't go to him."

A burning fury moved through me. I'd had enough. I refused to listen to more, to go along with Oma's mothering role now that my own mother was hardly functioning on her own. She needed Oma to assist her to the bathroom to clean herself, to dress and to eat. I was functioning well enough and didn't need Oma telling me what I could and couldn't do. My emotions got the best of me and I shot back, "You can't tell me who I can be friends with!"

"I'm not trying to."

"You just told me I can't go to Paul."

"Yes but I didn't say you can't be friends with him." She then told me she knew I'd insist on seeing him and what she had in mind was something other than my going to him at his house in Friedrichshafen, where he is known as a Jewish man. "We need to be very careful about what we do from here on."

She talked and I listened. The friend she received information from was in a fairly small group of German citizens opposed to the regime. Involved in low-key minimal overt resistance they weren't militant. A couple had infiltrated the regime as plants. That's how Oma's friend got his information.

She was smart to tell me what she knew because the knowledge helped me understand why it wouldn't be wise for me to go to Paul, which could endanger not just him and me but my entire family. Instead she had a plan to use her friend as a go-between. He was a businessman, who, like my father, freely traveled to Friedrichshafen among other places.

"He can relay oral messages from you."

That assuaged me, but only mildly for I wanted more than to send messages. I wanted to see him. To be with him. Before I opened my mouth to say what I'd just thought, Oma told me arrangements could be made for Paul to come to Ravensburg.

For the first time in days, I tasted the possibility something could be worked out especially with Oma and her friend helping. Further discussion pointed to the best time and place. Box factory on Sunday. With that, I told Oma to get a message to Paul to come Sunday, that I needed to see him. Time was of the essence for once the Games were over, it'd be harder to arrange.

Friday, I went to work while Oma tended to mother. As planned with Oma, I came home early to relieve her so she could visit her friend with my message. When she returned her rosy complexion had turned gray and she kept fidgeting with a button on her cardigan after she told me all went well.

Well? She looked troubled and that concerned me. "Oma are you feeling all right?"

"Me?" She twisted the button between her thumb and index finger pulling it off. "Don't you worry about me. I told you my friend will pass your message along."

"Oma." I gingerly prodded. "Did something happen? Is there something you're not telling me?"

"Christa. There are a lot of bad things happening out there." She looked out through the living room window. "A lot of things that young ears don't need to hear."

When and why did I revert to possessing young ears when a day ago I was adult enough to be let in on why I shouldn't go to Paul. Oma's selective choosing what was all right to say and what she shouldn't pass on didn't sit well with me. Out came my frustration. "I thought you were going to share things with me so I'd act more intelligently?" My sarcasm came out a little more grating than intended.

The infuriation she'd been holding in from whatever she'd just found out hit me between the eyes. "You asked. Here it is. Don't blame me if you have nightmares." Straining to keep her voice down, her neck veins bulged as she told me, "The handicapped aren't the only ones being euthanized. Undesirables are as well."

Undesirables, I thought of Paul. Jews were undesirable. Same with anyone going against the regime. They were being put to death! I gulped down the sob caught in my throat.

"That program Frau Vogt mentioned she was on loan from—"

"The Lebensborn Program?"

"Yes, you remember...children." Her voice grew gravelly and she fell into a fit of coughing.

I rushed off to get her a glass of water but when I'd returned her coughing had stopped and she waved it off. "What they are doing to children is despicable. Frau Vogt mentioned that one of her duties in the program involves work with a doctor. When children are found to be not racially valuable, she sends them to concentration camps."

Not racially valuable. My heart sank. The camps, a fate worse than death was what we at the BDM meetings had been told by Frau Schmidt to keep us in line. One of their scare tactics that worked. Were it not for the mishap with Jürgen and Arthur, the start of the debacle we lived, I'd probably be on board with Gertrude and Brigitte believing every piece of garbage they swallowed. "That's horrible."

"Yes it is and it's only going to get worse."

CHAPTER TWENTY

Friday night moved slowly. My mind was a rummage of conflicting emotions. Every titillating expectant thought concerning Paul came with oceans of tears for Jürgen, and that brought on more images, one particularly disturbing was of me holding a gun pointed at nurses in uniform ministering to innocent Aryan children. The world was upside down with those in power creating chaos while multitudes of Germans believed Germany would thrive without Jews and anyone else deemed unfit. My stomach cramped sending me to the bathroom to relieve myself.

I was doubled over in pain when I heard my mother walk down the hall calling Jürgen's name as if she was looking for him, thinking he was somewhere in the house. I had thought she'd been showing signs of improvement. She had seemed to watch my movements in her bedroom attentively, but when I recalled her actions more vividly, the way she had swayed her head smiling into space, I couldn't be sure of anything. Perhaps in the unreal place she seemed to exist in she was better off than me.

Hard as I tried to stop the barrage of mental images flooding my consciousness, I could no more control them than I could stop my heart from beating. But mixed in with the downside was good, and that was a saving grace. My lifesaver Oma. Paul. Other kindhearted people helping, like Oma's friend who'd delivered a message to Paul for me. That offered ample distraction to the uniforms in the streets.

As the sun streaked its orangish-yellow beam across the Saturday morning horizon, I awoke feeling better with tomorrow on my mind, the day Paul was to come to me. That feeling lessened on Sunday as trains arrived and there was no Paul. When I knew he wasn't coming, I asked Oma to repeat what her friend told her.

"The message had been delivered."

"Nothing else?"

"That's all."

I sank into a pit of despair. There was only one weekend left before the Olympics began, the clock was ticking and time was against me. So were my thoughts, like he's not interested, but my self-defeating thoughts always shifted to panic that when Games are over Paul will be rounded up. My desperation became all-consuming and I needed to help him.

"Oma, I need to send another message. I have a plan. I want to prepare a hiding place for him in the basement in the box factory and to tell him he must come to protect himself."

She whipped a hand across her chest. "You can't do that. Living that way with no fresh air, no sunlight and nothing to do eventually leads to rapid decline. It's worse than solitary confinement in prisons."

It's not worse than death, I thought, remembering what Paul mentioned about Dieter and his father. What he said about seeing Dieter after Bengle had been poisoned. The threats made to Nahum. I shivered thinking about what Dieter might do to Paul. I needed Oma on my side. I tried to convince her. "It could work. I've checked out all the areas and there's a bathroom in the basement no one ever uses. I could cover the door with a rack of supplies and equipment."

Oma knew about the bathroom with a rusted sink and stained toilet, and that it stopped being used when toilets and sinks were added to the main floor expansion.

"It could work," I repeated.

"No, Christa. It's one thing for him to come see you on a Sunday, but to hide him—"

"There's no one else to help him. If we don't, they'll find him. We have to do something!"

"Don't be melodramatic."

That last reply irritated me but I didn't want to say something that would alienate her. There was no time for that and I had to get her on my side. "There aren't many Jews in Ravensburg and like you said, Paul doesn't look Jewish. Who's going to suspect anything if they see him? He's my new beau from… we'll make up a story, that's if he's seen. Once he's out of sight in the bathroom, he can remain there until it's safe."

"Safe? And how long do you think that will be? Weeks? Months? You can't just hide him indefinitely. You can't take that on. It's way too dangerous. Not only for Paul, but also for our family and maybe even Herr König and the factory workers. Plus your mother will never go along with…" She caught herself, realizing there was no point bringing up my mother for only God knew how long she'd remain in her state.

To that I simply replied I felt the factory was a safe place and with mother not working I was taking on more functions. "Herr König leaves me alone to do my job. He's a good man, Oma. You know that. He shouldn't be a problem." I reiterated no one uses that bathroom and staff rarely go down to the basement anymore as most of the daily-use storage had shifted to the shelves at the back of the main floor.

"He is a good man. He stepped up and took care of his children when his wife died." Oma looked wistful as she recounted the story of how his wife had a healthy baby girl and a day later a clot dislodged from her uterus and moved to her lungs killing her instantly.

"That was a long time ago." I recalled how he'd bring his boy and girl around for factory Christmas celebrations.

"They are grown with their own families now." The forceful stance she held moments earlier shifted as she pensively took a minute to herself. "You are right, Christa."

"Right?"

"To want to help Paul."

Did remembering Herr König's loss soften her? Did Oma in her contemplation think about what had happened to Nahum? Perhaps she changed her mind because she didn't want to see what happened to him, a man she loved, happen to his son. "Are you telling me you're all right with him hiding there."

"Yes and no. I'm not in favor of it but I can't fault you for your feelings and wanting to help another human being even though it is extremely risky. Plus, how will you handle your father?"

"I won't tell him. When he's home he never goes to the factory."

"Hmm." Oma put her hand to her chin, lost in thought. "That's not a good idea."

"I don't disagree with you but what other options are there?"

"Christa, this is getting… it's too much. Way too dangerous." With each word of protestation she raised her voice.

"Stop reminding me how dangerous it is. I know it's dangerous but I don't know how I can live with myself if I sit back and do nothing to help him. What if the tables were turned?"

Again, she gave the matter some thought. Her history with Nahum made it hard for her to maintain a strict stance like she had in other situations. This with Paul hit too close to home and Oma simply couldn't put and keep her foot down. Under her breath, she said, "I hope I don't live to regret this. You do what you have to do but be careful."

"So you'll relay the message to your friend?"

"Yes."

"Please don't forget to have him include directions to the factory."

***

Sunday, July 26, only five days until the Games began and I was a nervous wreck. My message had been delivered with no response from Paul in return. Will he come or was I wrong about the connection I felt? Did I mistake how intimate it seemed when he opened up to me about the cruelty inflicted on Bengle? When he confided in me about Dieter? Was

I making a fool of myself going after him? I rubbed my throbbing temples willing myself to stop obsessing over Paul. Impossible.

The factory was a few long streets from our house, a decent distance to walk and my neighbor Frau Weber was pleased I offered to walk Max for the weekend, being that her husband was away and she couldn't manage walking the big dog on her own. I had the Sunday train arrival times memorized and knew how long it would take to get to the factory from the station. Not wanting to draw attention to myself, I had planned on walking Max for his normal twice-a-day outings, one after his midafternoon feeding and the other at night to correlate with the last train's arrival.

With some bread, boiled potatoes and water in my rucksack to give to Paul, I headed out with Max, who took his time–three steps forward before stopping to sniff the ground and bushes. Nose to the ground his snout wiggled and his tail went wild.

"Come on, boy." I tugged the leash to unglue his nose from the edge of the sidewalk next to a patch of grass that must have held scents left from other dogs and critters. He was onto something good and wasn't moving until his nostrils got their fill.

An elderly man with his German shorthaired pointer, a handsome dog with its sleek black and white roan coat and long slim body, was headed in our direction. Max's head shot up from the patch of grass he'd been sniffing, his tail picked up speed, and with uncontrolled excitement he pulled me over to them. The whining and barking dance began as Max hopped like a hare encircling the other dog who obediently greeted him with his hindside.

"Nice day for a walk," the man said. "All the better with a dog."

"Yes."

"I'm delegated to dog duty with the wife and children in Berlin visiting family. Awaiting the Games."

I didn't want to mention my father was there or engage in any personal conversation to draw attention to myself so I simply responded to the man's lead. "How nice for them. I guess nice for us as well to spend time with the dogs." I leaned down to pet his dog and discreetly pull Max away. When I stood separating the dogs, I told the man to have a nice walk and moved on.

When we arrived at the box factory I had hoped Max's intense sniffing and tugging on the leash meant he had sensed Paul's presence. No such luck. Crestfallen, we headed back.

CHAPTER TWENTY-ONE

Max's nighttime walk was faster. Not having the patience to wait for him to sniff every few steps, I kept the pace moving along at a rapid clip, rucksack in place. Max was a good boy heeling beside me until we approached the factory and he began whimpering and tugging on his leash.

"What is it, boy? You smell a squirrel?"

He pulled me around the side of the building that backed on a field covered in trees, bushes and other foliage making it hard to see if anyone was present. I heard what sounded like crunching leaves. A wisp of light from the crescent moon illuminated a rustling bush, and I stepped back to put distance between Max and whatever was lurking out there.

I'd seen an owl out in that field with a mouse in its talons. It gave me the creeps, the idea of the owl stalking and catching the prey, turning a living creature into a meal. I wasn't naïve about nature's laws and owls being opportunistic feeders but still it bothered me.

I grabbed hold of Max's collar and held tight waiting for the movement to stop, thinking of what I'd been taught and heard about the Nazi push for animal welfare. How could Hitler want to rid the world of Jews yet takes measures to ensure animals were protected? It was appalling animal hunting was banned, yet Nazis hunted down humans deemed lower than animals.

Random images sprang up and a surge of nostalgia moved through me as I thought of my brother, who I dearly missed for he understood my sensitive disposition. Of the two of us, he was the brave one. Like Max, Jürgen was a good teacher. He was brave when it came to being a friend and it pained me he lost his life for doing what I felt was a display of courage.

A bush rustled. Max jerked the leash. A muffled masculine cough sounded. My pulse sped. Could it be Paul? I waited but whoever coughed didn't move. I hadn't planned for this and I wasn't sure what to do so I whistled. If it wasn't Paul, I'd pretend I was whistling for my dog. Still nothing so I tied Max to a post and cautiously made my way into the field.

A cloud moved over the moon and everything turned dark. Eerie. I licked my dry lips, puckered and whistled again. Back came a trace of a whistle. The clouds moved and a centimeter of light broke through, but not enough to lighten my way. I waited for there to be just enough light to make my way safely to where the movement and sound came from.

My heart felt like it was going to explode from my chest when I saw him. Paul was crouched down on the ground and what I could see of him looked awful. He weakly raised a thin arm to me, trying to articulate something through his chapped lips.

I handed him the aluminum thermos I had in my rucksack. "Take some sips."

Once he was able to utter sensible sounds, he said, "I'm sorry."

He kept repeating that and wouldn't listen when I told him not to be and I wanted him to come. "I'm glad you're here, Paul. Now let's get you into my mother's factory."

He was wobbly on his feet, leaning on me as we made our way to get Max and head into the factory. I locked the door and secured Max to a table upstairs while I used a flashlight kept by the door to assist Paul down to the basement bathroom. Once I flipped on the bathroom light and got a good look at him, I felt sick. His clothes hung on him and his once rounded cheeks were now concave stressing his cheek bones. His skin was sallow and flaky. He needed hydration and nourishment. How he made it here on the train without being stopped or picked up was nothing shy of miraculous. He said he pretended to be reading a newspaper to cover himself, but still, this was not something I wanted to risk again.

"This isn't much but you should be fine here." I motioned to several pillows and blankets on the floor, and told him to sleep there until I could come up with something better. "The sink has not been used in a long time so it doesn't look too good but I ran the water and it's clean enough so you can use it to bathe."

He slid down atop the pillows and looked up at me. "It's perfect, Christa. You are an angel."

I didn't want to leave but had no choice. "Paul, I need to get Max back or his owner will worry." I gave him the food I brought. "You have enough food and water in the thermos to last a day. I'll bring more food and refill the thermos tomorrow night. I'll be without Max so we can catch up."

"I don't know how to thank you."

"You came. That's all I need."

Out the bathroom door I remembered something so I stuck my head back in. "Don't flush the toilet or run the sink unless you're with me and I tell you it's all right. For tonight you're safe, no one's here, but there are nights when Herr König and some of the staff work late." Responding to his puzzled look, I told him Herr König was the foreman.

He nodded he understood he needed to keep quiet.

I locked the door and moved a large rack filled with easy to move items against it then made my way upstairs to Max. I had him back to his concerned owner in ten minutes.

"I was getting worried about you." Hand on her hips, Frau Weber gave me a look like she suspected I was up to something. I disabused her of that notion when I told her Max took a long time to do his stuff and I was sorry to have worried her.

Back home, Oma was also concerned. "Well?"

"He's here!"

Out of habit, Oma told me to lower my voice even though Liddy wasn't there and my mother took sleeping pills to sleep at night. "And?"

She rubbed the side of her face red as she listened to me relay the night's events. There must have been a ton of things stuffed into that head of hers but it was late and she simply told me to go and try to get a good night's sleep. As if either of us would.

Morning couldn't come fast enough and once washed, dressed and fed, I packed my rucksack with a few items of Jürgen's clothes along with more drinking water and food–brown bread and three boiled potatoes– and rushed out the door, leaving Oma and Liddy to tend to mother and the house. On the way to the factory, I walked past Herr Meier's kiosk noticing the headlines on the papers, mostly all relating to the Games but something else on the front page caught my eye. Titled *Hitler Sends Planes to Support Spanish Nationals*, the following short, one-paragraph article mentioned twenty-six transport planes and other equipment had been sent to support the Nationalist side of the Spanish Civil War. I wondered what else was going on not being reported.

"Good morning, Herr Meier."

His round cheeks puffed out into a pleasant smile. "Off to work early?"

"Yes. Busy time." Why did I say that? When all of Germany was slowing down readying for sitting before radios in a few days why did I have to say something like that? I had to get ahold of my jumpiness and act normal. Speak normal.

I moved on, arriving at the box factory later than I wanted to, perturbed I wasn't the first one there. I didn't want to chance checking on Paul until the factory was empty therefore I would have to wait until everyone was gone for the day, which could be well into the evening.

The machinery making boxes buzzed while workers assembled orders for shipping. Everything was running smoothly, the staff were jovial, some singing while others hummed to the sounds of items moving along the assembly line. I went to the office to check in with Herr König and hang my rucksack on the hook. The bag was heavy and snapped the hook off the wall.

"Are you packing for a getaway?" Herr König joked.

"I wish. I would love to go to Berlin to see my father." I rambled on a few minutes while fumbling to reattach the hook and placing my bag under my desk.

"Everyone wants to be in Berlin. Just four more days."

"Yes."

"My neighbor purchased a radio and invited me over to listen to the Games." Herr König then told me it's the first time the Games were being televised by what was called closed-circuit television to over two dozen halls in Berlin and the Olympic Village. He was very chatty and continued on about reading an article on the new 100,000-seat track and field stadium.

His words led me to think of my father, madly involved in the final touches and preparations. My father in the city where the illusion of civility and tolerance reigned and my mother's dreams were shattered.

"That's very nice you'll listen on your neighbor's radio." I looked at the wall clock, my attention on the noise coming from the workers in the factory. Over nine hours to go and fingers crossed the place would empty. Up until that day I hadn't minded the ten-to-twelve-hour workday for I enjoyed what I was doing. That day my feelings changed. That day I appreciated the opposition to the long hours, six days a week. That day I understood the rumblings of protest from workers wanting to restore pre-Nazi rights.

The hours chugged along. Five more to go. I did some filing and paid bills. Three more to go. When the clock hit six and the workers left and Herr König cleared off his desk, I let out a sigh of relief. The day had passed uneventfully and I couldn't wait to lock up and check on Paul.

CHAPTER TWENTY-TWO

Paul stood with his arms out to me like a wounded child needing a parent, vulnerable and scared. What had he been through, I thought, locking the door behind me and going to him. In his arms, his body felt like an overworked engine with heat pouring from it. His chest was damp, his arms clammy.

"I'm here, Paul. You're safe."

His arms tightened around my waist. "Thank you, Christa."

It was hard to make out his words that were sounded through frightened whispers, mere wisps upon my cheek.

"Paul, you're trembling."

"I'm all right, just cold."

The room was warm and his body was hot, what wasn't he saying? The tension in the muscles in his arms and back belied his words.

"Let's sit." I moved back from him and lowered myself to the rumpled makeshift bed on the floor, pillows covered in stains of sweat. When he got down beside me I asked what had happened since I last saw him.

He looked at the door.

"It's closed, locked, and so is the upstairs factory. Just us here."

His eyes stayed fixed on the door.

"Other than me, Herr König is the only one who has a key to the factory and he's gone home with everyone else."

He lowered his head and spoke to the floor. "I don't know where to begin."

"Begin wherever you want. Say what you need to." I wanted him to open, to find the words to release the choked up sounds strangled in his throat but knew I had to give him time. Patience wasn't one of my virtues so the longer I sat there waiting for him to say something, anything, the more my stomach knotted yet I waited, rubbing my index finger against my thumb.

"First my father." A long pause followed with sniffing and wiping his face with the back of his hand. "The harassment. Losing his shop. More harassment. He feared more for my life than his and I am sure that's what ultimately killed him. His heart couldn't take it."

The air in that small bathroom felt thick, hard to breathe as I listened to him continue to pour his heart out.

"I saw things get better. You know, cleaning up slurs against us." The way he said us made me feel he didn't want to mention the word Jew. "Then I heard about a couple of thugs who picked on Jewish women on the streets with their children. One a small baby in a perambulator. The bullies tripped the mother and tipped the pram over. "Ran off laughing something about the woman being clumsy."

My hands turned into fists as I continued listening to him.

"I knew her. A good woman who gave so much to others. She and her husband waited years to have a child. Of all the people to pick on and one of the bullies, a young boy who couldn't be older than twelve, knew the mother. Knew she was a good woman. You didn't have food, she'd share the little she had." Paul's breathing sped like he was sprinting.

"That's awful." I stretched out my cramped hand, stiff from fisting it so tightly I cut off circulation, and reached for Paul's.

"Yes. I couldn't sit by hearing what had happened, not just to her but also others. Four instances were all I heard about but how many others had been harassed?" He turned to look at me but his cloudy eyes held a sullen faraway look. "I went after them. Got into a fistfight with one of them. Broke his nose. Dieter heard about it."

As he told me what happened, he actively motioned with a hand. It was then I noticed several of his nails were singed. My heart felt like it was going to race out of my chest. I tried to steady my shaking hands.

"Hell-bent on revenge, he came with a couple of his friends and set my house on fire. While I was asleep. I awoke to see them running away. I made it out with a little food and the money you gave me for train fare." He then said he hid out in a wooded area for several days until getting word the local police calmed the situation, handled the thugs according to orders to keep a lid on anti-Semitic disruptions until the Olympic Games ended. "I waited until dark to purchase a ticket for the last train on Sunday."

Lacking the aliveness he possessed the first time I met him, Paul looked as glum as the situation he'd briefly described.

"You made it. Everything will be all right now." The words were out before I could think of what I was saying. After all he'd been through, what we'd both been through, we both knew nothing would be all right. Not out there under the curtain of what the preparation for the Games was hiding and not in here in a bathroom hidden behind a rack of equipment in a box factory.

"I'd like to believe that."

My hand moved to my neck, to my good luck charm. "Here." I reached around to undo the clasp and handed him my necklace.

"What's this for?" He looked at the coiled chain and pendant in the palm of his hand.

"For good luck."

"I can't take your necklace."

"If it weren't for you, I wouldn't be wearing it. I want you to have it. Keep it in that pocket." I pointed to the one over his heart. "Better..." I reached into my rucksack, pulled out the few items of clean clothing I brought for him, and handed him a shirt. "You can put the necklace in this."

"Your brother's?" His eyes teared.

"Yes."

He closed his hand around my necklace and leaned over to kiss my forehead. His chapped lips felt warm on my skin. "As long as you reclaim it whenever you want, I accept."

While I was taking the food and water I'd brought for him out of my rucksack, he put the necklace in his pocket keeping a hand over his chest, the other on Jürgen's shirt on his lap. He looked down at my brother's shirt. "I'll have a wash later and put it on."

I stayed with him while he ate the bread and potatoes I brought and washed it down with water from the refilled thermos. "Won't Herr …" He hesitated, wrinkling his brow as if trying to remember a name.

"Herr König?"

"Yes, the foreman. Won't he get suspicious with your staying late?"

I thought about how kind Herr König had been to me since learning about mother's debility, commenting he thought I was staying late to lose myself in busyness to avoid going home and getting depressed. He knew me well, my likes and aversions. I appreciated his fatherly manner for he was a wonderful father to his children and me out of habit. I didn't mind him wanting to take me under his wing.

"No, Paul, he understands why…" I hadn't wanted to tell him about my mother and why Herr König felt I was staying late but with this slipping out, I didn't want Paul to feel I was not sharing something. I had encouraged him to open and felt I owed him the same so I told him about what happened to Jürgen and the state my mother was in as a result of the shock.

Paul put down the thermos he was sipping from and drew me to him. Words failed us as we held on to each other, our chests moving like waves on an ocean.

The following days repeated with everyone leaving before me, my locking up and bringing food and water to Paul. By Thursday, Olympic fever was at a high pitch as athletes and visitors arrived. Herr König and the factory staff, caught up in the fervor for the Games, left as soon as they could to rally around radios to hear the latest news about dignitaries and teams from various countries arriving along with celebrities.

Also by Thursday, Paul had settled in and looked more rested. He was tolerating the small, enclosed space better than I expected and didn't let an opportunity slip by when he didn't express his gratitude for our friendship.

Our friendship? Having been in his embrace and heating when his lips touched my skin, I wanted more. I wanted to live in a world where a German and a Jew could love each other and share that love openly in public. I told Paul if he were ever discovered to just say he's my beau. And to only mention his first name which is a common Christian name. I also thought about what Oma mentioned concerning Paul not looking Jewish and that it could keep him out of harm's way. "Who would question it? You don't look Jewish."

He pulled back, shoulders hyperextended, and took offense with my comment, mentioning the stereotypical faces drawn on posters with exaggerated noses and frizzy hair. One showing a rabbi with German citizens dangling from his mouth. "I don't look like the obscene version of a Jew?" He must have seen the hurt in my eyes when he blasted that at me for he quickly said, "I'm sorry. You mean to help and I—"

"I understand." I said that but wondered did I? How could I, a German girl, possibly know what he, a Jew, felt? I knew the feel of loss and pain but I didn't know persecution, not personally. How do I address the division between us? Tell the truth with loved ones for their hearts will understand, that was the answer I learned from Oma. "Actually, I don't know that I really understand. All I know is I care about you and want to help."

The tension he'd been holding in his shoulders appeared to ease. "You are helping, more than I can ever thank you for. What you said about my not looking Jewish. It struck a nerve. I'm sorry I lashed out at you."

I held out my hand accepting his apology. "Friends?"

He took hold of my hand and leaned in close, his lips against my hair. I turned my head and our lips met. In that sweet union I transcended everything that was wrong in Germany.

CHAPTER TWENTY-THREE

The buildup to the opening ceremonies spread through cities, towns and villages, large and small, and for citizens too poor to own a radio the newspapers provided them with coverage of the events. Anyone who dared to threaten and tarnish the Nazi's promotion of Germany being a strong and united country was hauled into prison or worse. Oma got word from her friend that a couple of dissidents slamming the façade–the cover-up that anti-Semitism was not an issue–were hauled away. God only knows where they landed. I couldn't get into the thrill buzzing through the streets as teams from over forty nations arrived, not while I was hiding Paul, not while I knew that no matter the presentation of a civil country, Germany under the Nazi rule was anything but civil. I knew about the abuses directly from Paul and indirectly from Oma, and instead of my arms jubilantly waving about, butterflies had taken residence in my stomach.

Lack of a good night's sleep had become a problem and I felt and looked worn down. Also because I hoarded some of my food to bring to Paul, I had lost weight I couldn't afford to lose. Although I felt it was a small sacrifice to keep him safe, Oma didn't agree and any goodwill she felt about my sheltering Paul was running thin.

"You need to find him another place to shelter." Oma began the day saying what she'd said every morning since Paul's arrival. She didn't let me forget that in a short time when the Games were over my father would return.

Find another place. How was I supposed to do that? "I am not sending him away." I dug my heels in.

"Christa—"

"Oma. Please. I don't have anywhere to send him. Nor do I know anyone who could help. Even if I did, I don't want to cast him out."

"Your mother is responding to me and if she gets better and returns to work what then? She won't keep it from your father."

"I don't think she'll find out. I'm being very careful."

"You think you're being careful but staying late every night is not normal for a girl your age. Herr König or another staff member will grow suspicious and that won't be kept from your father."

My belly cramped. "Has he said anything to you?"

"Not yet but once he's not preoccupied with all the fuss over the Games…" She didn't need to complete her sentence, stating the obvious.

Why had Oma changed from her earlier receptivity? Did she know something she wasn't telling me? Afraid to ask, I had to know. "You were all right with him coming here to begin with. I don't understand why you keep harping on me now that he needs to be moved."

"I was never all right with it and told you as much. I accepted you wanted to help him. For now. But seeing you come in late every night… look what you look like." She pulled my blouse up from my skirt to make her point. "You've lost weight and I see from the light on in your room in the middle of the night you're not sleeping well."

"It's just the first week, Oma. It'll get better now that I have a routine down."

She shook her head like she does when I'm being stubborn. I suspected a part of her, the part that felt guilty over what had happened to Nahum, kept her from saying more. She raised her arthritic hand to my cheek and her warm deformed fingers stroked my skin.

"I promise I'll be cautious, Oma."

Her eyes grew bloodshot and watery as she simply nodded.

***

On my Friday night visit to Paul, he was in the clothing I had brought. Taller and thinner than Jürgen, the shirt fit in the chest but rose up above his wrists so he rolled up the sleeves exposing his flaccid biceps. He told me it was fine and as for the pants a little excess material around the waist wasn't a problem.

"There's plenty more. My mother has kept my brother's things." A sorrowful draft moved up my spine. I needed a minute to let it pass. "Is there anything else you'd like me to bring?"

Paul's face empathetically softened, his lips loosened, as he motioned to the clean shirt and pants. "This is more than enough."

There was still a small bar of soap, enough to last him for several more days, but the towels needed cleaning. "The dirty towels need to be washed." As I reached for them, he stopped me.

"What will your cleaning woman say when she sees this?" He held up a filthy towel.

"I'll tell her I was gardening."

"No, Christa. You can't do that." His words were feeble, his eyelids dropped. "I don't want you to get caught in a lie and get in trouble. I can't allow that."

Earlier thoughts I'd had about not trusting what Liddy, a Hitler loyalist, would do if under pressure sank below an opaque web of denial. "I won't get in trouble. Liddy minds her own business and doesn't pry. She loves me."

"She may love you but she'll protect herself if she has to. Families are turning on families."

"You don't know her. How can you even talk about someone you don't know?"

"Christa." He shifted a pillow aside and moved closer to me on the floor where we'd been sitting. "I don't have to know this Liddy to know how people react. I've seen what people will do to protect themselves and it's not nice."

Paul yanked me out of my denial. I looked at the dirty towels, remembering the girl in my group who turned in her brother, and my certainty slipped away like tides receding. "You're right. How can I really know what Liddy or anyone would do? All I know is what I feel."

"How do you feel?" He inched closer, his body radiating a soothing warmth, his lips nestled on my neck.

"I really—"

"You don't need to say anything." He reached for my face, turned it to his, and gently put his lips on mine. Hungrily his mouth opened and he passionately kissed me. I never wanted the moment to end.

That night, I floated back home and when Oma saw me, she knew something was different. She didn't utter a word.

The next day, to musical fanfare the Führer arrived at the Olympic Stadium. Herr König was at his neighbor's house listening on the radio while the rest of the factory staff sat with their families gathered around other radios. Oma had the radio in our living room on and for a while I listened to the commotion, the announcement of hundreds of athletes marching into the stadium during the opening day regalia, the lone runner arriving bearing a torch by relay from the site of the Ancient Games in Olympia, Greece.

As the crowd roared and cheered, I thought of Paul, and my soul soared like an eagle.

CHAPTER TWENTY-FOUR

The next week while the regime soft-pedaled its anti-Semitic propaganda and bedazzled foreign visitors and journalists at the Games, my visits with Paul continued. With food I brought news of the Games, what Oma told me from listening to the radio. The schedule at the factory slowed only to get orders out on time, and other than that staff were allowed time off to follow the Games. It brought ease to the atmosphere in the basement bathroom where Paul had become restless.

"The upstairs door is locked?" He asked to reassure himself it was safe for him to leave the bathroom to stretch his legs.

"Yes."

Hesitant at the open door, he craned his neck to look at me standing at his side motioning for him to go on out. "I don't know."

"I'm sure no one else is here." I moved past him and directed my flashlight around the dark room. "Look." Boxes, old and broken equipment parts, cleaning supplies and other various items shone under the waving light.

Paul stepped out and stretched his arms and legs then followed me to a worn wooden table and bench where we sat. He reached for my hand, intertwining his fingers with mine, and asked about the Games. I told him the Führer had been jubilant about our teams doing well and capturing medals.

"Had been?" Paul was quick to pick up on my choice of words, on how my monotone voice lilted.

"Oma heard from a friend who returned from Berlin that Hitler wasn't pleased with an American black athlete who upstaged the German athletes by winning several gold medals in track and field."

"Really." Paul snickered.

"She said Hitler declined to congratulate anyone after the first day because of the American athlete. Supposedly, he was advised to treat all the athletes equally."

"I can see him fuming over that. I bet—" Paul stopped himself when he heard a creaking sound coming from the ceiling followed by a metallic bang. In a panic he rushed back to the bathroom, shut the door, and turned off the light, leaving me to move the rack over it and check out the noise. I tiptoed to the stairs and waited at the landing on the bottom for any more sounds. Nothing. The place was quiet.

I moved cautiously up the dark steps, slowly placing one foot down after another. Up at the door, I listened with my ear flush to its wooden surface. Again nothing. Noiselessly inhaling and exhaling I waited a couple more minutes before opening the door, and when I did the joists let out a popping vibration. It's just the building settling, I thought, remembering what Herr König had mentioned to me another time when the noise startled me. To be sure, I went to check if the front door was still locked. Satisfied no one had entered and we were safe, I returned to Paul.

I turned on the light, illuminating the room to see Paul sitting on the floor, arms wrapped around his knees up to his chest. "Building noise." I explained what I remembered and reaffirmed we were the only two in the building.

His biceps contracted, he didn't look reassured. "I think we better let it be for tonight."

The air between us filled with unspoken dread. I wanted Paul to reach for me, to hold me, but he was too wrapped up in holding himself, keeping his body from trembling. What held me back from reaching for him I'll never know for sure. I stood there watching him cowering on the floor, and I couldn't move beyond the emotional barrier he erected.

I ignored my gut telling me he needed time to himself, to leave him alone, when I asked, "Can I sit with you a while longer?"

"Not tonight, Christa."

I longed to tear down the unpassable boundary he placed between us. "Paul. Please don't shut me out."

He sat silently, arms still around his flexed knees, head down.

"Please." I took a small step forward but when I saw his back tense I stopped. "Do you really want me to leave?"

Another long silent pause from him then he finally turned his head to look up at me. "No. I'd like to be with you forever, but we can't."

I reached a hand toward him. He pulled back, shriveling. It hurt that my affectionate gesture created that reaction in him. "Please talk to me."

"It's no good, Christa."

He didn't allow me to get a word in before he told me he needed to be alone. Alone, I replayed, my body feeling like it was being squeezed by a vise. As I stood there a few more minutes, hoping he'd snap out of whatever he'd sunk into, the room grew cold. Any warmth we'd earlier shared had been eaten away by the oppressive monster looming on the horizon.

"I'll be back tomorrow. I hope you get some rest tonight." I ached to tell him how much I cared about him, what he meant to me and no matter the risk of sheltering him, to me it was worth it. He was worth it. I wanted to penetrate the fortress he hid behind but felt it best to let him be for now.

***

When I arrived home and heard my mother calling to me from the living room, I went into shock and dropped my rucksack. There she was sitting on a chair facing the door to the hallway, waiting like she had so many other nights before when I'd been out late. She had been improving but it was a slow process and the last thing I expected was to see her sitting there looking like a worried mother, the muted wavering tone gone from her voice. She sounded strong, looked present, and tapped her foot on the wooden floor—all the normal mannerisms of my mother before she descended into oblivion.

"Mother." I went to her, the initial shock from the blast of her calling my name receding. Unsure, I didn't know how to address this change in her. For days after she found out about Jürgen she forlornly paced, her depressed state inching away slowly in tiny steps so this strong-willed, shoulders erect woman now sitting before me was remarkable. It was also problematic for how was I to explain my late arrival home.

Had she spoken with Oma? I had to find out before I said the wrong thing and she caught me in a lie. "I need to go to the bathroom." I fibbed, hurrying off to go to Oma's room but before I could get through the door my mother raised her voice.

"One minute, young lady!"

A spasm of anxiety hit my abdomen. As I turned to face her, an odd mixture of emotions moved through me. I was relieved my mother had snapped out of the trance she'd been living in, but with her alertness came gut-wrenching worry over what this would mean for Paul when she returned to the factory.

"Can I just take a minute to—"

"Christa, come here." As if reading my mind, she told me she had spoken with Oma and knew what was going on.

I sat in the chair next to her, pushing my hands against its sides to steady them. My head was a whirlwind of thoughts trying to imagine what they talked about and how I would answer. Not sure what to say and not wanting to divulge something Oma might have held back, I asked, "What do you mean?"

"Don't play games with me. I know about the Landmann boy."

My reactivity took over throwing any well-thought-out logical response out the window. "He's not a boy," I muttered, instantly feeling stupid that was the first thing out of my mouth. I was on the defensive, and by the stern look my mother gave me I knew it wouldn't get me anywhere. The only thing left to do was what Oma had encouraged me to do when backed into a corner with my parents, tell the truth. Her words, don't dig yourself in deeper with untruths that can turn into a bigger mess, resonated.

There was no doubt my mother was back. Lucid as ever as she sat there not taking her eyes off mine waiting for me to respond.

I broke down in tears and told the truth.

CHAPTER TWENTY-FIVE

My mother shot up out of her seat and took hold of my arm leading me to Oma's room. "We're going to have a talk." My mother glared at Oma then me. Back to her old self, she meant business. "No more nonsense. Do you both hear me." She stomped to Oma and put a hand on her shoulder. "Look at me. I mean it. We can't afford your sympathies with—"

"That's quite enough!" Oma tossed my mother's hand from her shoulder and stood to face her. "I will not have you treating me like some impertinent child. I am your mother and I will favor who I please and act as I will in a kindhearted manner. I suggest you consider doing the same right here and now."

Oma ranted and my mother turned crimson. I stepped to them and apologized for putting them at odds with each other, feeling horrible to see them fighting like that. My apology fell on deaf ears for they both needed their rants, to offload what had been eating away at them. For months my mother held in her agonized concern over Jürgen's fate only to discover his demise. For as long a time, Oma grieved over the loss of Nahum only to find out he had died before she let him know how she felt. Compounding that loss for Oma was Jürgen's death and my mother's collapse. Now faced with the unpleasant choice of what to do with Paul, their emotions exploded.

I didn't want my mother to relapse. I didn't want Oma to be stricken down by a broken heart. There beside them I put an arm around each of their backs. "Please stop fighting." I wept and begged them to stop, feeling the moisture of their clothing sticking to my hands.

My mother stepped back and went to sit on the edge of Oma's bed. I joined her. Oma sat in a chair facing us.

"He has to go." The anger had left my mother's tone and her voice sounded weak and unconvincing.

"You can't put him out in the street, Inge."

When Oma addressed my mother with loving conviction, her wrinkled face softening, my mother broke down. She cried and cried, the tears she hadn't been able to shed for Jürgen. What she must have encountered in Rügen that shocked her into a near catatonic state. She cried and released and when she emptied the room grew silent. Too silent until the void was filled with her commenting. "What are we going to do?"

"Nothing." I found my voice. "Let him stay. Rarely does anyone go down there plus there's very little military presence in Ravensburg."

"Christa, he can't stay. It puts us at risk of—" She puffed out a shallow breath.

"Mother please listen to me. We can't put him out. He'll be killed."

"Your mother is right, Christa," Oma said. "He needs to go. I have expressed how I feel about his living for long underground. It can be nothing more than a temporary arrangement. We mustn't lose sight of how vulnerable this makes him. Think of his health. His well-being. We simply must—"

"Please." I didn't want to hear it. I didn't want to entertain the idea of setting him free only to have Dieter or some Jew-hungry soldier kill him. I couldn't explain that to them for fear they'd both insist that increased the overall danger to us of keeping him there. I stood and moved around the room, banging my feet on Oma's carpet. Dust particles flew into the air, circling like a cloudy weather front. "If he goes, I'll go with him."

Oma clapped her hands to get my attention. "Enough of that kind of talk." Her eyes and cheeks dropped. "Your mother doesn't want to lose you."

That got through to me. The whole darn situation was about loss. Who we had lost and who we were afraid to lose. In the semblance of clarity I was able to muster I told them what I needed to say, what was all that mattered to me in that moment. "I love him. He can't go. You'll be throwing him in the streets to his death."

"This is no easy matter." My mother sounded sympathetic, understanding the difficulties of both sides but ultimately she opted for the safety of our family when she repeated, "He has to go. You have up until your father arrives home to move your young man."

"That's only three days." I sank back down on the bed and with my head in my hands, repeated, "I don't know what to do." Once again I pleaded with my mother, then Oma, to please be reasonable, to please let him stay. I felt hopeless trepidation remembering how despondent Paul acted the last time I saw him.

Oma's attempt to soften the blow fell flat when she said, "You have three days. Your mother isn't telling you to kick him out now."

My core was torn asunder. What more was there to say? I lumbered to my room and spent the rest of the night tossing and turning, then up at my window looking at the expanse of Ravensburg. Gone was its glittering beauty that used to ignite me. Gone was everything in me that felt alive and happy.

The next morning I had no appetite nor any desire to sit beside mother and Oma who were at the breakfast table being served by Liddy. The two of them were eating their porridge like it was a normal morning, as if nothing had transpired between us last night.

"Come eat." My mother called to me with Liddy looking on expecting an order.

I said nothing and made my way out the front door. I left the house hopefully early enough to get to the factory before anyone else arrived, to have time to see Paul. But when I got there I was disappointed Herr

König and two other workers were already there readying an order to be shipped out.

"You're here so early." Herr König smiled and said a friendly hello. He looked at the other employees busy at work. "A delivery we need to get out so we can leave early to follow the Games."

The Games! The curtain of façade hanging over Germany was soon to lift after the final act. What then? More persecution. More deportations. My attention was riveted beneath the floor to the basement, to the old stuffy bathroom, where I wanted to be.

To make matters worse, near to an hour after I began work my mother arrived. Friendly nods and hellos came from the staff, along with a hearty welcome from Herr König. "It's good to have you back, Frau Becker."

"It's been a while, hasn't it Ulrich." Her lips slightly circled up but her eyes were flat. Those eyes had taken in too many things they didn't want to behold and there was no hiding my mother's suffering.

"You're back then?"

"Yes."

Herr König looked from my mother to me. "Christa has been working hard and doing well. Stays later than everyone else since we've lightened the staff's workload during the Games. I keep telling her the work will get done and not to take on too much."

My mother looked askance at me. "I'm glad to hear that Ulrich." She was anything but glad about the hours I was keeping for she knew why I'd been staying late.

I stood quietly taking in the back-and-forth catch-up between the two of them with Herr König informing my mother of important incomplete things on his plate.

My mother listened attentively commenting back there was nothing urgent that needed to be done and he could finish up and let the staff go home early.

"Thank you, Frau Becker." He slightly bowed his head showing the deference he had for my mother, a good owner who saw to the welfare of those working for her.

My mother's personality was a mixed bag, at times being stoic and cold, distant, while other times she was kind and considerate. On that day with Herr König, she manifested more kindness than I'd seen her do with him before. I attributed it to her being vulnerable from the loss, from what happened in Berlin.

The morning dragged on with me checking the wall clock frequently between tasks, my mother watching brusquely shaking her head. Once alone in the office with me, she leaned over my desk and whispered in my ear to stop looking at the clock. "It's rude and will only draw attention to you." She gave me a few chores to do in the office then went out to the factory floor.

Her tone had been sharp, prickling the back of my neck. The anticipation of waiting for everyone to leave so I could get to Paul was driving me mad, especially when I thought I had heard someone going down the basement steps. I blasted out of my seat pushing it back across the floor and rushed out to the factory floor where the staff were all accounted for. Herr König stopped what he was doing to inquire if I needed anything.

To cover up feeling foolish, I quickly told him, "I have a question for my mother." It was the only thing I could think to say but where was she?

Herr König did a circular intake of the area. "She was just here. Must have stepped out."

She wasn't outside where staff sometimes took breaks to eat or stretch their legs. The sound I heard earlier must have been my mother going down to the basement. I ground my teeth and went back to the office, sizzling.

The minutes dragged by like hours until my mother returned to the office, her face ashen, her eyes saucers. Then she started watching the clock and refused to answer any of my questions until Herr König and the staff left and she locked the factory door.

Before I could rush to the basement, she called to me. "He's not there." There was an edge in her voice, sharp and cutting.

"What!" I didn't wait to hear what she had to say before rushing down the basement steps two at a time. The rack by the bathroom was at an angle, wide enough for a body to get past and the bathroom door was ajar. Paul was gone! The clothes I'd given him to wear were neatly folded on the floor, all the other items next to them in an orderly fashion. I rummaged through the items, felt in the pockets of Jürgen's pants and shirts, looking for a note, anything to show where he went or what happened. Nothing. "Why didn't you leave me a note!" I cried out from deep in my throat, clinging to Jürgen's shirt. "Where did you go?"

"Shush." My mother was behind me at the bathroom door.

"What did you do!" I was livid at her and I didn't care if anyone heard me.

"He was already gone when I came down." She moved to me, her attention on my hand holding Jürgen's shirt. She picked up Jürgen's pants and held them to her chest.

His leaving hit me hard. My neck, pulsating like drumbeats, felt like it was going to burst open. My hand went to my neck. My necklace! I checked through the things once more looking for it, but it wasn't there. Paul had my necklace. Something about that calmed me a little.

My sniffling mother, still holding my brother's pants, looked like a lost soul. She reached a hand to mine. "Let's go home."

Heartsick as I was, how could I be mad at her? She'd done nothing but try to protect me. From her first surprised pale look to how grief-stricken she now appeared, I knew the empty room was not of her doing.

I cleaned the bathroom as my mother stood watching. Once outside we went to the trash receptacle to throw out the used items.

"Not Jürgen's." My mother grabbed hold of the rest of Jürgen's clothing and hugged them to her chest.

The walk home felt long and slow.

CHAPTER TWENTY-SIX

When we approached our street, I heard a dog barking. Incessant sharp explosive cries were followed by whimpering before another loud burst of howling and growling. "That's Max." Something was wrong and I needed to check it out. I told my mother I wanted to see if he was all right.

"You go on. I'll see you when you get home." She continued walking, clutching the bundle of Jürgen's clothes to her chest.

"Max." I called to him over the fence.

Delirious barking and scratching at the fence ensued.

"Calm down, boy." I yelled over the fence to him as I made my way around to the back gate to let myself into the yard. "I'm coming, Max."

Max was jumping against the gate, frantically trying to get my attention.

"Back up, Max. I can't open it."

Up against his resistance and wild motions, I side pushed my way in, surprised my immediate presence and reaching a hand to pet him didn't settle him. I grabbed hold of his collar to still him which only exacerbated his excitement. He continued barking, slipping loose from his collar.

"What are you telling me?" I followed him to a patch of garden not visible from the gate.

Max sat whining and pawing at the ground, next to Frau Weber's motionless body.

Quickly going through the first aid activities I'd learned at the girls' meetings, I felt her neck for a pulse. At first I thought I'd felt one but it was my own vibrating thumb. I switched to my index and middle fingers and checked several times on both sides. Her neck was cold, hard. It didn't feel like normal flesh. I raised her blouse and pressed my ear over her left breast, my heart galloping like a racehorse. I heard nothing. Her chest didn't raise and fall and there was no other bodily motion.

Max lowered his head to Frau Weber's bottom, sniffing what I also smelled, urine and bowel movement. Uncontrollably shaking and not sure what to do, I collared Max, found his leash, and rushed with him to my house to tell my mother and Oma.

The ambulance and police arrived around the same time determining she must have died of natural causes, a heart attack. Mother got ahold of Herr Weber who was out of town. "He asked if you could take care of Max until his return." Without waiting for my affirmative response, she added, "We'll keep Max at our place. Take a few days off to tend to him." My mother's voice was a gift, soft and tender, compassionately giving, quieting my shaking limbs.

The tragedy that befell Frau Weber turned into a miracle wrapped in a big black and brown fur coat landing at my door. Max's arrival changed all our moods, distracting us from the sorrow. I walked him several times a day and he slept in my room at the foot of my bed. Max, my best therapy, listened to me talk about my woes and cry my eyes out. He wouldn't leave my side. What a special friend he was and although he helped me feel better, I still felt physically and emotionally raw. I dreaded Herr Weber's return.

The last night I was to have Max, my mother came to me after work at the factory looking weary, the pressure she was under showing in her uncolored complexion, her limp stance. I didn't want to return Max the next day and was taken unawares when she told me we were going to keep him.

"Keep? As in a few days?"

"More than a few days." She told me Herr Weber was extremely busy with the regime and would be away too much to take care of Max. "He knows how much you love the dog."

Max was at my feet, looking up at me. It was the best thing that had happened to me in days, filling the vacuum loss had created. Although it didn't replace how I felt about Paul, wanting to find out what happened and where he was, I felt propped up. What I didn't understand was why my mother looked so miserable when she'd just given me good news.

Not wanting her to relapse, I asked, "Are you feeling well?"

A heaviness moved over her and she grew quiet. She looked down at the floor when she said, "Your father will be home tomorrow."

From the way she lowered her eyes and her voice cracked I realized something was amiss. Something must have happened in Berlin I knew nothing about. My mother had shut down and when I told her I was worried about her, she reached for my hand responding some things are best left unsaid.

Max whined interrupting us.

"He needs to go out. I'll find you when he's finished."

"I need to rest now." That was her way of letting me know the discussion had ended.

I wasn't comfortable trespassing into my parents' business, things they usually worked out between themselves. They'd been separated for many days now and I figured once he was home everything would return to normal.

Later that night, I awoke to the sound of my mother and Oma talking in my parents' bedroom. Max's ears perked up, his attention on me now up against the wall. I thought my heart would stop when I heard my mother ask Oma about her friend that knew Nahum.

Paul's father! What are they talking about? I leaned in pressing my ear harder against the wall, hearing only the whishing sound of my own heartbeat. Unable to make out what they were saying, I went to my parents' room and opened the door.

Four eyes gave me a look like you're going to land in trouble listening in where you don't belong. I instantly took responsibility. "You were talking so loudly you woke me."

"So of course you had to spy on us." Oma toned down her sarcasm with a wink. "Just what did you overhear?"

"Mother mentioned Paul's father. You knew him, mother?"

Oma answered for her. "Yes, she met him. On shopping excursions to Friedrichshafen we'd stop by his store."

"Why were you talking about him?"

When my mother found her voice she told me Oma had talked to her when she returned from Berlin. "She sat by my bed for hours talking about a lot of things. She mentioned your trip to get your necklace fixed. She thought I wasn't paying attention. Or perhaps your clever Oma wanted me to know."

What was she trying to tell me? My instincts told me to let them talk, don't interrupt because what I was hearing and how they looked was different and I didn't want it to stop.

"Inge, I wanted you to know." Oma shifted her glance from my mother to me. "I knew your mother was in a bad way with the loss of your brother and from whatever happened in Berlin. She needed to know that I understood. Not just from the loss of Opa but the recent shock and sorrow I felt over Nahum."

When she retold the story of our going to see Nahum and meeting up with Paul, I became frustrated because I didn't see what that had to do with Oma's friend, the local man who worked with a small group of dissidents. I'd been patient enough and wanted to know. "I heard mention of your friend Oma, the man who knew Paul's father."

"You heard that?" A distressed flush moved into Oma's face and neck.

"Yes. I heard that."

My mother nervously clicked her thumb fingernail against her middle one, looking at Oma waiting for how she'd answer.

"So, you heard that. He's a man we both know."

How was I going to get around her evasiveness without breaking down the communication or being disrespectful which never went over well with either of them?

Oma gave my mother an askance look like she wanted her to say something but when my mother remained mute, Oma did what she could to shut it down. "Christa, there's nothing more to discuss here. And I strongly advise you to stop eavesdropping."

I would not be deterred. Although Max had been a beneficial distraction, Paul's disappearance weighed on me. "If you know anything about Paul please tell me."

Oma was dug in and there was no digging her out. She would not tell me what they talked about. Nor would my mother who met my question about Paul with "enough!"

CHAPTER TWENTY-SEVEN

Enough, I thought about how my mother ended the conversation earlier that night. It wasn't enough for me, nor would it be until I knew Paul was safe. I replayed the conversation with my mother and Oma, sticking on the way Oma chided me with a wink about listening in. That wink meant something and I had to find out what.

I waited until I felt sure my mother was asleep, motioned with an outstretched palm for Max to stay, then slunk along the hallway and made my way to Oma's room. A dim light shone from under her door. Oma didn't look surprised to see me enter. In fact she patted her bed for me to join her as if she expected me.

I wasted no time playing on her sympathies, complaining I couldn't sleep. "I have to know if you know anything."

"What?" She leaned closer so she could hear me.

"Do you know anything about Paul?"

Oma let out a long sigh from the back of her throat. "Your mother doesn't want me talking to you, but you know me."

That's what she said whenever she was about to share a confidence with me, what she claimed in the past was the right thing to do. As far back as I can remember, Oma sided with me in many disagreements I had with my mother. She shared things with me she felt would help and most times what she shared had helped.

Pressure eased from my chest as I listened to her tell me her friend, who remained nameless, had put word out to locate Paul. "Your mother will kill me if she finds out I'm talking about this with you."

"I won't say a thing. But…" A light bulb went off in my mind. "You were talking to mother about the man. Does she know what he does? How he feels about—"

"Shh. Yes."

There was much more I wanted to ask, like how my mother felt with Oma having this friend, a man who opposed the regime and apparently helped Jews. When I began asking, Oma cut me off and told me to go to sleep.

I gave her a big thankful hug and went back to my room, to Max at the foot of my bed raising his eyes to mine, wagging his tail. I spent a long time watching him twitch and jerk, wondering what he was dreaming about. Somewhere in the middle of the night I drifted off, my feet touching Max.

***

The day my father was to arrive home the phone rang. I hoped it might be word about Paul. Instead, it was my father phoning to let my mother know he would be detained for several days. "Important business with higher-ups." She had a sour look on her face like she'd tasted something rancid when she told me.

The next three days I couldn't wait to return home to ask Oma if she'd heard anything.

"Nothing. Stop asking me every five minutes."

"Oma!"

"Come here, Christa." I moved closer to her. "I promise to let you know if I hear anything."

Her emphasis on *if* gave me a stomachache.

The following evening, I had been home for an hour when my father arrived. He walked through the door standing tall. He looked different. His receding hairline was more pronounced and he had more gray hair than the last time I'd seen him, plus he combed it with a left part, flattened over the top with pomade. Gone were the loose waves along with his inviting welcoming posture.

"Father!" I ran to him and wrapped my arms around him wanting to feel the warmth he brought to me so many times in the past when I was hurting. "I'm so glad you're home."

"Hello, Christa." His hello was clipped, not sounding like the affectionate father who left me a few weeks earlier. He stepped back and held his hands on my shoulders, keeping me at arm's length. "Where's your mother?"

"She's in your room," Oma said, moving to us. "Harald. Good to see you home."

"Helga." He nodded to Oma then made his way to find my mother.

It didn't take long for Oma and me to hear their raised voices, each becoming louder. Hers angry and his commanding. A cold chill ran through the house that not even Max rubbing up against me could defrost.

***

My father was home only briefly. He left early the next morning to go to Maybach and other jobs he'd been assigned to was all my mother told Oma and me at the breakfast table. Aware Liddy was serving us, we avoided sensitive conversations.

When he didn't come home that night I asked my mother if he'd be staying there.

"I don't know where he's staying."

What was going on? Did my father meet a woman in Berlin? Was he having an affair? His changed behavior and my mother's angry reaction was upsetting, and puzzling. Oma had no information on what was happening between them either. Apparently it was something my parents kept to themselves.

My father's distance when home, my mother's anger, and no news about Paul from Oma's friend had deflated my fleeting hope. Just when

I was about to give up, Oma told me she'd like to join me when I walked Max after the evening meal.

"You're sure?" I could hardly believe my ears when she told me Paul had been spotted in Friedrichshafen three days ago near where he had lived.

"Yes. He was seen with a man who did business with his father. Another good friend."

Friend. Good friend. Jargon for those Germans opposed to the Nazi regime, I thought.

The minute we were back in the house, I went to see my father who was working in the study. The door was closed so I knocked.

"Just a minute."

I heard papers shuffle and a filing cabinet drawer open and shut before he said enter. He locked the top drawer on the cabinet before taking the seat behind his desk.

"Sit." There was no smile. No asking what I wanted. Just a command to take a seat.

"Father." I plopped down in a padded wooden chair opposite him.

"Sit up straight, young lady." That wasn't a friendly request, like times in the past when he told me not to slouch. He had ordered me, with an obey me or else tone.

I straightened my posture and sat in a ladylike pose. "Father. Can I go with you to Friedrichshafen?"

"There's nothing for you to do there."

"I'd like to do a little shopping."

"Shopping." He let out a gruff laugh. "There is no extra money to shop."

His words felt like arrows pelting my body. "I don't need to spend money. I like to window-shop. Look at things. Also I'd love to take the ride with you."

He leaned back in his chair, seeming somewhat more relaxed and lowered his chin to his hand to give it some thought. "Clear it with your mother."

For a moment his tone softened. So did my heart for my father had always held a special place in my heart. The moment passed all too quickly when he waved me off, putting his attention back on the papers remaining on his desk.

"Thank you." I rose maintaining good posture and left.

My mother saw no problem in my going with him, in fact mentioned she thought it a good idea.

"Good idea?"

"Maybe it'll put him in a better frame of mind after spending some time with you."

The melancholy in her words and her slightly lowered brow made me feel sad. It pained me I didn't know what had happened between them, what had transpired in Berlin that stole my father and replaced him with a militant stranger.

CHAPTER TWENTY-EIGHT

"I will not!" My mother's words slammed through the wall of my bedroom, waking me.

"You have no choice."

My parents were arguing, at what the clock said was ten after three in the morning, making no attempt to muffle their words. Not one *shh Christa will hear us* which surprised me as I wiped the sleep from my eyes and sat up against the headboard.

Pieces of the Berlin puzzle came through the wall in snapping sentences.

"You could have gotten us all killed."

Killed! My father's anger scared me more than what was coming out of his mouth. Killed, he repeated giving me some clarity on what he had been referring to when he mentioned how my mother's slinking off on the ferry to Rügen had been reported up lines. "People have been shot for less!"

"You can't blame me for wanting to see our son!"

"And get us labeled Jew lovers! Are you crazy, Inge! Sacrifice our whole family, for what!" His loud voice rattled my insides, making me feel ill as he laid into her repeating, "For what!"

"For the love of my son, Harald." Her weepy voice let out a sorrowful beseeching. "Can't you understand that?"

"Snap out of it!"

What I heard next sounded like a hand slapping flesh. No, please no. My father had never taken a hand to my mother. His anger spread through the wall like a fast-moving infection into my body. Stop! Consumed with wanting to stop him, I rushed to their room, leaving Max in my bedroom with the door shut.

My mother was on the floor. Her left cheek dangerously close to her eye was red. My father was towering over her, his hand raised like he was going to strike her again.

"Don't hit her!" I moved impulsively in front of my father to help my mother up, noticing tiny burst blood vessels in her left eye. Once I assisted her to the bed I went for a cold cloth for her cheek.

My father stood there as I helped my mother, his face contorted, his mouth twisted into a repulsed grimace. "You two need to grow a spine."

"What!" I was beyond offended. I'd never felt animosity like that for him before but after hearing him, seeing what he'd done, I wanted to lash out at him, to do to him what he'd just done to my mother.

"You heard me. From now on you will hear me loud and clear and follow my orders. There will be no more talk in this house against the regime. Against the Nazi agenda. Not one word. Not one hint of a look. I will not hesitate to take action against anyone who violates the laws."

I couldn't believe my ears, and more significantly I couldn't believe my mother took it. That was not the strong-willed mother I knew, the woman who didn't cower or succumb to orders so timidly. There before my father she had turned into a hollow shell of her old self. Any strength she had possessed had transferred to my father, the imbalance deafening. Why?

"Father." As much as I wanted to cut his mean squinty eyes out, I had to reach him to find out if he was lost to me forever. "How could you hit her? What's happened to you?"

"Christa." My mother interjected. "Let it be."

My father nodded, and in that quiet agreeing reaction the closed-in space between us edged open.

"I'm going to work. I'll be back in a few days."

"It's not even light out." Rubbing her cheek, her left eye now bloodshot, my mother responded as if nothing had transpired between them. "At least wait for daylight."

He looked at her, then me, and shook his head.

My mother slumped, looking sadly resigned.

He left. As I heard his car pull out of the driveway, threads of anger drifted down my torso and knotted into bewilderment over what just happened. I asked my mother why she told me to let it be.

"Not now, Christa."

I would not drop it, not when too much had been planted in my brain, and I knew neither one of us would get any sleep. Not like Oma, who didn't hear the commotion and was sleeping through what had just transpired. "That's not fair, mother."

She moved her free hand to mine. "Yes, it's not fair, but it won't help you to know the facts. You just have to trust me."

It pained me she sounded weak, unconvincing. "May I be the judge of that? After all that's happened, I think I have a right to know. I'm not a child anymore."

The silence between us was interrupted by Max's scratching at my bedroom door to be let out.

"He'll ruin the door." My mother pulled her hand back.

"Let him ruin the door. I'm not leaving until you tell me what happened in Berlin."

More silence and Max stopped scratching. My mother knew I'd sit there all night if I had to, and because she was too emotionally spent to continue to resist me she told me what happened. The scene behind the big show put on for the world. My father didn't know that the only reason my mother had joined him in Berlin was not for the Games but to slip away to Rügen the first chance she could. It was there she found out my brother was dead, murdered as a Jew-loving invalid, a nurse let slip. The nurse didn't know it was the patient's mother she was talking to and when she found out all hell broke loose.

"I was reported to the Propaganda Minister."

My chest tightened. Minister Goebbels, a man I'd read and heard much about, one of Hitler's most devoted acolytes, was not someone to cross. I'm sure he had orders to keep any sign of dissension away from the crowds and out of the press for the duration of the Games.

My mother's words wobbled when she'd mentioned his name for she like the rest of German citizens knew that name and what he was capable of. She continued to sound shaky when she told me Goebbels knew, but he liked my father, a hardworking and as yet valued party member.

"Your father was infuriated when he found out what I'd done. I was held in Rügen while an investigation occurred. Goebbels himself contacted your father to discern what his position was on the matter."

On the matter? That sounded so cold. My grief-stricken mother, having just found out her son was murdered, was held hostage while the higher-ups arrogantly strutted their stuff around Berlin. The gall of it all was sickening. Worse was what she told me next.

"Your father assured Minister Goebbels it was a misunderstanding, that he and our entire family were Hitler adherents and Nazi party members. He lied swearing it was he who had turned Jürgen in to the authorities after the fight over Arthur."

"Do you think he was the one? Did he report what happened with Jürgen defending a Jewish boy?"

"I know for a fact he didn't. It was another boy who witnessed it. Your father tried to handle it but... I'm sure it wasn't your father."

"So why did he have to lie?"

"To save the rest of us."

That's when she told me any hint of a German citizen being a Jewish sympathizer or expressing an inkling of anti-Nazism sentimentality is an instant ticket to a concentration camp. My mother had painted a clear picture of what happened in Berlin. It helped me understand the state she was in when she had returned and now my father's behavior. I didn't like it, but at least I understood. Faced with the same excruciating situation, I'm not sure what I would have done.

I asked the only question left. "Does Oma know?"

"Yes, I told her when I was coming around. Talking to her is probably what helped pull me through."

What my mother told me explained why she wanted Paul to leave before my father returned from Berlin. It also gave me a better understanding of the compassion my mother had for she could have kicked Paul out the night she discovered he was hiding in the factory. Instead she gave me a few days to move him, ultimately to save his life. That made me feel a little better.

With the conversation ended, I got up to go to my room but before I was out the door my mother told me to be careful.

I turned back to her, loving her more than I can ever recall. Her words gave me permission to choose my own way, and to follow my heart.

"I will, mother." I pivoted to the door and looked back at her over my shoulder to see the smallest light back in her eyes. "Thank you."

CHAPTER TWENTY-NINE

My father was gone a few days and when he returned things were still distant between him and us but more tolerable. I had gained a new understanding about what needed to remain unsaid and to keep emotional outbursts in check. We all had to play our parts to maintain the proper image for Liddy and our neighbors. My father had made it clear that any whiff of anti-regime expression would not be tolerated.

At the dinner table my father engaged us with light chitchat focusing on how things were going at the factory, what Oma found to do around the house, and Max. Earlier that evening my father had seen me working with Max, training him to do tricks and it surprised me when he picked up a piece a bread and held it out for Max.

"Come."

Max went to him.

"Good dog."

Max stood wagging his tail by my father's side, wiggling his snout getting a sniff of the food. On command from my father, he gulped down the treat.

A thin smile shone on my mother who appreciated Max's antics. Max was the ever neutral consistent topic we could all turn to that broke the moments of awkward silence.

All eyes were on my father commanding Max to sit. "Good dog." He then broke off another piece of bread and told Max to stay before placing the food by his paws. One second passed. Two seconds. Three seconds and a few more before my father said, "Get it."

Again, Max inhaled the treat.

"Smart dog." Oma said.

The uplifted mood dropped instantly when my father said, "He obeys."

Obey, I thought, hating the sound of that word. Soldiers marching, boys in brown shirts, blond-haired and blue-eyed girls having Aryan babies, and a myriad of other images of Nazis obeying flashed in my head, tensing my neck.

After the meal, I went to my father's study and knocked.

"Enter."

I stood at attention in front of where he sat at his desk holding a piece of paper before he glanced over the edge to ask what I wanted. My heart sank at his cold treatment, and I feared he had changed his mind about letting me go with him when he went to Maybach.

"Father. I have tomorrow off and—"

He cut me off. "That's midweek."

"Mother said I could take tomorrow off and work Sunday. There's plenty for me to do and I would really like to join you on the ride." I kept talking, hoping to convince him when he cut me off again.

"I leave at seven sharp."

He held another piece of paper between us before I could say thank you.

***

My father stopped across the street from Herr Meier's kiosk, handed me some money and told me to get him the newspaper. Back in the car I watched him scan the headlines, mentioning proudly the repeating story about the German athletes capturing the most medals. "German hospitality praised by visitors. Good." He talked to the steering wheel, ignoring me as he thumbed through several more pages, smiling until he reached the second to last page. "What!" He spewed a few unapologetic cuss words before crinkling the paper in his fist and tossing it at me.

He gripped hold of the steering wheel, his knuckles turning pale, his lips tight, and continued on that way through the hilly countryside. As we passed dairy farms surrounded by resplendent natural beauty, I moved my hand over the crinkled newspaper in my lap wondering what he saw that got him so upset. When we headed into Friedrichshafen and he had to make a stop, I had my chance to look while he was out of the car.

On the second to last page was a headline he'd dug a nail into blocking one of the words. It was clear to me it said *Captain Wolfgang Fürstner, head of the Olympic village, committed suicide.* The article stated he killed himself when he was dismissed from his military service due to his Jewish ancestry.

My father had worked with him. I remembered a mention of him before my father left for Berlin. My head was spinning for my father's reaction was not one I expected, not after all his haranguing about following orders, showing no dissension. The man he once spoke highly of had Jewish blood in his arteries. A valuable man with a stellar history of service to his country had been reduced to a contaminated human being. My father showed no pleasure in the sad ending of the man, and that revealed something I am sure my father preferred I had not seen nor found out about.

In an odd twist of fate, the innocent act of stopping to purchase a newspaper told me something important about my father. He didn't go along with the party line and he certainly didn't hate Jews. Combined with what my mother told me, what happened in Berlin was making more sense as to my father's reaction to the family. He more than anyone had to have us believe he was with them because if we believed that then we would manifest that with relatives, friends and neighbors.

An ease moved through me when he approached the car and got in, the newspaper back on my lap like when he left. He grabbed hold of it and threw it in the back seat, most likely intending to keep it from me.

Paul was in my every thought as we drove through town. A few streets from his house, titillation rose in my thighs, it was hard for me to sit still. Please be there. His face appeared before me, bright and happy, his wavy hair cascading over his forehead emphasizing his expressive eyes, big and brown like Max's. I remembered how they lowered and turned sad when he mentioned his father and the plight of Jews, and also how they squinted anger at what the perpetrators were doing to his people and other unfortunates. Best of all was how his eyes shined when he displayed affection, when lost for words and his hands touched my flesh and our lips met. Please be there. I didn't want to entertain other options.

My father interrupted my daydreaming, his words indiscernible. I moved my tongue around to moisten my dry mouth. "What did you say?"

"I said, we're here."

Absorbed in fantasizing about Paul, I hadn't noticed we'd arrived at Maybach. "Yes." I dreamily responded.

"Christa. Get your head out of the clouds, young lady." He laid into me about my not acting like an upstanding German girl, sharp and attentive, posturing pride for our great nation.

It's what you read in the paper, I thought, certain he was taking his bad mood out on me. Despite my implicit understanding, it hurt to be on the receiving end of his vitriol and I shrank down in the passenger's seat. I wanted to reach for him to tell him to stop being so standoffish and mean. Mean was something unfamiliar in my father, nothing I wanted to get used to. I longed for him to return to how he was before Berlin.

"Sit up straight and look at me when I am talking to you!"

I wanted to yell at the top of my lungs for him to come back, to snap out of whatever he'd become, to stop projecting his anger over what he'd read in the paper on me. I wanted my father back. The narrow-eyed strict look on his face, his pursed lips, told me there was no reaching him. Straightening my posture, I simply said, "Yes, sir."

Yes, sir. No, sir. There was nothing more to say to his admonishments about my substandard behavior, my slack way of acting so I pretended like I did with others who have married the party line, I obeyed. Even though I'd gained an understanding from seeing his reaction to that newspaper article, it didn't assuage the sting. More than ever, I needed Paul, his comforting arms and kind personality.

"Three o'clock sharp." After telling me what time to return my father made his way to the factory and I walked off heading in the direction of downtown to give my father the impression that's where I was going should he be watching me. I kept on in that direction until I was out of sight from Maybach then backtracked up a few side streets and headed to Paul's house.

CHAPTER THIRTY

What I saw when I arrived in front of Paul's house nearly brought me to my knees. Charred destruction was all that remained of what was once a home sheltering a happy family, good productive people. I breathed in the burnt remains, wondering how long it took before the languid flames spread into torrents of destruction leaving in its wake blackened ruins. Ceiling beams rested horizontally across the front walkway blocking the door and a stack of seared vertical bricks which must have been the fireplace stood tall above a carpet of ash. Anything that might have been salvageable was ruined by the water damage. Paul did nothing to bring such a calamity to his life. The immensity of what I saw, Dieter's hateful act, boggled my mind.

As I looked at the pile of debris, broken glass fixtures, soot blanketing everything, my eyes caught a glimmer of a shiny object. A closer inspection brought me to tears. I bent down to touch the dog's bowl, what Paul must have kept after Bengle was killed. Paul, where are you? My upset turned to a fit of terror. Paul. I wasn't sure if the word escaped my mouth as I turned around and partially made my way down the driveway to see close-up the garage was mostly intact but not untouched by the fire as fingers of charcoal had scratched up the sides of the structure showing how close it came to being destroyed. A window with a cracked spider-like web spreading across its center looked like someone threw a rock at it.

You bastards. Every nasty word I'd ever heard ran through my shaking head as I moved closer to the garage, hoping for Paul to be in there.

"Fräulein."

The sound of an older woman's voice stopped me dead in my tracks. Fear inched up my quavering legs. She wouldn't know me. Should I run? If I was caught at Paul's house, a Jew's house, it wouldn't bode well for me or my family. Would I even have time to get away if she hollered?

"Fräulein." She reached a hand to my perspiring back. "Don't be afraid."

She sounded mellow, kind, but I'd seen the nice façade people with unworthy agendas used to get what they wanted. Surrounded by the ravage, I knew not to trust anyone whether packaged kindly or covered in a mean wrapping. I would take my chance to leave, to get back to Maybach as fast as I could, but just as I pivoted to get away I heard her say Paul's name.

"He's a good boy." Her eyes looked beyond me toward the garage.

A car drove by and she moved me further down the driveway telling me she knew Paul since he was a baby. "He played with my Horst, my son. They could have been twins, they looked so much alike." Her rheumy eyes dripped tears, and she reached for a handkerchief from her blouse breast pocket to wipe her runny nose.

From her reaction, the sincerity expressed in her voice, I knew she was no enemy and I had nothing to be afraid of. "Do you know where he is?" I asked overly anxious, playing with a loose strand of hair.

She must have mistook my urgency as being too inquisitive, perhaps thinking I might be a wolf in sheep's clothing. She backed up a little. "Why would I know that? I'm just the neighbor." Her flowing open posture tightened, the flex in her loose elbows stretched taut to her side. She stepped back a little more.

She knows something and I've made a mess of it. Think fast. She was just about to break away when I said, "If you've been his neighbor all these years, you must know my Oma."

Her shoulders lowered and she tilted her head to the side like Max does when listening to me. She waited, allowing me the space to explain myself.

"My Oma is Helga Koch."

That was all I needed to say before she reached her arm to mine, her fingers softly resting on my blouse. "I know your Oma. A fine woman. You must be Christa."

My imprisoned heart burst through its gates of confinement. "Yes. He's spoken to you of me?" I didn't wait for an answer before asking, "Is he all right?"

"It's terrible what they did." She spoke under her breath, clearly feeling I was a friend to be trusted.

"Yes, it is." I leaned in closer, and whispered in her ear. "Do you know if he's alive?"

She answered by looking at the garage and nodding. Then for show, in case another neighbor had seen us or anyone was around close enough to hear, she loudly said something about my looking to move into the neighborhood. "This lot can be cleaned up and rebuilt..." She held a finger up to her mouth directing me to go along. "The yard is still in good shape. Let's have a look."

I followed her through the gate to the yard where Bengle once ran and played. Ghostly barks cried in my brain as tears slipped down and off my chin. There, by the garage side window, I asked, "Do you know where he is now?" At first she was reluctant to answer, but when I said, "I love him. I have to help," she motioned to the garage, smiling.

Out through the window came a faint gasp. The elderly woman's smile widened.

I grabbed her into a hug. "Thank you."

"I hope we meet again."

She watched me sidle to the side door and out of her sight. Just inside the door, I heard her move back down the driveway to her house. I also heard something else. "Psst."

Paul! That's Paul. My heart leaped when I found him where he had moved from the door to behind a tall shelf filled with tools and odds and ends that no one thought to confiscate. He pulled me into his arms. "You love me?"

"You heard me?" I asked, smothering him in kisses, holding on to him, feeling the heat of his body against mine.

"Yes. Well?"

"I love you." My voice broke, betraying my aching heart. "But why'd you leave me?"

"I didn't leave you. Your Oma ..." He must have seen the horizontal wrinkles on my forehead, my jaw go slack, and surmised I didn't know what he was talking about. "What do you think happened?"

"I came to work worried. You weren't in a good place the last time I saw you and when I went to the bathroom you were gone."

"You thought I left you?"

"Yes. Why would I think anything else?"

"You silly thing. Don't you know how much I care about you."

After a long passionate lingering kiss I asked, "So what happened?"

Paul hesitated, seeming reluctant to answer. Instead, he digressed saying he spent most of his time in the loft in a hidden area behind a movable wooden wall. "I built that fake wall after Bengle was killed." His eyes clouded over for a couple of seconds then brightened when he said, "Ursula brings me food."

"Ursula?"

"The woman you were just outside with. My neighbor."

"Can you really trust her?"

"Yes. She's like a second mother to me. Her son Horst died in my arms after a rough bout of pneumonia a few years back. She told me I was her son now."

"She won't turn you in to the authorities? She's not worried about her own wellbeing?"

"I am her wellbeing. Her husband and son are dead and her extended family rejected her for sympathizing with those not, shall we say, diehards. She helps more than me. She's friends with your Oma."

"My Oma... you mentioned her a couple minutes ago then stopped. You never answered my question about what happened."

"She arranged for me to come here to hide where it is safer than in your mother's factory. She has friends. Like Ursula. There are others. I'll be fine up there." He motioned to the dark loft.

"Why didn't you tell me? Get word to me?"

"I didn't have a chance to. After the last time we were together, your Oma came to me in the middle of the night with a man who lives near you. He arranged transport for me to return here, next to Ursula who can help if I'm compromised or need to move again."

"I was sick with worry you might be—"

"Don't say it. Never think it. You're what's keeping me alive. Strong. Now you better go."

"I don't want to leave you."

"Christa." He held me tight, refueling our souls. "I'll be fine. I have your good luck necklace." When he released me, he pulled it out of his pocket to show me its bright shiny surface, a sparkling token of love.

I pressed it against my lips, then slid it back in the pocket over his heart. "Yes, you will be fine."

With his hands upon my cheeks, our final kiss was tender. Reassuring. As we let go of each other, I quietly slid out the door and made my way back down the driveway, replaying his words, *You're what's keeping me alive.*

CHAPTER THIRTY-ONE

On the ride back my father was quiet, holding the steering wheel less tense than the morning ride, particularly less rigid than he became after seeing the newspaper article. Busy productive time seemed to help his state of mind. I was glad for the respite, happy to enjoy the verdant countryside, no longer the blur out the window as on the earlier ride. Then I was too preoccupied with worry over Paul. Now I was filled with hope and dreams, savoring the sweet taste of satisfaction that the trip hadn't been in vain.

As we approached our house, a tickle of umbrage about what Oma did pulled me down. I didn't know whether to be mad at her or kiss her but either way I would have a word with her. After all the distress it caused, I wanted the secret planning behind my back to stop. Why didn't she tell me? Not a hint, and I was certain she said nothing to my mother either, not by her reaction to finding the room empty. She couldn't have faked her faded skin tone, the surprised reaction. Oma, what are you up to?

Dinner was uneventful with Liddy serving us as we engaged in light conversation about how our days went. I wanted the meal over with, for Liddy to clean up and leave, for my parents to retire to their bedroom and go to sleep so I could talk to Oma.

The clock ticked past twelve. My father was still in his study, my mother in her room most likely asleep as was Oma in hers. I counted the second hand movement on the clock, stared at shadows on the ceiling, and thought of Paul. His image infused me with strong feelings of sensual desire, a deep yearning to be near him. His touch and words had ignited something in me, and even though I had attention on what Oma had done, attention on what was going on in Germany with anti-Semitic escalations, I had a sense everything between us would work out and we'd have a future together. I didn't even want to entertain anything else. I needed that belief to sustain me.

My father's footsteps drew my thoughts from dancing shadows and visions of Paul. It was a little after two in the morning. I wondered what he was doing up so late and if it had anything to do with the article about Captain Wolfgang Fürstner. I waited for him to finish in the bathroom and go to bed, but was disappointed when I heard my mother say something to him.

"Not now, Inge. Go to sleep."

Yes, mother, please go to sleep.

She wasn't tired and wanted to talk, said she had gotten word about his friend. Without saying who had told her or specifically naming the friend, I knew when she mentioned suicide who she meant.

"Please go to sleep, Inge." That's all my father said but it was the way he said please in a resigned manner that sounded like what's the use talking, it can't change anything, what's done is done. The manner in which he spoke also told me something else, more importantly, he did still feel compassion. I knew that part of my father well, and sure as I was that Paul loved me I knew my father hadn't fallen off the edge of humanity into an unreachable chasm.

A brief amount of time passed before their room became quiet. I had no second thoughts about going to Oma's room and letting myself in. I edged my way to the side of her bed and turned on the bedside lamp. Not uttering a sound, rubbing sleep from her eyes, she squinted at the lamp. I was sure she knew why I was there. Sure she knew if I spent the day in Friedrichshafen and came back in good spirits, it meant I'd seen Paul.

Right to the point, I asked her what happened when she went to him in the box factory.

"He's safe?" Her sleep-ridden voice was raspy, phlegm gurgled in her throat.

"Of course he's safe. He's home. You know that."

She cleared her throat. "No. I hadn't gotten word back yet. I've not been able to get away to make contact."

"With your friend?"

"Yes."

"His last night in the box factory... what did you do?"

Oma told me she had contacted her friend to arrange transport for Paul and a safe place if possible. "I gather they weren't able to find a shelter for him."

I thought about that for a minute. "Either that or Paul wanted to go home. Never mind that, Oma. Why didn't you say anything to me?"

"My friend told me not to. Made me swear to keep it between us."

That stopped me for I respected her being trustworthy. I couldn't fault her that, not when I instantly understood it could cost her a precious connection that did in fact help get Paul to safety.

"Please don't keep things from me in the future."

"Christa, you know I can't make that promise to you. My word has to mean something."

"But you do share confidences from mother so why not this? You can trust me."

"That's different. Your mother will not abandon us if something accidentally slips, plus she understands I share things with you. But with my friend... if anything should accidentally slip and get back to him or he senses I'm violating his confidence that's much different. I can't afford to lose his connection or have word get out I have a loose tongue."

A wind picked up outside, rustling a tree branch against the window. Oma flinched and ended the conversation.

***

My father stopped making same-day trips to Friedrichshafen and refused to have me stay over with him. Desperate to find a solution to see Paul again, I went to Oma for help.

"What do you expect me to do?"

I felt frustrated trying to come up with an answer then I thought of her friend. "Perhaps your friend can take me there?"

"Absolutely not! You will not meet him, nor speak of him again! Do you hear me! You've got a lot of nerve!"

Oma was boiling mad that I was selfish enough to ask that of her and she laid into me the likes of which I'd never experienced from her. Not until her reaction had I contemplated an aspect of her friendship with the unnamed man I hadn't been aware of before. She valued and protected him, even at the expense of withholding communications and information from her own family. As I listened to her ranting about my self-serving needs, I saw something about my own naivety, how little I really comprehended about the magnitude of anti-Semitism and plans to rid not just Germany but the world of Jews. Oma had a wealth of information, and personal experience, I knew nothing about, not until she sat me down in her room and told me.

"You care about one individual, and yes, I see you love him in your own way, but the people I am friends with care about hundreds."

Offended and not yet grasping the magnitude of what she was saying, I couldn't unplug myself from thinking of Paul, one individual but he was my world. The hundreds Oma spoke of didn't register and that confused me. "Do you think I'm a bad person because my attention, my focus, is on Paul?"

"A bad person?" She shifted back, scrunching her forehead like she didn't understand why I'd asked that. "You are not a bad person, Christa. Your affections for …" Looking at the door to her room, and although Liddy was long gone and my parents asleep, she lowered her voice. "Your affections for Paul and wanting to be with him doesn't make you a bad person. But it is selfish to put your own desire above the welfare of many. You don't know all that is happening and what the future holds. Those gaining inside information are doing what they can to save lives. Some will be sacrificed for the greater good and that is why I will not allow you to connect with anyone involved in activities you may compromise."

"But Paul—"

"Keep your voice down."

"He needs help like everyone else. I want to help him."

"You can't, Christa. Let the people who know about him do their work. Let it be."

"I won't do what you—"

"What, Christa? What I did with Nahum? Not fight for our relationship? You silly girl."

I didn't like the way she talked down to me, and felt she wasn't being fair. I stomped a foot, not caring who I woke, not caring who I compromised, acting out like a spoiled child until Oma slapped me across the face.

"Stop it right now!"

My cheek burned a heated pain, and as I rubbed it, up bubbled the real problem. The root of hatred spreading through my marrow wasn't coming from my Oma, a woman who had nothing but my welfare and the welfare of decent others in her sights. The torrents of oppression moving through Germany, contaminating everything it touched, got to me and I collapsed against Oma's chest crying like a wounded animal.

"I'm sorry, Oma. I'm so sorry." I wept and thought I'd never stop.

She swept a hand back over my hair until I calmed down. Her voice a balm for my broken spirit. Her chest moved in a slow rhythmic motion, lifting my head with her inhalations and lowering it when she breathed out. Her breathing brought me back and so did her words.

"I told you I wouldn't connect you with my friend. But..." She paused, teasing me in the alluring way she did when she had good news, or something favorable to say.

"Oma." I elongated the *ma* begging her to say it.

"He can't help but I can."

As if on a coiled spring, my head shot up to face her. "Really!"

My heart pounded and sweat ran down my back as I listened to her tell me she'd work on something, even if it was to take me for a visit herself. "No one needs to know where we're going. A nice day off with my granddaughter."

"Oma, I love you."

"Even when you hate me?" She let out a chuckle, brief and contained, but amusement was in her shiny eyes. It was those eyes of hers that lit the way for me, lightening the heaviness surrounding us.

CHAPTER THIRTY-TWO

At my urging, and insisting I didn't want to wait until the weekend, Oma asked for us to have a day off together, again during the week and I would work Sunday in exchange. My mother was concerned about my wanting to take another day off during the week when all the staff were in the factory and she needed me most. She responded, "I will not allow it."

Oma stepped in and said it was the only time she could arrange a visit with a lady friend in Friedrichshafen. "Plus," she said, "everyone goes to church and spends time with family on Sunday."

Oma was fast on her feet, pulling that excuse out of her bag of tricks. However, the mention of people attending church on Sunday made me feel queasy because of what I'd learned earlier about Christians in Germany welcoming the rise of Nazism. How could I possibly forget what I'd been made to memorize backwards and forwards about positive Christianity as stated in an early Nazi platform. Article 24, yes, that's the one, and my mind went off reciting line after line, especially the part about demanding religious freedom so long as it doesn't interfere or conflict with manners and the moral sentiment of the Germanic race. Positive Christianity, I wanted to gag when I recalled how it incorporated propaganda about combating Jewish materialism at home and abroad. What hogwash!

I tuned back into Oma's guile, succeeding at convincing my mother to allow me go with one caveat. "Don't make a habit out of it, Christa."

We arranged our outing for the day after next, Wednesday, when my father would still be at Maybach and wouldn't know about our trip. That gave Oma time to plan, get our tickets, and finish a couple of things she said needed tending to in Ravensburg.

That night I was too excited to sleep, too full of dreams and plans filling the rest-of-my-life's calendar. In those trying days surrounded by so much fear and anger, I was a lucky one to have fallen in love, to have found someone I wanted to spend the rest of my days with. I couldn't imagine anything more wonderful. It sustained me when I saw SS in uniform, plainclothes Gestapo and sedans emblazoned with swastikas. It buoyed me up until the next day when I went home to walk Max on my lunch break and stopped by Herr Meier's kiosk to read the headline *Rome-Berlin Axis*. I didn't see beyond the first couple of sentences when Max bounded after a squirrel with me flying after him. What I did see mentioned a coalition had been formed between Germany and Italy. Not certain what it meant, I felt pretty sure it would not be favorable and that didn't sit well with me.

I was confident any remaining discomfort from having seen that headline would ease when tomorrow I would see Paul. In the meantime I did my duties animatedly, glad to do whatever my mother or Herr König asked of me, happily helping staff finish their tasks that needed doing before we could all go home.

I skipped along on the evening walk with Max, joy running through the pores in my skin. My mindset was as sweet as *Lebkuchen* at Christmastime, and just like I anticipated that mouthwatering honey-sweetened ginger cake I felt similarly about seeing Paul. The mood was not to last for as soon as I returned home I saw a dark sedan with swastika flags on each side parked in front.

Max got excited barking our presence alerting the visitor I was home. Gertrude opened the front door. "Christa, I've been waiting for you over an hour." Of course, she exaggerated for if she was with her father there was no way he'd be idling about with my father not home. My stomach roiled a bitter tasting upchuck into my throat.

I swallowed hard and coughed out her name. "Gertrude. This is a surprise."

Max jumped up on her nearly knocking her over.

"Get that beast off me." She pushed back against him, her hand swiping his saliva–dripping mouth. "Ick. He slobbered on my new dress."

As I watched her wipe her dress with a handkerchief, I held back a stressful laugh. I was nervous about why she was here and who drove her. "What's going on?" I wanted to get right to the point, to know if this had anything to do with Paul. Or Oma and her friend.

Gertrude, fast over her disgust at Max's saliva, bounced up and down when she told me her father had spoken with my father and he gave permission for me to spend tomorrow off with her to go shopping.

Not on my day off, the day I arranged to go with Oma to see Paul. I wanted to push her away and go find Oma to help me. Trapped and in no way wanting to spend my day off with Gertrude, I said the only thing I could think of. "I need to check with my Oma. I made plans with her and don't want to hurt her feelings."

"She can come with us." Gertrude was chomping at the bit to tell me what she had in mind and was fast with getting it in before I got to Oma. "I'm getting married. Günther is positively wonderful." She rattled on about her handsome SS fiancé, saying nothing of substance other than describing how good–looking he was. "You're going to be my bridesmaid! We'll go to Friedrichshafen to find me a dress."

For a moment I felt like I was with my old friend Gertrude, the girl I helped during physical education classes. The one I enjoyed spending time with. But there was no time for sentimentality when all I could think of was how in the world am I going to get out of this?

Gertrude grabbed hold of the sleeve of my sweater, sending Max into a protective barking fit.

"Calm that dog down!" Gertrude stepped back, distancing herself from Max.

I wished he'd have bitten her and sent her to the hospital too sick to ruin my day off.

"Let's go in and make plans."

Inside, Herr Hess was in the kitchen talking to my mother, who was preparing him a cup of coffee. Real coffee, he mentioned he brought for my mother, which concerned me almost as much as Gertrude stealing my day off. The wrench in the works was grinding on my nerves. My head was growing light, dizzy. I held onto the back of a kitchen chair to steady myself when I said I'd be right back that I had to use the bathroom.

I didn't need to go but needed an excuse to get to Oma, who was as equally surprised and upset as I was. She was also upset Herr Hess had been following my mother around the house with that pest Gertrude snooping through shelves in my father's study.

"What! Are they spying on him?"

"Shush!" She put a hand up. "Listen to me. I don't think that's what's going on. Gertrude is just a nosy rascal but Herr Hess… he arranged for your father to spend more time at Maybach and I don't like it. Not one bit, not after he's dawdling around here." She lowered her hand warning me to keep my voice to a whisper.

"Did you know about Gertrude getting married? My day off is now ruined because she wants me to go shopping with her."

"Yes. She told me. That girl can't keep her lips shut. And mind you, watch what you say to her."

As if the devil whispered in her ear, Gertrude was moving down the hall calling my name. "Christa, what's keeping you?"

"Oma, we'll have to figure something out."

Gertrude's eventful day had been planned. Her father would have someone drive us to Friedrichshafen and wait for us while we shopped then bring us back to Ravensburg. If Oma wanted to come that was fine with Gertrude. Once the time was established for the next day, she hassled her father about leaving. He took his time, seeming hesitant to go. That felt like a hot poker against my back.

My thoughts were a jumble. How am I going to get to Paul? Is there any way to get out of the day off with Gertrude? What's up with the way

Herr Hess looked at my mother? I watched them leave, the Nazi flags flying at right angles, and I wanted to run out the door to the train station and get to Paul as quickly as I could. It was an impossible situation.

Oma came through with a plan for her to see Paul. She would go with us but when we went shopping, she'd wander off to spend a little time with a lady friend she'd promised to visit. Of course, that was all made up, but who would check up on my innocent appearing Oma while I was out with a leading Gestapo official's daughter?

CHAPTER THIRTY-THREE

Underneath my smiles and agreeable nods to Gertrude on the ride to Friedrichshafen, I was in a sour mood, wanting to shut her up. Oma in the front passenger seat appeared reposed but I assumed from the way she'd avoided conversation earlier at breakfast her disposition was no brighter than mine. Yesterday when we spoke, she minced no words concerning how she felt about Gertrude and her father. Watch out for them, she told me with the caveat that she felt Gertrude acted out of selfish and immature means which could cause trouble but as for her father, he was a no-good scoundrel bent on doing evil to forward his own status.

Once I was close with the blue-eyed boy crazy Gertrude, along with Brigitte and Vera. We were an impenetrable foursome bound at our hips like sisters. I missed those carefree days of slumber parties and laughing ourselves silly until a parent came to the room to hush us. We'd hide our faces in pillows and continue carrying on listening to Gertrude talk about her latest crush while Brigitte held out her hands for us to see the nail polish she confiscated from her mother and how pretty it made her hands, hands that now wore an engagement ring. I missed Vera, my best friend, and it hurt never to have heard a thing about her or her family since they left.

Gertrude nudged my shoulder drawing me out of my reverie. "Where'd you go? I was talking."

I didn't like the way she commanded my attention, just like her father. Had she changed because of him, the big important Gestapo? Feeding into Gertrude's vanity, I replied, "Sorry, I was just thinking how lucky you are to be getting married." It wasn't hard to lie to her.

She continued talking and I pretended to listen while my mind wandered until I heard her mention something about seeing plans for a camp on Ettersberg hill near Weimar. She laughed then lowered her voice so the driver wouldn't hear. "My father forgot to lock his briefcase again."

At first I thought it might be a camp for Hitler Youth training but when she mentioned, "a concentration camp," I was sure it must be for something more sinister.

Gertrude rambled on, the only sound breaking her monotonous drool was Oma let slip a clicking of her tongue in disgust.

"Was that intended for me?" Gertrude directed her accusatory question to the back of Oma's head.

"Just an itch on my palate, dear." Oma emphasized dear, appeasement in her tone.

"Plate?"

Gertrude didn't hear or understand what Oma said, and I laughed trying to explain what the palate was. She didn't take well to my laughing at her and came down hard on me in a loud voice. "I'm trying to tell you about Buchenwald, where problems will be solved, and you find it funny!"

"Buchenwald?" I thought of the beech forest in Buchenwald, Germany, not understanding she was referring to the concentration camp she'd mentioned earlier. The whole conversation was confusing.

"That's what I was trying to tell you when she interrupted." Gertrude motioned a lifted chin toward Oma. "Buchenwald concentration camp should be up and running by next summer."

My interest was piqued. I wanted to know more of what she'd seen snooping in her father's things so I sat back and gave her my undivided attention, which was all she needed to prompt her along.

"For communists and other undesirables." She broke out in gleeful laughter when she continued. "I overheard my father on the phone talking about it, mentioning all the unwashed scum will be taken care of. The camp will be a place to stash Jews which will clean up our superior country."

Stash Jews! I wanted to wrap my quivering hands around her neck, and her father's. Instead, I gripped the seat of the car to steady them. I stretched my foot and tapped it under Oma's seat to be sure she was listening. Gertrude was too preoccupied with herself in telling me what she'd seen and heard to notice my gesture.

Gertrude went on about how wonderful everything will be when the camp removes the bad elements from society. I didn't want to hear another word and fall into a frenzied emotional state so I shifted the conversation, interrupting Gertrude's rant. "What kind of dress are you thinking about?"

Easily distracted, she was more than pleased to talk about herself, her clothes, her betrothed. On and on she went not leaving out a detail, including how handsome he'll look in his SS dress uniform. "They're tailored to project authority. My father said the black color fosters fear and no one will mess with a SS in uniform. I just love that."

Her father this, her father that, her father was turning her into a lunatic. She was never this obsessed with her father before he joined the Gestapo. It's as if he injected her brain with *Mein Kampf*. I dug a nail into the leather seat penetrating it, wanting her to shut up. There was no getting away from the machine's transformation of Hitler from common German soldier and politician to flawless deity. His word law.

It didn't matter what she said next, the writing was on the wall. I had to help Paul. The image of the ash and destruction that was once a home with a dog full of wagging life plagued me. His garage wasn't a safe place for him and his neighbor going there daily was way too risky. Oma understood that and hopefully she'd be able to do something about it when she went to him.

The last of Gertrude's nauseating babbling about the glorious SS and how she was going to make beautiful Aryan babies trilled through the car right up to its stop at the curbside of the dress shop. The driver got out and opened the back door, first letting Gertrude and me out before opening the front passenger door for Oma. That was rude, I thought, not tending to an elderly first, throwing out long-exercised civility. It was another thing I disagreed with the regime about, its emphasis on people's worth rested in their ability to work. Was my Oma being subjugated to a category of unworthy because of her age, in her early sixties? I resented the implication the driver minion made when he tended to Gertrude first.

As I moved past the driver, I swung my leg at a wide angle clipping his calf, a small comeuppance for his disdain to my Oma. "Excuse me, Sir." I feigned an apologetic tone and stood by Gertrude, waiting for my stiff rheumatic Oma to step onto the sidewalk.

The driver indicated he'd return for us in three hours and got back into the swastika waving sedan. As we watched him drive off, Oma stepped right up. "I'll be off on my own for a bit and back in time."

"You won't see me try on my dress." Gertrude sounded disappointed and looked a little crestfallen. It made me wonder where was her mother. She had no one to support her in her preparations.

"Gertrude, my dear, I have an ill friend expecting me. Plus, you and Christa can have your girl time together. Won't that be nice?" Without giving Gertrude a chance to rebuff her, Oma patted a hand on her back and told her to go shopping and enjoy herself.

I wanted to stop Oma to find out what she planned to do, but Gertrude was clinging to me like adhesive tape and I couldn't extricate myself from her. All I could do was talk in code.

"I hope you can help your friend… and, please be careful you don't catch anything."

***

Dress after dress, shoebox after shoebox, with accessories included, I sat, watched and listened, wanting to pull my hair out. At least there was no more talk about concentration camps or the SS, and for the first time I'd been with Gertrude I welcomed her mundane bickering. How she carried on with the salesladies trying to tell her she needed a larger size, but Gertrude insisted she had the right size and the seamstress would need to do a little waist adjustment. The seamstress agreed with the salesladies but they all lost the argument to pigheaded Gertrude.

As the seamstress was pinning the hem of the dress, Oma arrived looking grim, interrupting Gertrude's squealing about the length being too short.

"Did you fight with your friend, Frau Koch?" Gertrude tittered, looking down from the box platform she was standing on.

Oma tsked, not taking well to Gertrude's snickering. Neither did I, nor the pensive expression plastered over Oma's eyes-averted face, what she looks like when relaying bad news. Not being able to find out what had happened, my gut rumbled a loud belly cry threatening to bring up my last meal.

As I put up with Gertrude's incessant faultfinding blab, the rest of the day moved at a torturously slow pace. I stifled my anger until we arrived at my house and I tripped over myself getting out of the car. As the sedan moved away, I grabbed hold of Oma's sleeve, pulling a little too hard accidentally ripping it by the underarm. "I'm sorry."

"Never mind that."

We found a private spot in the yard, away from the house and Liddy's ears, to talk. Oma got right to it.

"He's all right for now."

I listened to her tell me Paul was in the neighbor's attic on a cot behind a stack of large trunks, but should anyone come looking for him there he's not safely hidden.

"Why's he there?"

"Ursula saw a youth hanging out across the street. She's worried he may be one of the troublemakers and will bring his friends around to do more damage. She convinced Paul to stay at her place where it's safer, said it's a temporary measure until other arrangements can be made." Oma drew her lips back like she'd eaten something distasteful. "After seeing the charred remains forcing him to live in an untenable space in his garage, I agree with her."

"I hate what's happening!" I wanted to hit something and scream from the top of my lungs how unfair it was, instead, I curbed my reaction. Oma looked shaken enough. She feared for Paul. So did I. "Now, he's at Ursula's… that's not much safer. What can she do? This is awful!"

Oma allayed my jangled nerves when she told me that similar to her friend in Ravensburg, "Ursula has friends in Friedrichshafen who will help."

"I want to help."

"You can help by staying put here and let the people who know what they're doing handle the situation."

"But Oma—"

"No, Christa, it's too dangerous. Not just for him but for you and our family. Stop thinking of yourself and think of what's best for Paul."

Before I could express my protest at being called selfish, and say why I wanted to be with him, and help, Oma told me it was Paul's wish for me not to be directly involved for the exact reason she had just expressed. It was too dangerous.

"Paul cares about you. Accept that's how he wants to show it."

When I heard he cared and that's how he wanted to show it, my objection thawed. "I know you're right. This is so hard, Oma."

"Yes it is." She reiterated Ursula was working on it now as we spoke, and reaffirmed she was a reliable, well-connected woman.

As I listened to her, I was on pins and needles and remained that way through dinner, moving my fork around on my plate to my mother's curious questioning. To cover up the real reason for my disaffection, I told her it was no fun being with Gertrude.

CHAPTER THIRTY-FOUR

After two days of sleepless nights, picking at my food, and looking like something Max dragged in from the gutter, an ominous appearing postcard came in the mail for Oma.

Upon arriving home and sifting through the day's mail, I stopped cold staring at the postcard with the image of soldiers in brown shirts and brown ties, wearing Nazi Stormtrooper kepi hats and holding poles flying swastika flags—the blood red from them standing out. I'd seen that before, the Nuremberg rally postcard, 1935.

"For Oma." I said aloud to myself, looking down the hallway for Liddy. "What in the…" I read the cryptic message about an unruly puppy being rehomed and how we all know how much the Führer loves Blonda. That was all it said but it was enough to rouse my ire.

"Pathetic!" I said that way too loudly and grew intensely aware a slipup like that could bring trouble. My reaction to Hitler's dog was an automatic response to the inequities of it all. There was Paul, an innocent Jew in hiding because he wasn't allowed to breathe freely the same air as Germany's leader's dog, Blonda!

As I stormed down the hallway, clutching the postcard in my sweaty hand, turning it into a soggy clot, I bumped right into Liddy coming out of the dining room.

"My apologies, Christa."

The tension over the last forty-eight hours broke loose and I fell into an uncontrollable bundle of tears, worrying Liddy she'd hurt me.

"I'm all right, Liddy. The fault was mine." Her face grew blurry then split into two heads. I blinked to regain a clearer vision and said the first innocuous thing I could think of. "I don't feel well. I think I'm coming down with something." I stealthily stuffed the postcard in my skirt pocket. "I'll go have a lie down before dinner."

"May I get you something to drink? Something nice and warm."

"No." I headed to Oma's room then turned back to see Liddy still standing where I left her. Remorseful I was short with her, I said, "Thank you, Liddy. I'm just not myself today. Hard day at work."

The expression she wore gave me no cause for concern she overheard my outburst or suspected anything.

Oma was in a chair looking out the window to our yard at the end of the year leaves falling and trees becoming bare. Bundles of gray rain clouds were forming into masses. The dismal sight matched how I felt. I pulled the ball of thin cardboard out of my pocket and tried to unroll it. More of the ink remained on my hand than the postcard but I remember every word.

Oma's smile made no sense to me. Not until she explained what the message on the postcard meant. "This is good news." Her eyes roamed to the door and she lowered her voice when she told me to make sure it's locked. Back beside her, I sat in a chair listening to her explain the postcard was from Ursula and the puppy referred to was Paul. "He must have been moved."

"He's safe?"

"I'm assuming yes, he's safe."

"How can we find out for sure?"

"Ursula told me she'd inform me when he'd been moved and we've heard nothing else from her. Using the P in his name we discussed the label puppy so I'd know who she was talking about. It can't be anything else but—"

"But what, Oma?"

"Unless I see something with my own eyes."

Her voice trailed off but I knew what she'd alluded to. That's what she always said when getting information secondhand, what she'd drilled into me about seeing things, hearing things, for myself. The postcard, the message, and Oma's explanation were good enough for me. I refused to entertain any ideas to the contrary.

"What now?"

"We wait for word, that's what."

Max's scratching at the door interrupted us. "You hungry, boy?"

Another couple of days brought a second postcard. The puppy had settled into his new home. Then more days with no message and endless handwringing. My bugging Oma to contact her friend too many times to her liking got me evicted from her room.

Work was hard, but being home with nothing to occupy my mind other than walking Max was not good for my sleeping and eating habits. I tossed food around on my plate drawing looks from my mother and Oma, and sat up against my bed's headboard night after night wondering where Paul was. Was he even in Germany?

The worst of distractions came the second Sunday after the last cryptic postcard arrived. Gertrude barged through our front door almost knocking Liddy over. Next entered her father all official with his right arm extended from the shoulder and hand-straightened *Sieg Heil* salute.

Gertrude giggled her way to me at the end of the hall as her father ordered Liddy, "Get Herr Becker."

Why so formal? He didn't even glance in my direction where Gertrude was smugly carrying on about something exciting soon to happen, hands on hips in an almighty stance like she knew something no one else did.

It was my father's first day off in weeks and he'd only arrived home a few hours earlier. His obsequious exhausted appearance was not met well by Herr Hess who told him to straighten up. As I moved to them, Gertrude pulled me back by my skirt. That was the first time her forcefulness intimidated me.

Liddy slipped away toward my parents' room, returning in a couple of minutes behind my mother, who was not happy with the scene nor was she about to be put off by Herr Hess.

"What is the meaning of this, Kurt?" She approached my father and Herr Hess, repeating the question emphasizing Herr Hess' first name. It didn't surprise me he treated my mother differently than he treated my father. For months I had suspected he had a special interest in her.

Herr Hess' tone became more cordial when he told my mother he had orders from Himmler himself. "Your husband is to go to Buchenwald today. I will escort him to his transportation."

Buchenwald? My brain felt like a beehive with a swarm of bees buzzing unintelligible sounds all at once.

The color drained from my father's face.

"Gertrude." I spoke into her ear. "What's going on?"

She didn't hesitate to tell me what her father was telling my parents. "Your father is needed to help with the final stages of the camp."

I jerked my skirt from her hold and went to the three adults by the front door, and told my mother to do something. She pushed me behind her and told me to be quiet then pled her case. "Kurt, he's only been home a few hours. Look at him. Let him rest and—"

Gone was any hint of friendliness when he indignantly cut her off. "You dare to question my orders!" Then he railed at my father to follow his orders or there would be consequences. "Get your bags packed!"

My father took control of the situation, quieting everyone down when he said he'd get ready and that there would be no further objections from anyone in his family. Herr Hess, seemingly satisfied, motioned Gertrude to him and together they strutted out to their chauffeur-driven black sedan. My father, who most likely hadn't unpacked from his trip to Maybach, followed them several minutes later leaving my mother, Liddy, and me standing by the open doorway watching them drive off.

My mother thanked Liddy for coming in on her day off to help with my father's return, telling her to take tomorrow off. When Oma returned from visiting a friend, who she earlier said was a woman she'd known from church, the house was quiet and a cold meal had been prepared by Liddy. Without asking what was happening, she set the meal out.

Once we were all at the table, Oma broke the silence. "Where's Harald?" She looked at my mother who held a spoonful of food midway to her mouth.

My mother put the spoon back down then caustically responded, "Where do you think he is!" She pushed her food away. "With them!" The lid was off the don't-say-anything jar and out came a tirade from months of withheld emotions. First she vented the frustration she had over not being able to speak her mind. Next came the anger at my father for going along with them, and lastly she broke down over the loss of her son, crying that every loss since then–every displaced Jew, handicapped citizen, or victim of awful circumstances–was a reminder of Jürgen.

Once her unleashed tearful words were out of her system, and she said she had no regrets speaking her mind, no one was eating. It was a powerful moment of coming together. From the look on my mother's face and the same serious nodding agreement from Oma I knew the regime hadn't won the battle of conformity in my family. Although we may have pretended to concur, they would never win over our hearts and minds. I also surmised from overhearing tidbits of conversations between my mother and father he felt the same.

To lighten things up, I threw the partially eaten piece of bread on my plate to Max, who was lying at my feet.

"Christa!" My mother laughed belying her punitive attempt to get me to not feed the dog from the table. "Oh, what's the use." She picked up a whole slice of bread from her plate and tossed it to Max.

We all broke out in laughter, releasing tension and enjoying the moment as Max wagged his stubby tail and sat up begging for more.

CHAPTER THIRTY-FIVE

When the dishes were cleared from the table and in the sink to be washed, Oma asked if Max had been out yet to do his stuff.

"Not yet."

"I'll go with you when you take him out. I need to stretch my legs." She spoke loudly looking out the kitchen door to where my mother was in the dining room folding the tablecloth, sounding as if she wanted my mother to hear why she wanted to go with me.

I followed her eyes toward the open door. "Do you want me to ask her to—"

Oma waved a hand to stop me then shook her head.

The mirth shared moments earlier dissipated like vapor coming off boiling water as we hurriedly washed, dried and put away the dishes and silverware. By then my mother had finished what she was doing, said goodnight and went to her room.

I leashed Max then opened the door to let him out. Oma followed.

Suspicious about why she wanted to be alone with me and to not include my mother, I asked if she had something to tell me.

"Not here." She motioned to a place in the yard, a distance from the house.

"You don't want to walk down the street?" That was where I usually walked Max to give him new places to smell.

"No."

Since we weren't going for a walk in the neighborhood, I let Max off the leash. Muzzle to the ground he found a spot to lift his leg, and after a snout sniffing operation across the lawn he circled and squatted to finish doing his stuff.

We were standing away from the house but still within range of the patio lights when Oma told me what she had to say. "I fibbed about where I was today." There was nothing coy in her words, nothing sheepish when she told me she wasn't with a woman friend from church. "However, I was with a friend."

I listened with bated breath as she told me a plan had been set in motion. Paul was going to be moved to Freiburg.

"No!" I squawked a little too loudly but caught myself and continued in an undertone. "That's so far away." I thought of the beautiful southwestern area where we'd once vacationed near the Black Forest, replete with vineyards where my parents enjoyed imbibing a glass or two with meals. I remembered my first taste, not to my liking, and how everyone laughed at my puckered lips. Also, not to my liking was how far away Paul would be.

"That's the point." Oma said he needed to get far away from where he's known and can be identified.

I couldn't argue that point but why so far I asked.

"Think for a minute, the geography of the region."

"It's warm. One of the warmest places in Germany. Wine country."

"That's correct but not why. It's on the main route to—"

"Oh!" It hit me like a sledgehammer coming down hard on cement. I didn't need to say Switzerland out loud, better not to. As to why that route, I remembered Paul mentioning Ursula had run-ins with Dieter's father at the ferry station Dieter frequented. Paul also told me if he ever planned on leaving Germany he wouldn't want to do it through Friedrichshafen. Like in the past, I felt it best not to mention what Paul had told me about Dieter to Oma. I figured if Oma didn't mention it she probably didn't know. I assumed all Paul told her was he was known and felt too unsafe to leave through Friedrichshafen and she understood what that meant. I wanted to cry over the unfairness that to keep Paul safe he had to be moved outside of Germany where nowhere was safe for a Jew.

Oma reached a hand to my shoulder and feeling me tense said, "I'm sorry. This is how it has to be."

"Has to be!" I whipped back, causing Max to erupt like the Düren earthquake in fits of disruptive barking.

It didn't take long for my mother to stick her head out the back door to find out what was going on, nor for Oma to say no more for now and we'd catch up later.

Later happened in a few hours with Max tucked away in the bed in my room and my going to Oma's, waking her to find out if she knew anything more like where was Paul now, when would he move, and most importantly could I see him before he left the country.

She explained it would take some time to get him fake identification and a story to go with it should he be stopped. In the meantime, he was still in a safe place in Friedrichshafen, where exactly she didn't know.

"Can you please get a message to him?"

"Yes. What's the message."

"I want to see him before he moves away."

"I don't think that can be arranged."

"Why not?"

"It increases the risk of him being discovered, not to mention putting you and our family in jeopardy."

"Oma, please try to make it happen. I love him and want to see him before he leaves. I'll be very careful."

"Careful?" She shook her head like that was a ridiculous thing for me to say. She ignored my request, instead commented I was young and would get over him. "What's important now is his safety. His making it out alive."

It hurt to hear her say I'd get over him, hurt to imagine a future without him, but I couldn't dispute the reality of the situation and the veracity of that last thing she said. "Of course that's important, the most important thing, but it's also important for us to have our goodbye together. He has no one else who cares about him like I do. Please don't deprive us of our one last chance to talk, to see each other before he's off on his own. At least send a message I want to see him. If he doesn't think it's a good idea, then I'll drop it."

"You need to drop it now. You could compromise him and everyone helping."

Despite her urging me to let it go, I couldn't. Not yet. I had to get word to Paul, to see if he needed to see me as much as I needed to see him. To perhaps plan some sort of future when… at that moment I couldn't even think of when and what that meant. To settle my heartache, I begged her, "Please just ask him. If he says no, I'll not bring it up again." I wiped my moistened eyes with the sleeve of my nightie.

"Christa, Christa, Christa, why do I always give in to you?"

***

Oma sent the message. The waiting game continued bringing with it troubling news about my father and my mother's upset over it. Now well into 1937 Buchenwald was near completion and due to open and the higher-ups, being extremely pleased with my father's engineering contribution, assigned him to Berlin for highly confidential work.

Oma put out feelers to see if she could find out anything other than the euphemistically laced superficial communications my mother received from my father. At night in my room when my mother was asleep, she came back with a mouthful of secondhand information leaked through a disaffected Nazi who felt the regime had gone too far, a member who turned spy to help small groups that were trying to rectify unjust situations.

"Too far?" I pumped her for specifics when she stopped, pink-cheeked and looking like she was thinking twice about mentioning more. There were things Oma told me earlier she didn't want to mention to my mother for fear she would let them slip in conversation with my father so I knew she was filtering those communications but up until now I hadn't felt her holding back from me.

She outright told me she was reluctant to continue.

That didn't sit well. The only reason she would clam up was if it was bad news and she wanted to spare me more stress. Sadly, it worked just the opposite instantly causing me to fear for Paul and I told her so.

"It's nothing involving him."

"Then tell me, Oma." I'm sure the aggravation at her evasiveness showed in my voice.

"This isn't good. Your father has been recruited into a committee working on getting rid of the Gypsy menace. Those were the exact words relayed to me with a terse elaboration."

She told me plans were underway to round up the entire Gypsy population and incarcerate them in concentration camps. I felt sick to my stomach. When she continued and said, "extermination," I vomited my soup dinner onto my nightgown. I had read *Mein Kampf,* had it jammed down my throat at school and in BDM meetings, and will never forget the ruckus that broke out when Frau Schmidt read, "The nationalization of our masses will succeed only when, aside from all the positive struggle for the soul of our people, their international poisoners are exterminated." To the few that went pale and were disgusted by the idea, Frau Schmidt scolded that anyone who disagreed could join the Jews' fate. She then forced us to memorize that section.

"Go clean yourself."

I knew it was just a matter of time before what was happening to the Romani people would happen to Jews, all Jewish people under Hitler's control. "I understand why you hesitated to say anything, and feel the increased urgency to get Paul out of Germany."

"Exactly. Now go clean yourself and get some sleep."

Sleep did not come. Nor did a response from Paul. What I heard from Oma was there was a snag in his getting falsified documentation, which those helping him insisted on before transporting him. As the year rolled on and my nineteenth birthday approached, I had all but lost hope of ever seeing Paul again.

CHAPTER THIRTY-SIX

My life turned into one long continuous drudge of work and home to spend time with my mother and Oma with breaks in the depressing monotony to walk Max. Although my father regularly phoned home, we hadn't seen him in months. In that time I had to put up with Gertrude's wedding preparations and her showing up at our home whenever it served her needs. The problem with that was she usually came with her father who had clearly taken a liking to my mother. There was nothing discreet in his alcoholic fawning over her.

My mother did herself proud when he showed up unannounced one night without Gertrude.

Herr Hess' loud disruptive knocks on the front door happened during our meal with Liddy serving us at the table. The pounding on the door was so violent Liddy dropped the Silesien floral serving dish my mother had received as a wedding gift that was filled with potatoes.

My mother looked down at the mess of broken porcelain and potatoes on the floor. "Clean that up, Liddy, I'll get the door." Enraged, she bounded to the door.

"You look delightful." Herr Hess loudly slurred his words.

I stuck my head out the dining room door to see him grab my mother by her waist. She pushed back against his chest. "Just what do you think you're doing here at this hour, Kurt!"

As he clumsily lunged for her neck, he lost his balance and stumbled against the decorative antique table holding our mail and the antique bowl knocking it over.

"That's too bad." He eyed the shattered bowl.

I looked back at Liddy down on her hands and knees cleaning up the dining room floor then at the mess by Herr Hess and my irate mother. Pushed beyond her limit, she slapped him across the face. "Out! Get out!"

He rubbed his puce cheek. "You bitch!" Spewing saliva and nostrils flaring, he grabbed hold of my mother's blouse catching her right breast in his hand.

My mother pulled back out of his grasp, staring him down, her eyes shooting daggers as she stood her ground. "I told you to leave and if you don't I will phone your wife! Then I will phone the authorities. Need I remind you that my husband is working with Himmler."

Himmler, I thought, recalling a conversation I overheard my parents having years ago when my mother asked my father who was Himmler. She certainly knew who he was now and the influence he wielded. She must have gotten through Herr Hess' drunken stupor for without saying another word he turned on his heel and tumbled out the door onto his behind on the porch, leaving us to clean the mess he left.

My mother slammed the door shut, locked the latch, tucked in her blouse and returned to the dining room.

Were it not such a precarious situation, I would have applauded my mother's fortitude. She showed more courage than Herr Hess, a man who called himself a Gestapo officer. Was it Himmler he didn't want to deal with or his wife? I knew Gertrude's bossy mother, radiantly beautiful and well connected, from old German money whose family helped finance Hitler's rise to power. You didn't tangle with her and all in the know in Ravensburg were well aware of who wore the pants in the Hess family. Frau Hess was a rare exception to the Nazi belief that women be subservient to men. Gertrude once told me even Herr Hess' cousin Rudolf Hess, deputy to the Führer, catered to Gertrude's mother, and warned his cousin Kurt to treat his wife with respect. My mother was smart to mention she would tell Frau Hess, but how long would it keep Herr Hess away from her, from us?

The next time Gertrude came to discuss her wedding plans, she was alone. When I listened to her talk about the event to occur next spring, it put a fire under me to find out what was happening with Paul.

I rubbed the empty hollow in my neck, thinking of my brother's present, the good luck necklace, and decided to use my birthday, which was a few days away, as leverage to convince Oma to help me. A new year was looming on the horizon and I didn't want to begin 1938 without contacting him. Too much time had already slipped by and I'd been patient enough, complying with Oma telling me to put Paul first and let everyone do their jobs. But what about me? Why hadn't he responded to me? Did he even get the message? I was losing faith in my connection to him and needed to regain a semblance of confidence that somehow, someway we'd end up together.

I made my way to Oma's room, thinking of what I'd say. Several muddled things came to me but none I felt were strong enough that would warrant risking my seeing Paul. Other than the one message she said she sent to him, she'd been uncompromising with me whenever I broached the topic of getting another message to him.

I opened the door to her room wanting to break through the fortresses of safe places and subterfuges preventing me from seeing Paul, but having already discarded several ideas of how to tackle my predicament, I didn't know what to say.

Oma was asleep when I entered and closed the door, but instantly woke when I stepped on a floorboard that creaked. She raised her head and rose against the headboard. "Christa." She rubbed her sleep-laden eyes and stretched her arms out. "Come here."

I sat beside her on the bed, coming right out with it. "I need to see him."

She sat there looking ahead, listening intently, not attempting to interrupt or stop me, which encouraged me to continue.

"I've been patient. Did what you asked but it's been weeks, Oma. Months."

More quiet. I hoped it meant I was getting somewhere.

"It's my birthday in a couple of days and all I want is to see him. Nothing else. Please help me."

"What is it you think I can do? I don't know where he is. There's nothing more I can do than send a message and we've done that." She sounded hoarse from sleep but her words were light.

"Send another message. Please."

"What do you want to say?"

"I want to see him."

"That's it? That's the message?"

"I want to see him," I repeated and added, "please arrange for that to happen."

"They won't do that, Christa. Your seeing Paul is not a priority for all who are helping him, in fact just the opposite. You would be a hindrance. If someone sees you leaving here, arriving there... eyes and ears are out everywhere looking for... you understand."

"Yes. I don't care how we make it happen. Please help me, Oma."

"I'll relay the message but please don't hold your breath waiting for a reply. We didn't get one the first time and I assume it means your man is watching out for you. Of that I approve."

It was a nice thought but what if he never got the first message? What if for some reason unknown to me, he didn't want to see me? What if something had already happened to him? More thoughts volleyed in my mind threatening to sink me into an emotional gutter.

The message was sent and my birthday came and went. The last week in December, after I returned home from work and fed Max, Oma wanted to go for a walk with us. This time Oma said she didn't need the backyard privacy so we walked down the street with Max tugging on the leash to get to his spot. We watched him raise his hind leg and walked on a few minutes more before Oma told me she had a reply.

"Don't stop walking. Don't draw attention." She spoke with lips closed like a ventriloquist. "He never got the first message. The person meant to deliver it was transferred to another location before the connection was made. That's why you've heard nothing."

"Did the last one get to him?"

"As far as I know, yes."

"Nothing else?"

"Not yet."

I liked how *not yet* sounded promising.

The next few days work was quiet and I slept better, then winter came with a blasting flurry of snow and freezing weather. Snow-covered limbs on bare trees cracked blocking already impassible streets and railways making it necessary for alerts to go out if you didn't need to be out on the road to stay home. As the temperature dropped and traffic remained limited to what was absolutely necessary for official business, I waited. The upside of the bad weather was Paul probably would not be transported to Freiburg even if his falsified documentation had arrived.

CHAPTER THIRTY-SEVEN

As the cold weather prevailed into March, the frost nipping at my nose moved into my throat. I stayed home from work a couple of days in the middle of the month with Liddy bringing me liquids for my sore throat and Oma keeping me company. March 13 was a date I wouldn't forget for a long time. It was the day when Oma brought two pieces of news, one good the other alarming.

Oma spoke quickly, hesitating mid-sentence when she told me she received word from Paul, but my enthusiasm was quickly curtailed by the strange look she had on her face like what she'd learned wasn't good news. She seemed distracted when she told me Paul responded he hadn't received his identification papers yet and was being moved every few days because of increased vigilance in locating Jews.

"Once he's in a space that is deemed relatively safe, he definitely wants to see you."

"That's wonderful, Oma."

"Yes. They'll get word to us when a visit can be arranged." Her little smile didn't reach her dulled eyes and for a couple of minutes she went elsewhere.

Although she tried to cheer me with the good news, her lack of direct eye contact and the sad tone in her voice was disheartening. I couldn't help asking what else was on her mind.

"Paul must get out of Germany." The sorrow in her tone changed to urgency. "Fast!"

"Oma." I coughed and blew my stuffed-up nose. My sore throat had moved into my nose and chest. A sip of water cleared the phlegm in my mouth and I finished what I wanted to say. "You're holding something back. Please don't do that to me."

"You don't need bad news when you're not well."

"Bad news?" Those two words sank into my lungs taking my breath away. "Tell me." I thought we were long through holding back information from each other. I'd done my part but Oma, to my disappointment, was still opting to protect me, spare me some unknown emotional reaction that could impact my health but that made me feel worse.

She pulled a folded newspaper out of a large apron pocket, unfolded it, and showed me the headline. *Anschluss–Austria.*

My nose caught a tickle watering my eyes. Two sneezes later and another blow of my nose my vision was still blurred. "It's hard for me to read that right now. What does it mean?"

She began reading the article which started with a little of the history at the beginning of the thirties when the German Nazi Party won no seats in the November 1930 Austrian general election. However, its popularity grew when Hitler came to power in Germany and the idea of the two countries joining also grew in popularity. A couple of years later Austria was eighty percent pro *Anschluss.* Then the terrorism campaign began toward anti-Nazi forces.

"So much for the July Agreement and Austria's full sovereignty."

We both knew that was an agreement signed a couple of years earlier but what I didn't fully understand was what that meant now. Oma explained the German occupation and annulment of the July Agreement reinforced Hitler's aggressive territorial ambitions.

"In plain words, Oma." I still didn't get the importance of what she'd read and explained to me.

"Austria is under German control. All anti-Semitic decrees now apply in Austria. Hitler's unleashing his aggression."

That news, painfully spoken, finally broke through: I felt like my stuffy head was about to explode. The article brought back the reality of Paul's situation, and I understood what Oma meant when she adamantly said he must get out of Germany fast. I now felt that urgency.

"The increased aggression doesn't look good for Paul."

"Correct." She then shared the last thing she'd held back from me about him. "I don't know what the documentation holdup is or why he's still in Friedrichshafen. It makes no sense—as long as he's there he's recognizable. If he is transported further away at least he has a chance of being mistaken for a German. He has that going for him."

"Then does he really need papers? Can't he just say he lost them?" Once that was out of my mouth I knew it wasn't well thought out, and I corrected myself before Oma did which I was sure she would. "That wasn't very smart. Why do you think there's a problem getting him documentation?"

"It's possible that the small number in civil service who initially were keen to provide documentation to help Jews get out has thinned with the heightened aggression toward anyone assisting Jews. Could be many reasons but ultimately I'm not sure. Why speculate on the wealth of garbage I can easily come up with. We just have to be patient."

I grabbed hold of my blanket and squeezed the corner. It did nothing to relieve the dismay I felt, which lasted long after my sore throat and congestion cleared.

***

As the days moved on, I became exhausted from lack of sleep from awful and weird dreams that taunted me. Some I couldn't make sense out of such as the one I dreamed about two babies playing together. Aryan babies but they both had dark hair and brown eyes. They happily giggled at a woman moving a wooden car around the floor where they all sat. Even though I couldn't make out the woman's face, she seemed familiar. I remembered waking up in a cold sweat, my nightgown drenched, wondering who she was. Unlike other onetime dreams and nightmares, the baby dream kept repeating.

When Gertrude showed up at my house in tears one day after I had the dream, I thought it had something to do with her. She was waiting for me on my front steps when I arrived home from walking Max. He wiggled his backside silly as we approached, and I could see her eyes were bloodshot from crying. Her hair was a mess with loose strands flopping over her forehead and cheeks as if she hadn't properly brushed it. It was the end of April and the weather was still nippy.

"Why didn't you go inside? It's cold out."

"I saw you coming down the street and wanted to wait for you here." She hugged her arms around her chest and her teeth chattered when she said, "I'm too upset to see anyone but you."

It'd been a long time since I'd seen her vulnerable, with no chip on her self-righteous shoulder. Max, sensing her woe, moved up the steps to sit beside her. At that moment I loved them both. Gone was the feeling she was a thorn in my side. "Come on in." I reached my hand to hers to help her up.

"Christa, I'm so ashamed."

"Come on, let's get you in where it's warm."

"No, can't you stay here with me for a minute?"

A minute? When had it ever taken her a short time to say anything? I was cold and a wind had picked up dropping the temperature even more. I had recently gotten over a cold and with my lack of sleep I didn't want to get sick again, but I wanted to be there for her so I sat close to Max to feel his body heat which helped. "What happened?"

"The wedding's off. My dress is sitting in the store and I'll never wear it. My beautiful dress—"

"That's what you're upset about?" Just as I was becoming annoyed she landed on my porch and insisted I stay out in the cold with her so she could complain about not wearing the dress, she dropped a bomb.

"I am upset about that but it's not the real..." Tears poured from her eyes, mucus dribbled from her nose, and she dry heaved.

"Are you sick?"

"No. I'm pregnant."

She cried, wiping her eyes and nose with her hand as she told me her fiancé had lured her to his bed. She missed her next period and knew it wasn't late when she had morning sickness and couldn't keep food down. I was shivering as I listened to her tell me after she told Günther he confessed he also got another girl pregnant and didn't want to marry either of them.

"I told him he'd have no choice and once my parents found out they'd insist on his marrying me."

"You said the wedding is off."

"Yes. He talked to my father and told him he had done his duty for the Reich and was proud of what he'd done, but he wasn't in love with me and never planned to go through with a wedding." She sobbed and sniffed then continued. "My father, at my mother's insistence, did not make waves. Neither wanted to risk the consequences of appearing to challenge a program that Günther was involved in."

"The Lebensborn program?" As I remembered what Oma told me about Frau Vogt's role in the program Himmler established a couple of years earlier, to provide welfare to unmarried women in unwed mother homes and put the babies up for adoption to upstanding Nazi families, a wave of nausea moved through me. The thought of children deemed not racially valuable being sent to camps lingered a few seconds before Gertrude's voice drew me back.

"Yes and because of that they reluctantly accepted Günther's decision not to marry me. Also my parents told me since the baby is racially pure, if it's healthy they will raise it and I am not to mention another word about it to anyone. They're concerned my upset will be taken the wrong way and cause them problems. You won't tell anyone?"

"Of course I won't."

Boy crazy Gertrude having been brought to her knees let out a wail I was sure would bring my family out of the house and the neighbors running over. The front door opened and Liddy stuck her head out asking if everything was all right. Gertrude turned away wiping her disheveled hair from her face, not wanting Liddy to see her grief-stricken state.

"Yes, thank you, Liddy. I'll be right in."

The door shut and Gertrude lamented how embarrassing it was she was brought up not to have a baby out of wedlock and now it's all the rage.

Have a baby no matter what. If it enhances the Aryan population, morals and decency be damned. We were all victims of circumstances, some threatened with worse situations than others but none of us were unscathed. It was a rude awakening for Gertrude. Gone was the hubris she lorded over me. She had joined the ranks of the wounded. What price would we all pay?

She went on her way, head down, crying and bemoaning the unfairness of it all. For once I agreed with what she'd said but compared to what Paul was going through, and others deemed undesirable, it was hard to muster much sympathy for her.

My dreams about the two babies and the woman playing with them repeated. With certainty I knew it had nothing to do with Gertrude and her being pregnant. She was not the loving friendly woman in my dream, plus I wasn't even sure if the brown-eyed, dark-haired babies were Aryan. Funny how things you never think connect come to you in dreams, which is exactly what I thought when I wondered if the woman in my dream was Ursula.

CHAPTER THIRTY-EIGHT

Something about the two–babies–and–a–woman dream kept bringing Ursula to mind, niggling at me but nothing substantial came to my consciousness to bring it back to reality. Nothing until April moved into May and my mother mentioned my father said something to her during a phone conversation about needing to replace his damaged passport.

It was odd that thinking about my father replacing his passport reminded me of what Ursula had said to me about her deceased son and Paul looking alike. The image of them playing together as babies, just like in my dream, flashed through my brain, tying a piece of the puzzle into a clearer picture. No wonder the dream made me think of Ursula.

Ideas sparked like a welder working on metal, fusing fragmented parts–the dream, Ursula, my father's passport–into a solid plan. It might just be able to help Paul, but first I had to get to Friedrichshafen to talk with Ursula and Oma needed to help me.

"I need to go to see Ursula. It's important. I have a plan—"

Oma cut me off like a guillotine. "I don't care what your plan is."

"Please hear me out." When she didn't protest further, I told her what I had in mind was to use Ursula's deceased son's passport for Paul. "Horst and Paul grew up together. That makes them around the same age. Paul doesn't look Jewish and if Ursula still has Horst's passport, we could replace his photo with Paul's."

"That's a crazy idea."

I didn't think Oma would be in favor of any plan I had to see Ursula or to connect with Paul on my own. Regardless of her opposition, I felt strongly I had to pursue it, plus no one had come through for him with falsified documentation. My waiting days were over, and I was determined to get my way.

Oma opened her mouth to say something else and then stopped herself. Was she giving me the benefit of the doubt it was a good idea and could work? I didn't wait to hear what she was thinking and give her a chance to slam her foot on the brake. "What do we have to lose by talking with Ursula?"

Oma rubbed the side of her head causing dandruff to fall on her shoulder. "If he's caught and a matchup with Horst's passport to his death certificate turns up that won't bode well for Paul."

That was a good point, however was there any plan without peril? I acknowledged that was a possible pitfall, but I still wanted to talk with Ursula to see if it was even possible and if so have it presented to Paul. "Let him decide." I then reiterated what she had mentioned to me earlier about all that had been happening in the last few months. The increasing street violence against Jewish people and their property. The Gestapo and police officials rounding up anyone unwilling to work and incarcerating them in concentration camps. The Flossenbürg concentration camp opening. The government requiring all Jews to report property over 5,000 Reichsmarks. I kept at it, chiseling away at her rock-hard resistance to my getting involved.

Oma looked distracted, contemplating what I'd said. "All that money going to Göring." She grumbled about Hitler's entrusted money man and Jews' money going to support the German economy. "They work and sweat to make a living and their reward is it's used against them, to their death."

My last barrage got to her and she was on board with my plan. Haste was of the essence but convincing my mother about taking the next day off would not be easy. Unprepared with an excuse, I pled my case.

"I want to take tomorrow off, mother."

"Again in the middle of the week. No, I need you at the factory. I have some errands to run."

"I need to do something as well. Can you run your errands the next day and please give me tomorrow off?"

"What do you need to do?" She splashed a few more suspicious words at me.

I didn't like the sound of the mistrust in her voice nor her asking me what was really going on.

We were in the kitchen and Oma came in from the dining room with the dirty plates. "Liddy is gone. I told her to go home early."

My mother watched Oma put the dishes in the sink and turn to us, inserting herself into the conversation.

"Just tell her."

My mother did not like what was going on. With arms akimbo, she said, "Tell me what?" She tapped a foot on the wood floor waiting for the answer.

I was cornered with no way out but to pray for my mother's mercy. "I want to go with Oma to Friedrichshafen tomorrow. To pay a visit to Ursula–Paul's neighbor."

"Absolutely not!" My mother slammed her foot down.

"Hear me out. He's not there. He's…" I faltered, not comfortable saying anything more, fretting that whatever I said would cause my mother to shut any doors I was planning to go through. Just as I needed Oma on my side, I needed my mother, but I already felt I'd said enough and by the way she looked she wasn't having any of it.

Oma seeing me struggle came to my rescue. "Perhaps we all better sit down." She ushered us to the table in the kitchen. "Inge. The boy's in hiding in a safe location unknown to us, but most likely nowhere near where he lived next to Ursula. Christa has an idea that might help him and she needs Ursula to implement it. That's all."

"That's too dangerous. I don't want you helping a Jew. End of discussion."

Helping a Jew! That hit me the wrong way and I was up on my feet, voice raised when I responded. "He's a man! A person! More than a bad label a power-hungry group of men pin on people who don't deserve it. He's a live, warm-blooded human being who I care about. Deeply. If you refuse my request, I'll go anyway."

The healthy sheen left my mother's face, and her forceful verbal protestation turned to a deep sadness when she lowered her head to her hands and spoke to the table. "Not again. Christa please, I can't lose you."

I sat back down and reached for my mother's hand. "And I can't lose him. Please understand."

Oma was so still it looked like she'd stopped breathing.

My mother raised her head, rivers of bereavement streaming down the valleys and grooves in her fleshy cheeks. There it was, what no mother would ever get over, now a wall separating her from anything that would replicate what happened to Jürgen.

I had to tear that wall down. How was the question. There was only one answer and it wasn't far from the truth. "I don't know what I'll do if anything happens to him." She had to have heard the desperation in my words, the intimation I wasn't beyond hurting myself, doing what she feared the most, causing her to lose me one way or another. Coupled with the dark cloud I'd been engulfed in for days, the message hit home.

Her face was a sad tome of loss, her lowered eyelids tense, when she yielded and gave Oma a stern warning. "If anything happens to her, I'll hold you responsible. You had no business condoning this in the first place."

Oma was smart to keep quiet while I hugged and thanked my mother.

A little later in her room, away from my mother, we planned. When all the planning was completed Oma told me to wait a moment before leaving. She went to her armoire and reached up to the top shelf to retrieve a hatbox. Under a wide-brimmed hat with a cluster of faux flowers on the crown was a smaller box wrapped in an embroidered handkerchief with the initials MK on it. She unfolded the linen fabric, removed the smaller box's top, and brought out a simple but elegant diamond necklace.

The bedside lamp cast a light on the sparkling surfaces of multiple diamonds strung together on a choker necklace, one of the most beautiful pieces of jewelry I'd ever seen. The light's dance-like movement and the way the sparkling diamonds' rainbow colors came alive brought me to the present moment. Gone was yesterday. Absent was tomorrow. Right then in that moment of captivated awe, my insides went quiet.

I ran a finger over the MK initials. "It's absolutely exquisite. Oma, where—"

"It was a gift to me from my mother, Mahthildis Kranz. It's been in the family for generations."

It's the first thing I'd looked at in days that shifted me out of my doldrums. Is that why she showed it to me?

As if sensing my thought, she said, "It's for you."

I pulled back. "I can't take your necklace. Besides, where would I ever wear it?"

A wry smile came to her lips. "Who said anything about you wearing it?"

As if the heavens opened and angels alighted on my shoulders, I understood exactly what she had in mind. It was a spellbinding gift and although it needed no further words she did say it would help Paul leave the country.

The warmth of Oma's generosity lingered through the night as I slept with that beautiful necklace on the pillow next to me, feeling the love it passed along. Another necklace for Paul, the first for good luck–the second for a chance at life.

CHAPTER THIRTY-NINE

With the diamond necklace tucked into a pouch hidden inside my skirt's waistband, we made our way to the station. As we passed Herr Meier's kiosk, something in a newspaper caught Oma's attention. She stopped to glance through an article about a large German minority living in Czechoslovakia, mainly in Sudetenland, wanting autonomy. As I stood beside her, in a faint whisper she falteringly said, "This isn't good."

Herr Meier, busy with a customer at the other end of his stand, didn't give any sign he heard her.

When we were beyond his earshot I asked her what she'd just read.

"There are a considerable number of Germans living in Sudetenland claiming they are being oppressed by the national government."

I didn't understand why she'd said that wasn't good and asked.

"First Austria. Then…" She looked disturbed, speeding her pace.

"You think Czechoslovakia is next?"

She nodded and said, "*Lebensraum.*" Every German citizen old enough to read knew the geopolitical goal of Germany since the Great War was for territorial expansion. *Lebensraum* ricocheted between my ears, what wars are made of. Oma's nod and answer in response to my question sent a shiver through me.

Minutes later we entered the station and boarded the train for Friedrichshafen, distracting us from any portentous ideas. That didn't last long for behind us sat two men who although trying to talk in an undertone were audible. I couldn't help overhearing one say to the other, "I've heard enough to know things will not get better. I've decided to leave."

Heard enough? I wondered what he was referring to, which was cleared up the minute the man with him responded. "It broke my heart to see the Müllers so upset at losing you as their doctor. But to leave your home… isn't there some other place a little calmer?"

"I've made up my mind. There is no place calm enough, no place in this country for me to practice medicine. No place to feel safe. It's time to leave."

The other man with him said someone might be listening and to lower his voice.

"Lower my voice! What voice? What voice am I allowed to have?" He gurgled from deep in his throat as if talking through clenched teeth.

I felt bad listening, but worse at what I was hearing. He must be a Jewish doctor–now forbidden to practice in Germany.

"Ben, please." The man's voice trailed off like a wisp of cigarette smoke.

Oma must have heard what they were saying for she craned her neck to look behind her before bravely standing and moving around to them. "Excuse me, gentlemen."

The two men became silent as Oma's peaceable posture and soft inoffensive voice told them she overheard them.

Lips smacked into a gasp. "We…" The one not named Ben meekly stammered. "We… meant no disrespect to—"

"Please do not worry. I am merely pointing out these friendly ears overheard you and perhaps you may want to wait for solid walls before continuing."

"Yes. Absolutely."

The rest of the way to Friedrichshafen they remained quiet. Once we arrived, Oma leaned around to the two men who remained seated. "Good luck in your travels."

I wanted to say something as well but what? Too perplexed, I attempted an accepting smile as we passed them, wondering how long before they were no longer safe in public.

**

Ursula's house was quiet and no inside activity was visible through the opened front curtains. To my left the blackened burned-out remains from the menacing flames were a reminder of why we were there. There hoping that a near stranger would be willing to further endanger herself if the passport was available, which would tie her to Paul if he was found out. It was a lot to ask of anyone, but Paul had mentioned she told him he was her son now. What actions would those words translate to?

My heart thumped in my chest as we approached the door, Oma mumbling about how horrible it was what "they did to Paul's house."

I hesitated to knock, waiting a minute to listen for any noise inside and perhaps around back. Whether out of fear she wouldn't be there or fear she would be there and we'd dead-end, my hand wouldn't raise to her solid wooden door, a barrier if crossed could either offer a step in the right direction or a broken heart. I didn't know how much more disappointment I could tolerate.

Oma, who up till that moment at the door had been patient with me for she knew how on edge and fragile my emotions were, grew impatient with my stalling and rapped on the door with her palm. She winced, drawing her hand back, rubbing it against her hip.

Another minute passed and when Ursula didn't arrive at the door, I pounded it with my fist. That did the trick for within a couple of seconds I heard Ursula shuffle to the door, saying, "I'm coming." The minute her sleep-crusted eyes saw us, her brows bewilderedly furrowed. "Christa. Helga, you're here too?" She wiped the dry crusts from the corners of her eyes.

"We need to talk to you." Concerned with time and having to be back to the train station in a couple of hours to catch our return ride, I rushed my words. "It's important."

"Yes, I imagine if you're both here it is." She ushered us in, locked the door behind her, and brought us to her modest living room where we had a seat as she closed the curtains and turned the overhead light on. She sat then moved to get up. "My manners... would you like something to drink? I have a little—"

"Nothing, Ursula." Oma thanked her for her offer, tersely stating we didn't have a lot of time. "Christa will explain why we're here–the plan."

She settled back in her chair. "Plan?"

"Yes. I..." It didn't feel right to get directly to the point, to not say a few words of salutation and to give thanks for all she'd done to help Paul. "You've done so much. Thank you." I repeated myself before telling her I loved Paul and wanted to help him.

"I know, dear. We all do."

We? I wondered who that meant? We three? Whoever was housing Paul? Everyone who had helped him along the way? Or some wider vaster network of Germans helping Jews? I didn't know the answer but whoever the collective we was for them I was grateful.

"I had a dream about two babies." I explained the dream and that she came to my mind, mentioning when my father talked about needing to replace his damaged passport all the pieces of the mystery jelled into a cohesive whole.

Ursula listened intently. When I got to the part about Horst's passport her eyes teared yet she continued to give me her undivided attention. When I was finished with everything I wanted to say and Oma had nothing further to add, Ursula stood and left the room.

My pulse raced. "She's upset about this," I said softly. "I feel bad upsetting her when she's done nothing but help."

Oma held up her hand for me to stop. "I don't think so."

Oma was right for when Ursula returned her eyes were moist, but in her hand she held a brownish-maroon passport. "With a new photo I think this will work." She blinked away tears pooling in her eyes.

That must have been an extremely difficult thing for her to do. Nothing about this was easy for her. For any of us. By her actions she had indeed honored her word, her commitment to Paul.

When Oma and I had a look at the passport, my heart regained its normal rhythm. I felt like I could breathe again. I relaxed even more when I gave the necklace to Ursula to help with any expenses for Paul. It was then I learned a thing or two about my Oma, who was more involved with helping than I was aware of. The diamond necklace wasn't the first time she'd donated jewelry to help a Jew. She had given other valuables, items that would be traded for money. Money to feed people. Money to help with forged identification. Money to help people, like Paul, flee Germany. My Oma, my righteous Oma, was more of a heroine than I ever imagined.

After we said our goodbyes and left, I told Oma I was proud of her.

"When we can do something then we do something."

"We? You did it, Oma. You stuck your neck out. You helped. You gave your—"

"Hush." That was all she said, for in her beautiful inimitable way she didn't want to take credit for stepping up to help another. All the more reason I respected Oma.

CHAPTER FORTY

That visit to Ursula was a high for me, and I stayed on that hill of excited anticipation riding out the next few days right up to the time I received a postcard from her, one addressed to Oma but intended for me. The image on the postcard wasn't a political statement like the earlier one with soldiers and Nazi flags. Instead, it was a landscape of a wide open gray-green field with white puffy cumulus clouds hovering over forest-covered mountains, reminiscent of Freiburg. I thought of Freiburg, the place earlier mentioned that would be Paul's last destination in Germany before he'd cross the Swiss border.

Ursula told us any messages she sent would be cryptic, similar to communications in the past but clear enough we would understand the inherent message. "Card inspired me to take photography lessons. We're having a temperate June with sprinkles and spring vibrancy fading. Soon another visit?"

She was clever to mention photography, obviously referring to a photo of Paul for the passport. The mention of the weather and changing season meant things were moving and plans were underway. When I read about another visit, I felt like my head disappeared along with all the worries it stored. The expansive feeling was liberating, pushing away doubt and fear, and for the first time I envisioned Paul a free man–with me by his side.

Oma agreed with my interpretation. We kept the news from my mother who remained stable and was doing better emotionally and physically, even regarding her conversations with my father. She had only recently expressed affectionate things he said to her that made her smile. Sharing her lightness lifted the rest of us. That was not a balloon I wanted to stick a needle in.

***

Although the good feeling from that last postcard lingered for several days breaking up the continuous thread of ticking minutes and waiting, a blur of the same routine of work, home and time with Max divided by sun and moon risings, it didn't last. Not when everything around me was going to hell, a hell not far removed from Paul's existence. It wasn't enough that he and the Jewish population in general and other enemies of the state had been isolated, segregated and impoverished. No, now they were being rounded up and incarcerated with rumors spreading of their harsh treatment, some I even found unbelievable–like mass shootings. For what? Civil and criminal laws had been flushed down sewage lines along with innocent offenders being considered less than the accompanying human waste.

It was hard for me to keep meals down when I had just overheard Oma telling my mother about a circumcised baby boy being ripped from his mother's arms, dragged away with legs flailing, relentlessly and inconsolably crying for his mother. What on God's earth had motivated someone to do that to a baby? What had gotten into my fellow Germans? My neighbors? My classmates? I once believed Hitler capable of turning Germany around but I never believed, not deep in my soul, that Jews caused all the economic problems he had attributed to them.

Every story, news report, radio update spoke of escalating harsh treatment against Jews. It all pointed back to the first words I read by Hitler, something to the effect that the world would be better off without the existence of any Jews. We heard more talk concerning death camps. Was my father involved in their construction?

With everything that was coming back to me from my family, from seeing news articles, and talk in the factory, how could I possibly escape from my worry about Paul? There was the occasional rare event that distracted my attention, such as the night the phone rang and Oma rushed to wake me to tell me there was an urgent phone call from Gertrude's mother.

In my half asleep state, I tried to comprehend the bitter reproachful words coming from Frau Hess, not directed at me but not easy to receive. She was in an outraged huff and when she calmed down enough to make some sense, she told me Gertrude was in the hospital in critical condition.

"Why? Frau Hess, what happened?"

More unintelligible blather came from her before I interrupted and as politely as I could muster asked her to please slow down and explain what happened.

"What happened!" She screamed, probably mad because she felt I hadn't been paying attention.

I wanted to scream it was the darn middle of the night and if she didn't have the courtesy to be clearer with her communication I was going to hang up. That's what I wanted to do but knew better, knew there was no speaking back to that woman and I had to let her have her way figuring I'd head to the hospital and find out what happened once there. As calmly as I could I told her I'd head to the hospital right away and thanked her for phoning.

After Oma told me there was a phone call, she went to wake my mother who was now up and dressed, car keys and purse in hand. "Oma told me about Gertrude."

"Where's Oma?"

"In the bathroom."

"What'd she say?" I asked my mother to see if Oma told her more than I'd heard. Once she said all Oma knew was Gertrude was in critical care and we needed to get to the hospital, I went to get cleaned up and dressed.

The streets were empty of other vehicles, but the ambulance bay at the hospital was busy with two ambulances waiting to unload their patients. What could have happened to Gertrude? She was in a bad way the last time I saw her, left crying and I hadn't seen nor spoken to her since then. I felt guilty about it but I didn't want to get embroiled in her messy situation.

Mother dropped me off by the entrance and went to park. I didn't see Frau Hess in the emergency room waiting area, and assumed she was in with Gertrude. What smelled like urine soaked clothing, rotten apples and fetid vomit mixed with an antiseptic odor filled the room. No one answered my knock on the glass window partition that separated the waiting room from the treatment area, nor did anyone appear behind it. When the door to the treatment area opened to admit a patient at the same time as two ambulance drivers blasted into the area with metal wheels clanking on the worn gray concrete floor transporting a very ill-looking jaundiced woman on a gurney, I snuck in.

I peeked through curtains making my way around the rows of hospital beds. None contained Gertrude. A harassed appearing nurse at the main nursing station banged the handset down. "Stop phoning!" She mumbled a few disgusted words to no one in particular.

I conservatively approached her and in a small voice said, "Excuse me."

Without giving me a second's chance to say another word, she indignantly asked, "Who let you in! You need to wait in the waiting area!" She rapidly swept past me heading to a bed.

"Please." I called after her.

She turned around to face me and before she could order me out again, I asked if she could direct me to where Gertrude Hess was. She must have known that name, the family, for her sharp edge dulled when she told me intensive care.

I expected to find Frau Hess with her daughter, instead I found only an ashen Gertrude asleep in a bed all alone, a bottle of blood hanging from a metal tree attached to one arm while another with a reddish tinge labeled Prontosil went into her other arm. A blood transfusion and what I remembered was a new antimicrobial drug from my BDM first-aid classes meant something really serious had happened.

Her wrists were clean. No cuts or other visible suicide attempt apparent, which was my first thought for I had wondered if the pregnancy and rejection from her fiancé had done her in. Other observable skin areas were also devoid of cuts or inflicted self-harm. If this wasn't her reason for being in such dire straits then what had happened and where was her mother?

"Christa, there you are." My mother entered looking as distressed as I felt. "What in the world…" Her voice trailed off as she looked around the single bed occupancy room, white and clean. The neat lonely room had two chairs, a bed with a nightstand, a bed table and metal medicine trees.

As she sat, my mother asked, "Where's her mother?"

"I thought she'd be here but now that you ask, I'm not sure where she phoned from."

"Hmm." My mother did not look happy about us being the only two visiting and not having a clue what had happened to Gertrude, who helplessly slept while we sat by her side waiting for someone to arrive who we could ask. That didn't happen for nearly two hours when an exhausted appearing surgeon entered in his blood-covered surgical gown waking my mother who'd fallen asleep in the chair.

"It has been a night. My apologies for not making it here sooner but your daughter will be all right. We got to her just in time."

My mother didn't have a second to correct him from the mistaken identity before he explained what had happened.

"She lost a lot of blood but the transfusion will take care of that. I'm sorry we couldn't save the baby but we got the tumor out."

"Tumor!" That was out my mouth faster than a fired bullet. I didn't know Gertrude had any medical problems let alone cancer, which is what I assumed the doctor meant by getting the tumor out.

"Yes. I thought my nurse spoke with you earlier?"

My mother's neck flushed a flustered pink for she had let him talk, let him believe she was Frau Hess who his nurse must have relayed information to on his behalf earlier. "I'm not Gertrude's mother. My daughter here, Christa," she motioned to me, "is her best friend. Frau Hess phoned us to come."

"I see." He thought for a minute, contemplating his next move. "Well then, no harm in what's been said but I should finish this conversation with the patient's mother if you'll excuse me." He left immediately, leaving us in a vortex of confusion, sorrow, and questions.

We gave the surgeon enough time to make the phone call to Frau Hess before my mother phoned using a hospital phone to get in touch with her. Frau Hess' earlier frantic, ill-tempered manner became understandable when my mother returned and told me what she'd found out.

"She began bleeding and lost a lot of blood. Her mother phoned for an ambulance and followed it in. In the surgery they found a large mass extending from the left ovary into the tube and uterus. No need for biopsy as it looked like tissue-eating cancer that disrupted the pregnancy and would have kept hemorrhaging if her female organs remained intact."

"That's going to kill Gertrude." Again, my lips moved faster than my brain engaged and the comment upset my mother.

"Don't talk foolish. They just saved her life and she will go on like the rest of us. Time will heal her."

Maybe for you, mother, I thought, but Gertrude's life was all about meeting her handsome SS dream man and having Aryan babies. The German fantasy of living the good life, happily ever after. Gertrude had no other aspirations. In that lonely room I watched Gertrude's shallow breathing, wondering why Frau Hess was not there. I recalled Gertrude once told me her mother–a Nazi party woman to the hilt–threatened to ostracize her if she didn't have Aryan babies.

Sadly, it looked like her mother's threat came to fruition for a very depressed Gertrude never made it back home before she was shipped off to a sanatorium. Too far away from Ravensburg for me to visit. Just like my brother was lost to me, so was she. Although some of her recent actions rubbed me the wrong way, she was a longtime friend who despite all that had transpired I still cared about.

CHAPTER FORTY-ONE

There was no time for me to process my heartsick reaction to what happened to Gertrude for I got word arrangements had been made for me to go to see Paul. As delighted as I was, the message frightened me as it carried a dire foreshadowing by informing me to hurry. Although he had a target on his back for being a Jew and his presence in Friedrichshafen was dangerous, a part of me didn't want him to leave. The physical proximity with him—a quick train ride away—lent to a sense of connectedness, a closeness, I feared we'd lose once he moved away. No matter what he had said to me before about his feelings, I knew what time and distance could do to relationships. Would his leaving be a one-way road out of my life? There were no guarantees and the more I thought about it the more I wished he could stay put closer to me, close enough for me to see him from time to time.

I abhorred those in charge who had created this untenable situation that ripped lives asunder. What made matters worse was the abject helplessness I felt over all options other than for him to flee and make it out of Germany alive. When I weighed all my emotions, one after another, the only right action was to do whatever necessary to keep him alive. What about me? My life? My love for him? Darn it! I fisted my hands, digging my nails deep into my palms, drawing a trace of blood.

I pled depression to my mother as my excuse for more time off. Oma also told her, "She needs the time." Gertrude was fresh on everyone's minds which I didn't hesitate to mention had really gotten me down. Plus the box factory was running smoothly with Herr König handling production matters and my mother managing orders, bills, other office paperwork and phone calls. She understood my need as she had been through her own psychological trauma.

One last thing to tend to. "Can you feed and let Max out?"

"Where are you going that you can't tend to Max?"

"Oma has a nice friend she wants to visit. I want to go with her."

"Are you going to that Ursula woman's place again?" An accusative edge entered my mother's tone.

Was there another easy lie I could tell? No, there wasn't, not with Oma scowling behind my mother's back, how she looks when urging me to spit it out.

"Yes."

I knew what was coming next.

She slapped a hand on her thigh "The boy's neighbor!" As if she thought him tainted, she couldn't bring herself to say his name.

"Paul, mother."

"No, Christa. This must stop. It's way too dangerous."

"Ursula is a kind German woman in good standing. What is the harm in our visiting her?"

She ignored my response and the entire topic of Paul when she turned to Oma and told her we should go somewhere else. "I've no problem with Christa having a little more time off but I'm not in favor of her visiting that woman or being anywhere near that boy."

"He has a name, Inge." Oma's castigating tone matched my mother's. "I must say that in this matter you are being unreasonable. Let your daughter have her visit with the kind woman with whom she can at least talk about Paul."

My mother looked from Oma back to me then back to Oma again appearing head-tilted flummoxed, rubbing her hand up and down her thigh. "Why are you condoning this?"

"I'm hardly condoning anything. You're overly sensitive… understandably so, perhaps if you better understand your reaction you will understand Christa's need to spend time with people who know Paul."

I stood there loving Oma, holding my breath.

"I don't know." The weakened resolve in my mother's voice told me Oma got through to her. Perhaps the lineage bond from mother to daughter to granddaughter was stronger than my mother's opposition. Deep inside we three were coming from the same book just different pages. I knew when my mother didn't instantly have another knee-jerk reaction that she was seriously looking at what Oma had said. When she moved from her head to her heart, she stopped resisting and simply said, "Please be careful."

I went to her, arms stretched out for a hug. "I love you."

She breathed back, "The feeling is mutual," and said she'd take care of Max.

***

Ursula opened her front door before we knocked, and ushered us in. Seated in the living room was a man in coveralls and a beige pullover that had smudges on the sleeves that looked like where he had wiped his dirty hands. His dry cracked weathered skin was tanned from working outside. A farmer who worked in the fields, I thought.

No time was wasted with lengthy introductions and small talk. As we walked to the back of the house and out through the kitchen's backdoor to the yard, he told us he was a local farmer who owned a potato farm on the outskirts of Friedrichshafen that also had several cows and a couple of horses. He was an old friend of Ursula's deceased husband who after Horst's death often stopped by to see how she was doing, what he would tell anyone if seen and questioned why his farm truck pulled into her driveway. Parked in the back was his truck holding silage for the cows and horses. The silage smelled like a communal latrine, which was the point. He lowered his voice when he said, "The SS don't like to sully themselves with the fetid aroma." For my comfort, he lowered his voice again to barely audible when he said it hadn't ceased to work to protect anyone in the hidden compartment under the silage.

He explained I would go in the compartment used for transporting people and to remain quiet. When I looked down at my skirt and nice brown and green argyle sweater he assured me there would be a blanket to keep me clean and an oiled canvas tarp over the compartment that tended to keep the odors off clothing. At any rate, now was not the time to worry about soiling my clothes or smelling badly. My only opportunity to visit Paul was in the farmer's truck and that was good enough for me.

The last thing he told me was his name. "Everyone calls me Erwin."

Oma gave me a goodbye hug and told me to do whatever Erwin instructed me to do. "I'll be here when you return."

I nodded to Oma and reached a hand to Ursula. "Thank you."

"We need to get going." Erwin pulled down a three-step wooden ladder attached to the side of the truck and I stepped on. The compartment was obvious the minute I got to the top of the ladder. It looked like a wooden casket attached to the right side of the truck. The lid was open and I got in on top of a clean wool blanket. Once the lid was tightly closed, I saw the air hole through the side of the truck, just large enough for my nose to inhale fresh air. Erwin placed the oiled canvas tarp over the lid then shoveled silage on top and smoothed out the surface. He had described the procedure to me before I got in, which saved me an attack of nerves.

Paul, is this how they transported you? Images of his face, his wavey hair swept across his forehead, the way his brown eyes lit up when listening to me, kept my mind from reeling in the claustrophobic space, kept me from going off into a hundred different dark mental gyrations. He was on my mind as the truck bumped and bounced over uneven surfaces, which I imagined were countryside roads. I struggled to steady my position so I wouldn't make a sound, which was impossible as my head kept banging against the side of the compartment. By the time we arrived I had a mammoth headache. Getting out of the wooden box was awkward and I fell back on a mound of silage. Once my feet were planted on the ground, my head felt like it was ready to explode, my vision was blurred, my eyes tearing, and I stank like dung.

There was no time to clean up, no time for anything but to move hastily to the farmhouse. My shoes were rubbing and I hoped blisters weren't forming on my feet. I was annoyed at myself for wearing shoes with a little heel to look fashionable instead of dressing with utility in mind.

The air was fresh, farm soil fresh, and the property had a wide expansive view of hectares of planted potato fields in every direction. The farmhouse was off the beaten path, down a long unpaved dirt road, open for anyone in the farm to see someone approaching. It put my mind at ease to know Paul was somewhere relatively safe. Even better was his actual hideout up in the attic. Erwin told me it was behind a false wooden wall. "Built with the help of some of my local friends who also want to help those needing to hide or escape from Germany."

In the attic I couldn't figure out where the hidden room was. The space was packed with boxes, trunks, old furniture, some of which were up against the fake wall that we needed to move. Erwin told me his wife and children were out working the fields and wouldn't be bothering us while I was here. He explained while moving chairs away from the wall that his wife knew what he was up to but the less seen or talked about the better for all involved.

Not a single peep came from the space Paul was in. As Erwin moved the last box, I held a hand up to the wall. My unsteady hand grew hot and sweaty on the wooden surface, all that separated us.

CHAPTER FORTY-TWO

Paul didn't look the same and to see him so thin with skin hanging from his bony arms, arms that were well-built the first time I'd met him, was not what I expected. It hurt to see his hands spasmed like an old man with a neurological disorder as they reached out for me. "You're really here." His voice broke, his tongue moved over his dry, cracked lips. Was it lack of food, lack of vitamins, minerals and the sustenance he needed? Or was it lack of appetite?

The space was small, too confined with nothing other than a thin narrow mattress, a blanket, one pillow, and a smelly pot on the floor by the foot of the bed. On a shelf above the head of the bed was a pitcher with water, a cup and few eating utensils, and a pencil and paper for him to write or sketch on to occupy his time. There were no windows, but a couple centimeters knot in the siding had been removed for him to be able to see outside. That helped to alert him to anyone coming and going, also to give him something to watch to break the monotony of confinement.

Confinement, I thought as he embraced me, was what he'd been reduced to. Our heads almost touched the slanted roofline. The walls were an arm's distance away leaving no space to exercise or walk to stretch his legs. Was this what it was like being in the camps? With the feel of his breath on my neck any selfish ideas I had about him staying in

Friedrichshafen vanished. This was no existence for anyone, the injustice of being driven to near death for no crime was appalling.

As lousy as I smelled from the silage and as poorly as he looked, our embrace was invigorating. It was the stuff of love, of what I'd never fully comprehended until that moment. It's what I had witnessed for many years between my parents but never felt beyond a yearning. I longed for the fulfilled sheen I'd seen in their eyes when they looked at each other at the dinner table, in the car, on outings, and when involved in mundane activities. The light within had clearly shone with them, and my Oma and Opa before them, also what I imagined Oma felt with Nahum. Now, I understood on a cellular level. Now, I knew I would do just about anything to keep Paul alive.

He kept repeating, "You're really here." His lips moved on my neck as he continued to speak. "We have little time."

He wouldn't let me pull away to look at him, to gaze in his soulful brown eyes. He held me tighter, his bony arms digging into my ribcage. The physical ache was nothing compared to the pain I felt over the minutes ticking away. His tight hold on me told me he felt the same.

"How much time do we have?" It wasn't what I wanted to talk about but since it was on his mind, I needed to know. Would I have enough time to fill our moments with everything I needed to say?

"Only twenty minutes is what Erwin told me."

"Twenty minutes?" That was so little time. Too little time. In that moment I couldn't bear to separate from him. The push-pull hit me. He had to leave but I desperately wanted to be with him. How? "I want to go with you."

Desire wrestled with sensibility. Rational thought surfaced. I didn't have a passport, plus if I went missing it would tag both Paul and me for death for us to be found together. I couldn't count on his non-Jewish looks and his forged passport to hold up under intense Gestapo scrutiny. Plus what would it do to my family were I to do something rash?

"How I wish… you need to stay here. I don't want to bring harm to you or your family."

"I want to be with you." I couldn't think of anything else important to say.

"I want to be with you also, my love. And when this is over I'll come for you. I have this." He reached a hand into his shirt pocket and pulled out my gold necklace.

He called me his love. My heart fluttered and skipped a beat–the power of his word was mesmerizing. "Our good luck necklace."

"Yes. It has been working."

Not good enough, I thought, and then another idea hit me. As bizarre as it sounded, I thought of Gertrude. Why in the world would she pop into my head at this time when I was with Paul? His leg moved against mine, and my heart skipped another beat reminding me of the clock ticking away burning our time together, drawing me back. "I don't know if I can wait for you to come—"

Paul tensed and pulled away from me. "What are you telling me? This can't be it for us. I love you."

"I love you too, Paul."

"Then why—"

"I need to finish what I was about to say."

His sad look reminded me of Max the night Frau Weber died, the look that I wanted to make better. I loved Max but I would leave him with Oma and my mother to be with Paul. I would leave everything to be with Paul, but to wait endlessly for some unknown future to arrive, to live with the tyranny that drove him away, that I didn't want to do. Beyond a month or two, I needed something tangible to hold on to, and doubted he'd ever be able to return to Germany once he left. "I will come to you."

His tightened shoulders dropped a little lower. "You can't. It's too risky."

"Paul, listen to me. Once you are in Switzerland, you'll be safe. I'm a German citizen and can travel. I'll think of something. There has to be a way. I just need an excuse, something to keep me safe while traveling and to protect my family."

He sounded like Oma and my mother when he cautioned it wasn't safe.

"I refuse to stay here and be lined up as a baby producer for some SS officer. That is not my future. I want to be with you. I want you to be my first and only love. I will make it happen someway. I just need to think of a plan." Again, I thought of Gertrude and the seed that had earlier been planted sprouted.

He knew not to pursue the topic any longer for my attitude made it clear I would do what I needed to do and there was nothing he could say to discourage me. My presence with him in that cramped, musty space had shown him who I was and it wasn't someone to let our love slip away. There was no way I was going to spend the rest of my days kowtowing to those who dared to control me. I was done endeavoring to placate the powers that be.

In the little time we had left, he told me about Basel, where he'd be going in Switzerland. As he spoke, a softness moved onto his face. I felt warm and comforted when he mentioned he'll be safe there. Those few brief moments of dreaming of his safety were interrupted when footsteps approached and there was a knock on the door. Two taps followed by a silence then three taps was code to open.

"Christa, I love you."

"I love you. Mark my words, I'll find a way."

The door opened. Erwin was there to take me back.

"A minute more, please." I grasped hold of Paul's gangly arms and pulled him back into an embrace.

Paul's breath warmed my neck. "Thank you, Christa, for the necklace."

"It'll bring you good luck."

"Not that necklace. The other one."

"That was Oma's gift."

"Please thank her for me. Tell her that someday I will repay her."

"Stay alive, Paul. Stay alive and we will reunite and make babies. That's payment for my Oma."

"Make babies. Little Landmanns. I like the sound of that."

He gently pulled out of our embrace and smiled, his sad longing eyes betraying his real feelings. With arms outstretched, fingertips touching, I backed out the doorway slowly, mouthing I will come to you. I love you.

Once out of the farmhouse and back in the compartment in the truck, ideas flowed through me like melting butter. As we moved along the bumpy road away from the farm, up bubbled an image of Gertrude and a full-fledged solution to my problem. "Something good will come from your tragic situation, Gertrude."

CHAPTER FORTY-THREE

I couldn't talk freely to Oma on the train ride back. Once home and out of my dirty clothes which Ursula had sponged off and spritzed to reduce the smell for the train ride, while mother was still at the factory, I went to her. Oma's reaction to the first few words of my idea was expected. "Absolutely not!"

"Just hear me out."

She kept interrupting me making it hard to explain the whole plan. "Gertrude's situation was one thing. A real emergency in a real hospital. Real surgery. It was a life-threatening situation that demanded action. I'm sorry she can't have babies now but it's not the end of the world for her. In time she'll snap out of her doldrums and return home."

"I know all that but what I'm proposing is not to actually do anything other than to get paperwork that says I can't have babies."

"That's not a good idea. Besides who in God's name do you think would do such a thing?"

"Your friend must know a doctor? Perhaps Ursula knows one?"

"You want me to go to my friend to see if he knows a doctor who will write up a fake medical diagnosis for you that says you can't get pregnant? So you can flee Germany and join Paul? Even if I were to go along with your harebrained idea, you have nothing earlier in any of your medical records to warrant this."

"I know that and what I plan on—"

"Forget it, Christa. This is where I draw the line. Paul's on his way out, let it be."

"I will not let it be, Oma. I can't." It was hard to see the pained expression on her weary face, how the skin on the outer corners of her hazel eyes crinkled into new crow's feet, and more gray hair had taken up residence on her head. I watched her expression when I told her my life would be over without him and despite her attempt to cut me off with a lip smacking don't-be-histrionic look, I kept at it. "Put yourself in my place. What if it was Nahum? What if you had a chance to be with him?" I looked up at the ceiling, envisioning where I imagined he along with Opa and Jürgen were watching over us.

She extended her neck as her eyes followed mine, and she crossed her chest, something she had rarely done in the last couple of years. I figured I must have gotten to her when she went quiet and sat at the edge of her bed, motioning for me to sit by her. Her adamant assertive tone, the way she sharply said *no* earlier, turned feeble, weepy, when she reached a hand to mine and said, "What am I going to do with you?" She rhetorically repeated *what am I going to do with her* to the room as if expecting an answer from the ethers, for our angels in heaven to descend and give guidance.

I listened to her mumble a few more things that made no sense to me as her attention shifted to some unknown time and her eyes became hazed.

"If only… to think of what could have been." Her body shook like a chill ran through her, snapping her back from wherever she had just drifted off to. She let out a deep long sigh and looked at me. Her wrinkled countenance held a sea of sorrow. Her lips parted but nothing came out, no words, nothing to help me understand why she looked so troubled.

"What's the matter, Oma?"

She spoke softly, her voice shaky. "I have a confession. I would…" She stumbled and paused, struggling. "What exactly is it you want me to do?"

"Oma. Thank you. Thank you but what were you going to say?"

"It's not important now."

"I'd like to hear."

Out came the tears. She put a pillow behind her back, shifted her position, but not satisfied with it changed it again seemingly more uncomfortable with whatever was bothering her than her physical position. A few more maneuvers with the pillow and she opened up. "If it were me…"

"Yes." I gently prompted her.

"If given the chance to keep Nahum alive and be with him, I would do the same thing. I didn't want it to end, but he sent me away because he felt my associating with him could only cause me misery."

"Because he was Jewish?"

"Yes."

We sat together, side by side, my hip up against Oma's thigh, as close as can be, not saying a thing for a long time. We remained still until Max came scratching at the door. I got up to let him in, breaking the stillness and the mood.

Oma smiled at Max's wagging stub. "You found us. Is it time for your walk?" His tail picked up speed, throwing his rump into wiggling excited anticipation. Oma looked from Max to me. "Go ahead and take him for a walk. I've some thinking I need to do."

She hadn't agreed but from what she'd said and how she looked, I knew she'd help. The questions now were would her friend want to help and could he find a doctor willing to help?

***

That night Oma came to my room when my mother was asleep. She wanted to know the specifics of what I planned to do to get the paperwork.

I whispered I would fake abdominal pain and tell my mother I needed to see a doctor. I stopped for a minute to formulate what I wanted to say. "Once there I would ask the doctor for paperwork to show I can't get pregnant because I am infertile. Something like that. I wouldn't need an exam, simply the medical report."

"How did you learn about that?"

I told her that when training in the BDM meetings I had learned some things about female anatomy, including reasons prohibiting pregnancy like when undernourished women stop having their periods. Frau Schmidt emphasized the need for proper nutrition to maintain a healthy monthly cycle for being able to get pregnant. What I didn't pick up there, I found in the library.

"That diagnosis would give me an excuse to go away. To leave because I feel a failure not being able to produce Aryan babies like my friends at the BDM. Now that we know what happened with Gertrude, it's not unfathomable for me to have something wrong and want to hide my face. My leaving would spare me and the family the humiliation we'd all face were I not to be able to produce babies."

Without expressing disagreement, she pondered what I'd said. "How'd you come up with this?"

"I remembered someone mentioning their aunt had something, I didn't remember the exact word, but whatever the condition was she couldn't have babies. So I went to the library and looked up causes for not being able to get pregnant. Infertility seemed the most plausible."

"This is what you want the doctor to diagnose for you? Do you even know what's required to do that workup?"

"No but I wouldn't actually receive an exam. I just want to get the written diagnosis. That's so you and mother have something to show father and anyone else who wants to know why I suddenly left."

"You're planning on doing this before your father returns? It will upset him, and your mother will be devastated." She fell back into resisting my plan, telling me it wouldn't work, that I'd be found out and our entire family would end up in a camp.

"Let's just take it one step at a time. First, I need a doctor."

"If we can't find one, you'll let go of this idea?"

That was a fair question, but I didn't want Oma to get the notion that if she came up blank I'd give up because I wouldn't. "First let's tackle getting a doctor. I can't think beyond that."

Oma indulged me saying she would ask her friend to see what, if anything, he could arrange.

***

Like in the past when working through Oma's friend meant delays, again I had to wait. Each night when I returned home from work and saw no mail or phone messages or heard any word from Oma, my spirits dropped. Then something came but it wasn't from Oma's friend. It was a postcard from Ursula. All it said was she was on her way to vacation in Freiburg with family from Basel.

My heart hammered in my chest as I thought of Paul moving through the rolling hills of southern Germany's wine country, taking in the steepled churches and old stone buildings. I remembered how much I loved visiting the lush countryside bordering the Black Forest and listening to waterfalls cascading into rainbows arching over trickling brooks. The man I loved was passing through a place I loved, making his way to safety in Basel.

I knew nothing about Basel other than it was a city in northwestern Switzerland on the Rhine and what Paul had told me the last time I saw him. He said it was a populous city whose inhabitants speak mainly German. Once there he had an address to go to where people would help him. He told me he knew it was the right place for him for his father once mentioned that if he ever needed to flee Germany to go to Basel, a safe harbor. It had a long history of being supportive of Jewish people. What Paul said about the Basel Program promoting Zionism relaxed my taut back muscles. He planned to wait in Basel until we were reunited.

I read and reread that postcard a hundred times, fraying the edges, smudging the ink with my anxious moist fingers, feeling like I'd grown wings. Wings that I hoped would take me to him.

CHAPTER FORTY-FOUR

At the same time I got confirmation from Ursula through Oma that Paul had arrived in Basel, Oma also told me she might have good news for me.

Might? That put a damper on my enthusiasm for when she explained she had the name of a doctor, which of course made me happy, she also said he had been warned by the authorities not to help Jews directly or indirectly. He had been close to being found out when he helped deliver a Jewish baby which had put him on edge.

Not wanting to buy into any stops, I asserted, "I am German, not Jewish. So why wouldn't he help?"

"What you would ask him to do is illegal. If he asks why you need him to help with a highly questionable matter, it goes to him helping a Jew indirectly."

"I'm will not bring that up."

"If he asks?"

"I've thought this through. If he's a compassionate man who at one time helped Jews, I will rely on that compassion and tell him I don't want to be a vehicle for making babies. I will fall on my knees if I have to and beg him, tell him I want to wait for love to be intimate with a man. I will tell him I'd rather die and I will kill—"

"Enough, Christa. You've made your point." She then told me the doctor's name and address which I memorized. When I turned to leave her room, she told me to wait a minute then went to her armoire, reached up to her storage place and pulled out a radiant bejeweled brooch, a floral design with petals made of rubies and sapphires with an emerald stem.

"Here." Oma held out the brooch.

"No, Oma, I can't take that."

"Do you see me wearing it?" Her lips moved into a soft smile, raising her cheeks. "You'll need money to help with the doctor… and other things."

"I don't know what to say, Oma."

"Then say nothing."

My heart was full as I reached to hug her, grasping the beautiful gift in my hand.

***

Dr. Joseph Hauser, a tall thin man with a receding hairline, wearing dark horn-rimmed eyeglasses, entered the room where I sat upon the edge of an exam table. A draft from his opening the door slid under the open-backed patient's gown I had on. I hoped the doctor would be warmer than the cool environment. He spoke in a welcoming soft voice as he approached me holding a chart in one hand and extending the other in a greeting, putting me at ease. "Christa, I understand a mutual friend referred you to me."

"Yes, doctor."

"So how can I help you?"

"I have a problem and…" I'd rehearsed what I wanted to say but now in front of him the words stuck in my throat, my tongue felt too fat to move.

Chart in hand, he sat in a chair facing me patiently waiting for me to express what brought me there.

It was harder than I thought it would be when I stepped into my discomfort to state what I needed. I took a breath and then in the most diplomatic way I could conjure up, said "I understand what happens here is confidential, but I'm not comfortable with what I am about to say going in a chart for..." How do I say I want nothing written that could label me as a dissident? The pervasiveness of distrust spreading through Germany had escalated once the Olympic Games ended with the regime growing more violent to the point where no one was safe and nothing was sacred. I wasn't sure how much I could tell this doctor. Where was the limit for what would and wouldn't be acceptable to him? He was a German doctor and knew what was going on, knew he had an obligation to report anyone disaffected with authority. Would he sell me out or did he stand on a higher moral ground, one where he saw people for who they were—human beings and not some horrific entity labeled this or that?

He put the chart in his lap. "I hope you feel safe here. Because of who referred you, it is tacitly understood there may be some sensitive matters you want to discuss with me. I will use discretion in what I document."

That was exactly what I wanted to hear, exactly what I needed from him. "Thank you. That makes this a little easier. I need something in writing from you that states I can't have children."

"I see." He paused and the conversation stopped there for a minute with him running a hand through his hair as if deciding what to do. He looked to the door as if something beyond it was influencing his response, which we both knew to be the case. Mostly, those out there did control and influence what happened in private rooms. "Please tell me why you need this?"

The idea of discussing such an intimate matter with a stranger, albeit a doctor, sent a hot flush through my body, telling me to tread lightly. "I'm a virgin. I desperately want my first time to be when I marry, with a man I love."

He leaned back in his chair, easing his posture. "You know the Lebensborn Program? You know your obligation... for what you are asking me to do is… " His sentence broke into fragments, his words blurred, his lips were moving but I couldn't make out the end of that last sentence.

I understood enough of what he'd said to respond. "Yes."

"It's that important?"

"Yes. I'd rather die than have to—" I stopped myself when I saw that seemed to have gotten to him for his attention went elsewhere for a moment and a worried countenance moved across his face, the look a doctor shows when telling his patients bad news.

"Do you have someone, Christa?"

There on the precipice of perhaps my only chance to be with Paul and not expecting what he'd just asked, I burst into tears. Sobs came forth as I choked out another yes.

Doctor Hauser gently handed me a linen handkerchief and waited for me to get a control of my emotional outburst before asking me what exact documentation I thought would accomplish what I needed done.

I placed the handkerchief on the exam table. "I need a diagnosis and report validating that I can't have babies. I had a friend who had a hysterectomy because of a miscarriage."

"That's a rather extreme solution for a miscarriage."

"When they were operating on her they found a tumor."

Again, he said, "I see."

"Of course, if I want children in the future, I need to come up with something nonsurgical and I thought of… I heard about infertility."

"You want me to write a note that you are infertile?"

"Yes." The way he asked put doubt in me and I felt sick inside, losing hope of him helping.

"And if someone investigates this and there's nothing to back it up?"

"That's why I came to you. Why the discreet referral. Is it possible to use another patient's lab work or X-ray report and put my name on it?" The more I explained what I needed from him the sicker I felt.

Just then someone walked by the room and he held up his hand for me to wait a moment. When the footsteps moved out of earshot, he said he thought he could help.

Really? Did he really say that? I knew I wasn't dreaming when his furrowed forehead and lowered eyelids told me he was dead serious. Instantly my body felt lighter like I could fly through the ceiling and float away.

He flexed his elbows on his knees and leaned in close to me when he said he had a lovely patient who is no longer alive who had that diagnosis. "I still have her diagnostic workup."

Perplexed, I asked, "She passed away from being infertile?"

"No. She was in the wrong place at the wrong time."

From the sorrow etched on his wrinkled brow and the judicious way he brought her up, I figured she was Jewish. I also imagined that was why he was willing to help, because of what happened to a patient he cared about. Now in an indirect way he would put her data to good use to help me. That unfortunate patient's circumstances would open a door for me. Hopefully, the door to freedom and not demise.

Bless that kind doctor who told me he'd get the documentation to me through our mutual friend. He also refused to accept any payment from me, money I would have gladly paid out of the proceeds from the sale of Oma's brooch. I left feeling lighthearted. My list of decent people had expanded.

CHAPTER FORTY-FIVE

It was with a newfound appreciation for those who risked helping others despite the consequences they could incur that I navigated through the toasty July weather, thankful for the shade trees gave, thankful for the help offered. While Oma wasn't surprised with the outcome of my visit to Dr. Hauser, I was. During a conversation with her about the doctor, I gained an understanding about why she wasn't surprised he agreed to help me. Perhaps she needed to get a few things off her chest to someone she trusted, so she opened up like never before when she told me of her connection with Dr. Hauser. It also helped me comprehend the doctor's forthright communication during my visit.

"You needed his services?" I repeated what Oma had just said about her encounter with the doctor, what she never told anyone. She had been his patient. "Were you ill?"

"I wasn't ill, Christa. Not in the way you're thinking."

"But you saw him as a patient?" A dim lightbulb flickered in my consciousness. "Oma, were you—"

"Yes." She reached for her abdomen, below the umbilicus, right over her womb. Her cheeks puffed out like she was going to be sick and her eyes welled up. "I was with baby."

Stunned and saddened, I was confused about the timing and whether it was from Opa or with Nahum. If with Nahum, she would have been into her fifties and from what I knew from my studies that would have been beyond the safe birthing age, the window when healthy babies are born, and is an age when problems with pregnancy can arise. Being this was such a sensitive matter and Oma was visibly upset mentioning it, I didn't ask her to explain. I was itching with curiosity but this was not an itch I wanted to scratch.

Oma took notice of my reaction, how my body moved back at the news, how my attention wandered off. "It was with Nahum." She told me if she had a healthy report on the pregnancy she would have kept it, but he insisted it was wrong, wrong for her to have a Jewish baby even if it were possible for her at that age. "We fought. He won."

"He wanted to protect you." The whole situation stank. What came from loving someone, what must have been the joy they shared, was made dirty by government dictate. I wanted to scream about how wrong it was. How wrong it was to interfere with the love of a man and woman, how wrong it was to sentence an unborn child to death.

"I procrastinated about going to a doctor or doing anything about it for several weeks." Oma then told me when she saw Dr. Hauser, she found out it wasn't a viable pregnancy. "The heartbeat can be heard at six weeks. When I saw him I was in my eighth week. There was no heartbeat."

The room grew dark and dreary as she continued telling me that the doctor offered her medication.

"He said the pill contained several ingredients. I distinctly recall ergot, aloe and Black Hellebore. I'll never forget his words about those drugs and what he said about their safety and effectiveness being unknown. It was that or wait it out for I wasn't going under the knife." Oma took a minute to slow her breathing, to wipe a tear from the corner of her eye.

Feeling like the air had been sucked out of my lungs, I remained quiet.

"It happened right here in this room." She didn't say how long after she took the medication nor did she explain anything else. The baby she made with Nahum, the product of their forbidden love, was dead. Expunged.

We sat together, sad there was no homage for the fetus, a life that came to the wrong couple at the wrong time. In that length of solitude with Oma, her undying attitude about staying connected with undesirables, her protestations against the regime, and ultimately her agreeing to help me despite the danger involved became crystal clear. I recalled the look on her face when she gave me the diamond necklace for Paul and then that same look when she gave me her brooch. It was a poignant look that said things mean nothing, life matters most. Above all else. As long as I live I'll never forget that look in her eyes, deep from her soul. What it meant became my north star.

***

Life was cruel but it was also beautiful, like when out with Max and appreciating his wonderment at the simplest of doggie pleasures. A good sniff. A friendly pat on the back. Food. My boy constantly reminded me it's the little things that hold a ton of meaning. Max, my friend, my teacher, had taken care of me and I had to be sure he'd be well taken care of when I left.

Despite her arthritic limitations and past hesitation, Oma offered to walk and feed him, and, although begrudgingly, she said she would let Max sleep in her room so he didn't get lonely. I think it was so she wouldn't get lonely but she'd never admit it. She'd always gotten a kick out of Max and he would see to protecting her.

Once I'd received my documentation, which included travel paperwork, I gave Oma the medical information to show my parents and anyone else who questioned my sudden departure. Dr. Hauser had supporting data at his office. To be able to leave cleanly, I knew the only communication I could have with my mother had to be written for she'd never consent to what I was doing even if it was to run away from the shame of not being able to get pregnant, if that were true. She wouldn't care, nor would she turn me out like Frau Hess did to Gertrude. Poor

Gertrude out somewhere tending to her wounds didn't deserve the hand she'd been dealt. My mother said as much. Someday, I hoped to return and tell her the truth but until that time, I'd stay in touch via mail so she'd know I was safe and sound.

One important thing to tend to was letting Max know, which I suspected he probably already did. I don't know how that dog understood so much on his own. How when I was down, he'd come to me and offer a paw, or simply stay close until I felt better and then as if I told him I was all right he'd wander off somewhere, and how he wagged his tail when I had experienced something pleasant. My intuitive furry friend knew me inside out, and I couldn't love him more.

"I'm really going to miss you, Max." We were out on a walk in an isolated field when I sat on a fallen tree limb. "You're my best boy."

He looked up at me with his big brown eyes and raised ears, his stub swinging.

"I'm going away for a while."

He sat beside me, tilting his head to the left then the right, his breath warming my thigh. The look on his face warmed my aching heart for as much as I longed to be with Paul, I wished Max could come with me. He had been one of the best things in my life for the last several years and I didn't want to leave him. He still had a few good years left to live, but all things going well his lifespan wouldn't exceed mine and I didn't want to think of this as a final goodbye. It was with that intention I told him, "I hope to see you soon." It was my sincerest hope that something would happen and things in Germany would return to a civil way of harmonious living. A way of living that would allow me to return with Paul.

We walked back home and that night I slept fitfully, listening to Max breathe and whimper dreamfully. I cried knowing how much I'd miss him.

Too restless to stay in bed, I got up and looked at my documentation. I read through the medical transportation paperwork showing I needed time off work to rest, to acclimate from a recent medical trauma. The trauma of course was the diagnosis of not being able to have babies, which any official reviewing my documentation could sympathize with. The irony that I'd gain sympathy for being infertile when Jewish babies were being murdered was sickening.

I couldn't help thinking of the woman who belonged to the official report and what she went through when she discovered she couldn't have children. Then to have her life torn away. As my thoughts drifted from her to Paul, my sorrow dissipated.

CHAPTER FORTY-SIX

My loving Paul had brought me to a place I never knew existed, an inner strength to grab onto a dream and take the next step. To do what I needed to do for myself, even at the cost of hurting my parents. The hardest thing I ever did was write the letter to them, one Oma would give to my mother when she woke up. One I prayed would not irretrievably break her heart. My father was resilient and I bargained on him understanding. My letter to them stated I had been having some physical complaints and saw a doctor who discovered I was unable to have babies, and Oma had the medical report to show them. I explained I now felt I understood what Gertrude must have felt over the disgrace of not being able to get pregnant and having to be sent away because of it. Nausea rose to my throat as my hand wrote those words, but my disgust at lying was far more palpable than the truth. There was no way under the Germany sun that the truth would be accepted. My lying was to smooth the way for me but it was also to protect my family. As I wrote the words, I thought of Gertrude and wished her well, thinking that her loss became my gain. From the well of her sorrow sprang something good.

Fortified by what Oma had painfully shared about what happened to her, her words resonated with me as I wrote line after line of fabrication promising when I overcame feeling ashamed, feeling a failure, I would come home. In the meantime, I would go to a place I loved and recuperate from the shock. Oma confidently reassured me she would be able to handle my mother. But what if my mother suspected it was all a lie and I really left to be with Paul? Oma assertively reiterated she would handle my mother and for me not to worry about it.

***

Way before sunrise I fed and walked Max, weeping. He knew I was sad because he stayed flush to my side not doing his usual interminable sniffing. "I'll be back, my boy. You take good care of Oma."

When I handed him over to Oma, his tail wagged and I thanked him for understanding. My brave big boy greeted her with licks and a raised paw. What a good boy!

Oma's eyes were red, her shoulders lowered. She must have been up during the night shedding tears like me, and I imagined all she went through with Nahum was probably fresh in her mind. She gave me a great gift telling me about what had happened to her, a selfless act of kindness. It was more significant than the jewelry that helped finance Paul's travel and now mine. It was exactly what I needed to remove the doubt that was churning my stomach and make way for the love that would help me step into my future.

I handed her the envelope addressed to my father and mother, gave her a hug, and told her no words would ever express my gratitude, my love and appreciation. In her endearing way she responded like I knew she would.

"Enough with the sentimental mush. Be on your way." She winked at Max and he wagged his agreement.

Oma's words repeated with images of Paul telling me he wanted me to take the same train route as him. He feared Dieter may have seen me at his house and if he was at any of the exit places in Friedrichshafen, especially the ferry station where his father worked, they wouldn't be safe for me to use. Without knowing the specifics about Dieter, Oma understood Paul's fear and why I planned my route the way he had insisted.

With rucksack stuffed to the brim, a purse over my arm, money in a pouch attached to my undergarments, and a bag with bread and jam, I stepped out the front door of my home in Ravensburg. My place of protection. Now, protected only by my overcoat, I was prepared to face the crisp morning air, prepared to take my next step to the rolling green and purple wine country hills, a short distance across the border from Paul.

The taste of freedom was sweet as I strolled at a leisurely pace feeling the rucksack's weight on my back, aware of the paperwork in my purse. I passed Herr Meier's dark kiosk, a couple of hours yet from opening. News headlines flashed before me like captions on a motion picture screen, the unfolding of events in Germany over the last several years. Time had become events of escalating hostilities. I remembered when I was fourteen and heard about the Jewish people being barred from holding civil service, university and state positions. Jürgen warned me worse was to come. I didn't believe him, for I was at the birthing stage of formulating my own opinions about the regime and to go against it was forbidden. Then tragedy stuck and I was shaken, my beliefs pried from their foundation. You were right, Jürgen, I thought, the heaviness on my back taking on more weight. A few steps beyond the kiosk, another headline flashed, and I smiled recalling Oma's comment that the Nuremberg Laws were hogwash. At that time I was a naïve sixteen year old, and she must have been devastated over what had happened with her and Nahum.

So many memories flew by as I made my way and arrived at the train station. The waiting area was empty when I purchased a one-way ticket and had a seat on a wooden bench next to the boarding door. Emotions flooded my head but I refused to dwell in the past when I was embarking on something new, something good. Paul's image sustained me, the way his eyes met mine as if no one else existed. The way his hands caressing my face made me feel alive. His promise of a future, a good life together where love is not suppressed, buoyed me as the clock ticked and daylight reared her sunny face.

A few people drifted in and bought tickets. I was glad no one sat near me in the waiting room or once I boarded the train and found a seat at the rear of a car. The ride with stopovers would get me there at night when Oma's friend had arranged for a contact to meet me. I hoped to avoid someone sitting next to me and asking a bunch of questions, or worse recognizing me. I settled into my seat and stretched out, my belongings hanging over into the seat next to me.

An hour in and the landscape was flush with bushes against a densely wooded area. Cauliflower clouds filled the baby blue sky. It'd been a long time since I appreciated the spectacular views, the crescendo of scenery as we traveled through the forest. No one disturbed me through the trip and the conductor kindly checked my ticket. I regained the appetite I had lost earlier back at home before leaving when I didn't want to make noise and wake my mother, consequently I was able to enjoy the bread and jam I'd brought. Two times to the toilet were all I allowed myself for the dangers of leaving my seat and being seen by someone who might know me or someone suspicious of my traveling alone far outweighed my leg stiffness and cramping muscles. I took care of that by stretching out my legs and staying put.

As the day progressed and the sun rose and descended into an array of orange, red and yellow streaks across the horizon, I welcomed the clickety-clack of the wheels rolling over the rails, distracting me from the chitter-chatter going on a few seats away, a man and woman traveling with two youngish boys, each boisterously raising his voice above the other. It was an odd juxtaposition to a quiet woman wearing a headscarf holding her golden-blond hair back who sat with her head lowered. From time to time she would shake her head as if the noise was disturbing her. Like me, she said nothing and I wondered if, also like me, she didn't want to draw attention to herself.

I must have nodded off for my head jerked up from my chest when I heard the wheels squeal as we rounded a curve. I slid toward the window and witnessed the full moon casting a bright glow on the countryside. Then the glow turned dark as we entered a tunnel causing turbulence. My father, ever the engineer, told me it was the air displacement of the train that caused the turbulence. My father, I thought, burdened by what his reaction would be.

I didn't like his involvement in helping with the design and construction of Buchenwald, and wondered what else he was working on, but what choice did he have? If he went down, so would my mother, Oma and me. When the decision was between follow or die, the only choice was obvious. I felt for him. I felt for my mother who had been impacted by his position more deeply than the rest of us. I knew he was a good man inside, a good man doing what he needed to do in an extremely undesirable situation, what any good man would do to stay alive and keep his family safe.

I stayed awake for the rest of the ride, through the tunnel and another several kilometers until the train rumbled, slowed down and stopped. I gathered my belongings and quickly exited, thankful I could walk the kinks out of my legs.

At the platform, a bushel of faces looked on. Voices raised and arms extended to family and friends. All I knew was someone would meet me but I did not know if it was going to be a man or woman. I stood at the platform waiting for someone to approach me, but after a long time, when no one did, I made my way to a singular wooden bench outside the building.

There I was in Freiburg on a fairly warm July night, sweating in my overcoat, feeling very alone, praying someone would come for me.

CHAPTER FORTY-SEVEN

Two hours after I had arrived, sitting outside in the brisk night, a wind picked up slapping my face. After waiting there for well in excess of what I felt was a reasonable amount of time I panicked. Panicked that something had happened to the person I was to connect with, and worse something might have happened to Paul that drew the authorities to those who were to help me cross the border. How could I trust anything I'd been told, all secondhand information passed along from various links in the chain? What if a link in that chain sold someone out? Dictated by fear, awful thoughts ran rampant sending me into a cold sweat.

Another half hour passed when I heard unobtrusive footsteps move around the corner of the building and approach. The poorly lit outside cast a glow on a woman with flat-heeled shoes and a dark skirt revealing stout lower legs. She took a few steps in the direction opposite where I sat then waited before pivoting around and rushing over to me.

"Quick. We need to go." A robust woman with brown hair, carrying extra weight in her midsection, stood before me anxiously looking around. "Quick!"

Without question or saying a word, I did what she said, following her to an old beat-up Opel that had seen days of accidents and rough driving. She opened the passenger door and placed my rucksack on the floor then had me get in. Once she was inside with the door shut and locked, out of earshot of anyone, I piped up before she started the car. "I'm not comfortable going anywhere with you before you tell me you know who I am."

"Christa." She stepped on the self-starter pedal and pulled away. "I may have been followed." She raised her voice above the noisy engine. "There's been a complication." Her attention shifted from what she was saying to the bumpy dirt road, to what looked like a fallen limb from a tree, which she clumsily maneuvered around sending us off the road into a small gully. "That must have just fallen." She grumbled something about it not being in the road when she drove to the station.

My mouth went dry as the car's wheels spun and continued spinning. I kept quiet, holding my breath and clutching the car seat until the tires crunched and groaned over the countryside debris and hiccupped back to the road.

"I loathe driving these dirt roads at night but we've no choice." She spoke with her head leaning over the steering wheel, squinting to see the road ahead.

It was disconcerting we ran into trouble just when she had mentioned there had been a complication. "You said something about complication."

"Yes, but first things first. My name is Margit. I am not the person who was supposed to come for you but... just a moment." Again her attention went to the road. Her breathing sped up. She looked straight ahead, but nothing other than dirt, twigs and potholes were visible.

As I wondered what she was looking at, panting about, acid ate away at my stomach.

"I'm a little nervous," she finally said, glancing sideways at me. "I've never done this before."

That didn't help my nerves, nor did it give me any confidence in her ability to get me to where I needed to be. I'd been patient enough and before my stomach eroded into an ulcer, I asked her, "Can you please tell me what happened, the complication?"

"Yes. Yes, I'm a mess. My humble apologies." She slowed the car and turned into a curve in the road. "The man who was to get you met with a bad situation."

The more she beat around the bush, the worse I felt, physically and emotionally. "What happened!" I knew my tone was too harsh, but my nerves were frayed and I had a right to know exactly what she was so frazzled about. "Please, just tell me." I toned my attitude down.

"I'm really sorry I don't know the whole story but here's what I do know. The man who helped get Paul across the border was followed."

I thought about the confirmation I'd received earlier Paul was in Basel. What if that was wrong? "What happened to Paul?" Please God, don't do this to me!

"He's across the border but the man who helped him was on another mission, helping a Jewish woman. They never made it across. Since he's been compromised most of the people he worked with went into hiding, fearing he would give their names to the authorities. The couple of men left were desperate to recruit new people. I volunteered."

I felt for that nameless man and the unfortunate Jewish woman. Concerned the plan to connect me with Paul had gone off the rails, I needed to know more. "Thank you, Margit. Is there anything else you can tell me? Do you know about the plans for me to reach Paul?"

"No."

My heart dropped to my feet, my body sank down in the passenger's seat. "Then where are you taking me? And what from there?"

"I'm to await instructions. In the meantime, you can stay with me but you have to stay indoors."

"Why?"

"All I was told is because your papers have your real name, and the authorities may be looking for you. I need to hide you or we could have the Gestapo breathing down our necks."

"I do have official papers. I'm a German citizen and—"

She cut me off with a swift incision. "I have my orders."

"So that's it then? We're going to your house and we wait."

"Exactly."

What I had hoped would be a blissful reunion in a day, maybe two, had become a nightmare. Did I make a mistake coming ran through my head. My definitive answer was no. I had to come, to do my part, for if I didn't try to be with Paul, make the effort regardless of the outcome, I didn't know how I'd live with myself. I didn't want to end up like Oma, regretting letting Nahum get away, never to see him again.

Margit lived alone in a small two-bedroom house. Her deceased husband had lost his life during the Great War. Not a woman of many words, she showed me to a small bedroom that contained a single bed, armoire, dresser, and chair by a window overlooking a backyard. "We share the bathroom across the hall. I put out a washcloth and towel for you." She swept a few loose tendrils of hair back into one of the buns on the side of her head. "I leave for work early and will return home in time to make us something for the evening meal. If you are asleep when I leave help yourself to some bread and jam. There's also some milk from a neighboring farm's cow I'm happy to share with you. Food is sparse but there's enough for us to make do for a few days."

A few days? I swallowed down what felt like a ball of clay stuck in my throat. "Do you have a minute?" I shot the question at her back when she turned to leave. I needed to connect with her, to insert some warmth into the terribly awkward and distant situation, my frightened state.

She turned to make eye contact.

Another hard swallow and I asked what she did for work. I wasn't ready to be left alone in this stranger's house.

"I work for a German officer, doing some cooking and cleaning his house."

From what she said, I assumed she worked for someone in the SS. What the hell did I get myself into? "Doesn't…" My stuttering words caught in my dry throat. I took a couple of second to compose my words, to compose myself. "Doesn't where you work make it unsafe for you to help me?" Moisture bubbled on my forehead.

"It's probably safer. Who would suspect me?"

I wiped my forehead with the back of my hand.

She must have noticed how nervous I was to have said, "The man is rarely home. It's his young wife and child I'm there with. She's pleasant enough." When I didn't reply instantly, she told me to sleep well and turned to the door.

"Wait. Please."

She stopped. Half-turning, she gave me a straight-lipped serious look she wasn't in the mood for socializing at close to midnight. "Christa, I can well imagine how you must feel but I need to get my rest. I don't have more to tell you. When I hear something, I'll let you know. Now get some sleep." She had said her piece and that was that.

For what seemed like hours I stared at the shut wooden door, at the splintering grooves, trying to convince myself things would work out. A heated sensation ran up my arms. I didn't sleep. I didn't think I would. I listened to the sounds of the night. The wind upon a window. Leaves swirling. Critters foraging. Then came the disappearance of ambient noise. In the stillness my heart beat erratically in my ear, engulfing me in fear. There was no getting away from it, the pulsing rush of blood through my arteries, my restless legs, and sweat pouring from my underarms. Breathe, I told myself, as I moved air in through my nose.

The next morning I heard Margit rise, use the bathroom, make herself breakfast and leave. Once she was gone, I tried to keep my fearful thoughts at bay. I went to look around the five-room home comprising, in addition to the two bedrooms and bathroom, a living room and snug four-seat table in a dining room next to the kitchen. A few knickknacks, a worn somewhat tattered quilt over the living room couch, throw rugs that had footstep lines through them, and dishes with more chips than solid surfaces, all told she was a woman of little means.

While she was out cooking and cleaning for the SS' family, I made myself useful dusting and sweeping her place. By the time she came home everything had been neatened to her smiling satisfaction.

As we sat down to dinner, she said she forgot to mention something last night. "When word comes it will be from the mail carrier. A friend." Like Oma's back in Ravensburg, I thought, and that thought made me feel better.

The next day I peered through a thin slit in the living room curtains looking for the mail carrier's arrival. After he dropped a parcel in the mailbox, I ran outside to get it, and to see if there was a message for me, only to feel guilty I had acted on impulse and done what she advised against by going outside. Once I saw there was nothing for me, I brought the parcel in, feeling antsy. I paced off and on until Margit returned home. One look at how chagrined I must have appeared when I told her I got excited seeing the mail carrier and didn't think before rushing out, she kept quiet. Not a word of rebuke came.

We shared a meal talking about the weather getting unusually warm for that time of the year and how welcomed the brisk nights were. She asked if I wanted to read the local newspaper, one the family she worked for gave her to dispose of. "I keep it to read at night, to stay up with the news."

"Thank you." I wasn't very thankful when I got to my room and turned on the lamp to look at the news. There on the front page was an article about Italy enacting a manifesto of race which stated Italians belonged to the Aryan race, and Jews did not. The malignancy was spreading. What was the sentiment in Switzerland? Was Paul really safe? Was I safe? Would I make it to my twentieth birthday in December?

CHAPTER FORTY-EIGHT

On day three at Margit's, my morning was spent looking out the window for the mail carrier's arrival. I missed Ravensburg and my family, yearned to see Paul, and sank into lonely despair. If I could have at least gotten out, perhaps made a trip to the Black Forest or a vineyard to distract myself, it might have helped. I tried to busy myself around her house to no avail for whatever I involved myself with my mind followed. What was my mother's reaction to my letter and my father's response? Not knowing deeply troubled me.

Was Oma all right? Was it fair for me to leave her to handle my mother, and who knew what else? I felt guilty imagining the consequences from what I'd done, sure there were unhappy faces, arguments with no good endings.

I was mad at myself. Angry at what I knew hurt people I loved and complicated their lives. Nothing felt right about the situation I'd gotten myself into, nothing until the mail carrier came and put a few pieces of mail into the mailbox. One I thought looked like a note and that played in my mind for the rest of the day as I gazed out the window like a dog awaiting its owner, my breath fogging the window. I ran my index finger over the fogged glass, and the line I'd made turned into droplets, tears reflecting how I felt.

The minute Margit was through the door with mail in hand, I was at her side.

She shuffled through two pieces then, sure enough, she opened a note and looked up. A nod and lit eyes emptied my head and filled me with excitement. "Here." She handed it to me.

My eyes moved over the words, come for a visit. An address was listed with a time. Tonight at 6 p.m. Margit stayed beside me as I read and reread the note. "It's really going to happen."

Margit's complexion regained some of the color she'd lost over the last few days. I was glad the burden would soon lift from this kind stranger who risked so much to help me. "Yes." She looked at a wall clock. "Now we must hurry." It was ten minutes past five, which meant fifty minutes to get to the meeting.

"How do I get there?"

"I'll take you. Now go pack your things."

In no time, I got my things together and found her in the kitchen. "That was fast." She put a half-loaf of brown bread and two boiled potatoes into a bag, smiling at me. "I don't know if they'll have food for you." She looked down at the bag then back at me, her eyes glistening. "I made this for you." She handed me the bag, gently patting my hand.

A huge lump of gratitude stuck in my throat, and I was at a loss for words, overwhelmed by her kindness.

In the car I asked if she knew the location where she was taking me.

"Schallstadt. There's a well-known vineyard there. I'm familiar with the area."

"I've been to Schallstadt." I spoke with voice-raised eagerness, adrenaline coursing through me, my heart racing. "I vacationed there with my family."

The drive was slow, taking longer due to the hard-to-maneuver backroads she had to take. Once past rolling hills of vineyards resplendent with vines dangling clusters of purple, plump grapes, we came to a house. Margit waited in the car while I went to the door and knocked. A middle-aged man with short graying hair and thick black-rimmed glasses opened it. He nodded to Margit and she drove off.

"Come. Come in, my dear girl." He showed me to a cubbyhole of a room I assumed must have been a converted storage closet. "Leave your things there." He motioned to a cot, comprising a thin, worn mattress atop a sagging wire frame that had seen better days.

At his small kitchen table, sharing the food I'd brought, he told me his name was Klaus. No last name was given. He was a jovial, chatty man, who'd lost his wife to typhus during the epidemic during the Great War. "She was a nurse." His voice cracked when he spoke of her and his two grown sons who were in the German military.

"Is anyone unscathed by war?" I was surprised I felt comfortable enough to express my thoughts aloud but saw no harm in commiserating with him over such a sad loss, and for what? For retribution, territorial expansion, power grabs that got the depraved perpetrators more than they bargained for in deaths, hunger and disease. I knew about some of the statistics from the rantings that brought Hitler to power, what Frau Schmidt jammed down our throats. I also knew Hitler blamed the loss of the war and Germany's financial problems on the Jews. What madness.

I listened to Klaus bitterly restate what I'd read and learned, growing angrier and angrier before he caught himself. "Enough of my ranting. There is good in life." He switched the topic to his job, helping at the vineyard which was within walking distance. "Put me out there with the grapes and I'm a happy man." He kissed his purple stained finger tips then fanned his hand out to make his point. "The different fruity, sweet flavors...I haven't met a wine I didn't like." He laughed, then got up and went to a cupboard where he pulled out a bottle of pinot noir. "Have a toast with me. To no more wars."

I wasn't one much for liquor but wouldn't refuse his hospitality nor the benevolent toast to a worthy cause. We raised our quarter-full glasses and lightly clinked them together. The dry wine tingled my tongue and warmed my belly. A few sips and I felt the buzz. Time for me to stop for I needed to be alert for the rest of the conversation, especially when he told me that in the morning before he went to work he'd take me to the train station in Freiburg, where he'd see I got a ticket to Basel. He was familiar with my route, mentioning a friend of his had recently transported a man from Friedrichshafen. Paul! Klaus' friend must have been the man who helped Paul! Sadly, he told me his friend had been caught, confirming what Margit had mentioned earlier.

What he said sent my heart beating into my throat. I nearly jumped out of my seat wanting to ask if he knew anything else, but something in the way he spoke, not giving any more information, told me to let it be. He didn't have to mention the transport of a man from Friedrichshafen. I felt that was his way of letting me know Paul made it out and I was in good hands. It was kind of him to say what he had and that was good enough for me.

"You don't want to finish your wine?"

Not wanting to offend, and with the conversation ending, I drank the rest, feeling its effect by the time I was in my room falling upon the concave cot. The wine had taken the edge off my adrenaline pumping arteries and I instantly fell asleep.

Morning came and I stumbled up, legs stiff, back strained. Still in my clothes from the day before, I stretched my limbs and back, went to the bathroom to wash my face, then sat in the kitchen where we had our meal last night. It was 4 a.m. Sunrise was another hour and half away. Fifteen minutes later, Klaus was up, dressed and after a quick bite to eat ready to transport me in a vineyard vehicle he had brought home with him last night.

The morning air was fresh and aside from a wisp of wind rustling leaves it was quiet. Soon the slumbering world would wake to the sun's rich tapestry of hues, igniting activity. Although my attention was never far from Ravensburg, what I felt in that moment making my way to Paul was gratitude. I had much to be grateful for, the list growing, including the two new strangers who taught me volumes about courageous service.

CHAPTER FORTY-NINE

Paul welcomed me to Basel with a warm, friendly smile. I never wanted to let go of our first embrace under the umbrella of disbelief we'd finally been reunited. That disbelief stayed for days to follow in the simple one-bedroom apartment he'd rented while working for a jeweler, a man who knew and respected Nahum, a Jew who left Germany with his family in April, 1933 when his brother-in-law was let go from his employment in a university. The smart Jewish professor told the jeweler to get his family out fast and so he did.

Nahum had remained in touch with the family through the years and Paul was deeply moved when the jeweler found out Nahum had died and offered him a place to live if ever needed. He was a kind man with a welcoming family who spared nothing to help Paul with work. With the money he had left over from Oma's diamond necklace and the little he made helping the man with his jewelry business, Paul was able to make do.

Our being together was everything I had dreamed it would be. We felt safe. Happy. That lasted until the beginning of November when a German-born Polish Jew living in Paris assassinated a German diplomat, then everything fell apart.

Kristallnacht. On November 9-10 Nazi leaders in Germany and other newly incorporated areas retaliated for one man's assassination by carrying out a series of pogroms against Jews. Jewish homes, hospitals, schools and other places of business and worship were demolished. Thousands of Jewish men were arrested and sent to camps. Bodies of women who protested, trying to protect their husbands, were left battered and bloody in the streets with their crying children clinging to them.

There was no hiding the devastation to life and property the SS, SA, Hitler Youth and German civilians throughout Germany had carried out. No denying the stories told by the downcast and bloodied few who made it across the highly guarded border into Switzerland. One man who was hidden under bales of straw in a farm wagon arrived at Paul's boss' shop picking straw off his suit. In a terrible state of sweat and worry, Paul came home from work that night panting about what the man had told him and his boss.

"The man was crying." Paul wiped a runaway tear off his cheek. "He arrived home to learn his wife and children were sent to a concentration camp. He hid and waited for things to calm down. After two days, hungry and thirsty, he snuck through back alleys to a reliable friend who helped him escape."

I listened, stunned, and just as I was about to open my mouth to respond how sick and scared that made me feel, Paul said, "We're lucky to be here."

Lucky? My lips curled in a disbelieving contortion. Paul and I had talked about the Anschluss and Sudetenland. As Germany had annexed its neighbor Austria and occupied Czechoslovakia, I felt sure Switzerland was no longer safe. "How can you say that?" From what he'd just told me about the family of the man who escaped, all I could think about was how that would be our fate as well if we remained so close to Germany.

"Switzerland is neutral. It's safe."

There was nothing Paul could say, no reassurance to give, that would cast out of my head the horrible things I'd learned. I feared for us. I also feared for my family with whom I was unable to establish communication. With family turning on family and neighbor turning on neighbor, and no one could be trusted, what if someone who helped me make it to Paul let slip to the wrong person I was with a Jew in Switzerland? I hated to think of what would happen to my family, but I was helpless to do anything about it. When my anxiety stretched to the breaking point, I begged Paul to leave, to find a place further away from German borders.

I continued to plead with Paul for days then, miraculously, I'd got my wish.

"We're really leaving?" I had to be certain I heard him right, that I wasn't deluding myself. It was too good to be true and I needed convincing.

"Yes, Christa, my boss agrees."

The relief from hearing those words and seeing the tender look he gave me was immense. "Really?"

"He's heard enough. Seen enough and his wife shares your fears. He's decided to sell his shop and leave Switzerland." Paul grabbed me in his arms, and in the warmth of his embrace he told me his boss invited us to join them and said he would handle everything.

Again, not convinced I'd heard right, I pulled back. "For sure?"

The tenderness in his eyes spread to his upturned lips. "Yes, for sure."

Paul mentioned no plan, any future geography, and when he finally did, I thought he must have somehow misheard his boss. "America?"

"Yes, darling. America."

Things moved quickly after that. Paul's boss turned his shop over to a Christian friend who said he'd forward the money for the sale when he had it. We had ten days to pack before leaving to board a ship and in those days my emotions bounced all over the place.

I wasn't able to get through to my mother or Oma to let them know I decided to go to America. I sent a letter but received no reply. The regrets and chagrin I felt over not having said goodbye to my parents had been eating away at me, turning into a profound sorrow. Somehow being in the next country, only a border away, lent to a sense of being close to them. But an ocean? The cold vast expanse of the Atlantic Ocean felt like an unbridgeable distance that tore at my heart. The choices I had to make for the love of one man were never easy. Were it not for that love, the completion I felt with Paul, I would have fallen into irretrievable despair.

In those few days of tending to the business of settling our affairs and packing, Paul was gentle with me. Gentle and kind. He exuded infectious gratitude for the gifts we'd been given, from Oma's necklace and brooch to his boss financing the trip for us so we'd have a little of our savings left over once settled in New York. Gratitude for all our good fortune was a soothing balm.

CHAPTER FIFTY

At the end of December 1938, heading into a new year, we boarded a ship for New York.

How Paul's boss arranged visas and space on a ship for us was beyond my comprehension. The man had connections, Paul told me, emphasizing that the combination of money and good deeds didn't hurt. Turns out Paul was right about what he'd said to me earlier about being lucky. We were lucky with each other and with his kindhearted boss who took us in as part of his family.

Although I enjoyed Paul's boss, his wife and their two young sons, I spent most of my time in the cabin in a horizontal position on my bunk holding my belly and wishing for the seasickness to go away. Paul rubbed my neck, my back, my feet and did his best to help me get a few bites of food and sips of liquid to stay down. He placed his hand on my abdomen and talked to my stomach, telling it to feel better to keep me strong. Those bitter hours were sweetened by his attentiveness and, at times, humor. With his hand on my belly and a mischievous grin, he asked, "Are you sure it's seasickness and not morning sickness."

Those moments of sweetness soured as Paul kept me abreast of the stories he'd heard during walks and meals.

"Refugees are being turned away?"

To answer my question, Paul relayed what he had learned from a man who'd earlier traveled to the United States on business. "Roosevelt knows about the spreading refugee crisis in Europe. There was hope for a while he would raise the immigrant quotas but unfortunately their Congress refused to raise them."

The topic wasn't helping my nausea. "What's going to happen to us if we land and are turned away?" I swallowed down the bile rising to the back of my throat.

"My boss assured me we will not have a problem."

Paul was optimistic, at times to a fault. Me, I was much more skeptical. "How can anyone assure you of such a thing?"

"We simply have to place our trust and faith in our visas and the assurance all the proper arrangements have been made."

Faith? Trust? Big empty words when there is so much pointing me away from believing in what isn't immediately tangible. We were in a precarious situation with our lives on the line. How could I possibly rely on some invisible unknown? I just didn't have it in me.

A swell of the ocean slanted the ship and I held onto the bunk to avoid slipping out. The bile I attempted to keep down came up with a gush all over Paul, ending our conversation.

If worry about being turned away when we arrived in America wasn't enough, I almost went into a panic when Paul mentioned a man on board had frantically started a rumor he saw a German U-boat surface near our ship. His attempts to persuade me it was an unconfirmed rumor fell on deaf ears for the seed had been planted and I was sure the Nazis were after us. That kept me awake at night.

After two days at sea and hardly able to keep dried bread and sips of water down, I went up to the main deck for some fresh air. Paul had convinced me it would help. He was right for it was then in seeing the wide open ocean, pearls of rippling white cascading over rolling waves, and the absence of any other seacrafts that I believed we probably were beyond Hitler's reach.

Finally, a week of pitching and rolling on my bunk, of fighting dry heaves and timidly stretching my legs on deck passed, and a beautiful sight came into view. The Statue of Liberty stood at what I'd learned was over ninety meters high, including the pedestal. Tall and proud in her raised right hand she held a torch. What a sight it was. I took in the ripples on her gown, the blue-green color, her majestic crown, and glanced over to her left hand.

"What's in her left hand?"

"I don't know."

A man wearing a faded brown cap standing near us overheard my question and answered. "If I may... Inscribed on the tablet is July 4, 1776. The date the Declaration of Independence was signed. It is a declaration of freedom." He had a kind smile and worn eyes. To not intrude further, he backed away.

There was something in his expression and the way he said freedom that stabbed at my heart, right in the raw area that hurt from missing my family. My Oma, my father and my mother. And Max. It was strange that although I missed them all, it was missing Max that hurt the most. Max was the living being I could talk to about anything, the one who never let me down. Oh Max, I'm so sorry I had to leave you. I also missed Oma a lot but it felt different, not final like it somehow felt with Max. I loved my parents but in the last few years I had a different emotional connection with them, especially my father. I tolerated the distance from them better than I did for Oma and Max.

As I watched the clustered landscape of statuesque buildings pass before me, the face of the man in a faded brown cap lingered. It was the face I'd seen on Jewish people and others who had escaped the dangers of oppression, but not before scars were etched in their memory. When Lady Liberty was in hindsight, I wondered how many more emotionally scarred faces I'd run into in the land of the free.

When the ship slowed and docked and my feet were planted on firm ground, my stomach settled. It stayed settled as we were flawlessly processed and driven to an apartment building on the Lower East Side, a neighborhood in the southeastern part of Manhattan in New York City, where Paul's boss' relatives lived. We were right at home with cousins and uncles from a long line of jewelers. Men who worked hard to make a good living to support their families, which included extended family like Paul's boss.

"Eat. Eat. Eat." A buxom woman with wisps of bone-white hair escaping a clasp and falling over her face kept insisting I was too thin and needed to eat more. At night in the one-room apartment that had been rented for us, Paul laughed about the Yiddish-speaking grandma who kept trying to fatten me up. It was so good to hear him laugh, something that had become more frequent since landing in America.

More smiles entered as the days moved along, and Paul worked along with his boss to help his cousin, who owned a lucrative jewelry business that catered to the rich and famous. People who escaped the Great Depression and could still afford to purchase extravagant items like diamond brooches.

Through 1939 and 1940 life was good in America, but with all the goodness the sorrow over not being with my family, not sharing my new life with them, was a burden I could not rid myself of. A burden that got heavier as refugees arrived with stories of the horrors the Nazis were committing in Germany and their occupied territories. Territories that were expanding like Poland, Luxembourg, Holland, Denmark and France.

News spread of families targeted for concentration camps being ripped from their homes with those protesting being shot. Weepy voices cried over horrifying stories of people packed into trucks and windowless trains to double, triple and four times the number that would ensure a safe capacity. I couldn't imagine cattle cars filled with tens of people, sometimes over seventy Paul told me, with no latrine, no food or water and fetid air. Already malnourished and in poor health before the transportation began many died on the trains. Their bodies were left to rot at the feet of those struggling to stay alive. As if that wasn't bad enough once at the camps, families were separated. The earth-shattering cruelty was something I'd never been able to wrap my wits around.

The stories fueled my fear about my family's safety. With no way for me to figure out how to contact them, in writing or by phone, I worried something happened to them. Did word get out about my being with a Jew? Were they considered sympathizers because of what happened with Jürgen? As long as Hitler remained in power, they would never be safe. A million horrible thoughts wouldn't let me think otherwise.

Like with all things, the adage time heals proved to be true for although my family was not out of my mind for a day, the pain lessened. So did the fear. I had Paul's love to thank for that. He never let me down.

***

Years later I found out the lines of communication were tightly guarded and my letter never reached my family. It was also years later, when settled in New York and pregnant with my first child, I found out more about the magnitude of what had happened in Ravensburg, and Germany, and the world. Much of the horrors didn't make it into the American press and the only reliable information we received was from the stragglers who fled to America like we had. As if the things we'd already heard about the crowded trains and poor conditions in the camps weren't horrible enough, the expanded reports were hard to believe. The bad news kept coming until the tide turned with the Normandy landings and associated airborne operations. I was hesitant to allow myself to feel optimistic until the Allied victories continued and the end was in sight. When it came, I felt like I woke up from a nightmare.

After the war, with the help of the Red Cross, my mother was able to contact me. I recall how my heart soared when the first envelope arrived. How I yearned for her touch as I moved my hand over her neat writing wishing it was her hand, wishing I could feel the warmth of her skin. My heart felt light until I opened and read what she wrote. It was then I learned about all the bombings and devastation. All the displaced people. I read on holding my breath and not able to release it until I came to the part about our home and the factory. They remained unscathed.

I teared up when I read, *We were among the fortunate ones but it is hard to feel good about what we have when so many lost so much. Some days when the wind picks up it is impossible to see from the house to the street through all the flying dust from debris. But enough of that for I must learn to keep my focus on what remains.* My mother must have been teary eyed as well when she wrote those lines for a couple of words ran together as if water dripped on them.

World War II was a dreadful business, the death and destruction, families ripped asunder, devastating.

CHAPTER FIFTY-ONE

It's been five years since the war ended, five years filled with joy and sorrow. In the light of my beloved, a shadow follows me for I dearly miss my family and what was before. Before a radical man rose to power, an evil man who told lies that enraptured a hungry nation, there was much good. Most German people were a strong and good lot, citizens wanting nothing more than a roof over their heads and food on their tables. That's the Germany I care to remember, not the one that took the lives of Jürgen and Nahum. Not the one that persecuted Jews and undesirables. Not the one that caused me to flee to be with the man I love.

Despite the hardship, the years have been good to me. Eventually and with his family's blessing, Paul's boss set up his own jewelry shop in New York and within several months had enough customers to bring Paul in with him part-time. Paul insisted the money from the part-time work was enough to keep us going, but in reality we struggled to make ends meet. We lived off of our savings and I did part-time work cleaning houses. My work stopped when I had my first child. I think it was then my mother forgave my lie about not being able to have children for she wrote frequently asking me to send more photos. She lived for those photos. So did Oma.

Little Nahum is a joyful, pudgy bundle of energy and by the fluttering in my belly my next one will most likely be active as well.

When I last spoke on the telephone with Oma and she asked if I wanted a girl I told her I'd love a girl then added, I'd love another boy as well. I would happily bring either into a world where he or she is free to grow and experience the riches a life without oppression offers. In the background of our conversation, I heard a dog's bark. It saddened me I did not get to be with Max on his passing away. Oma assured me after refusing food and water, he went peacefully. The dog barked again and Oma hollered for my mother to feed her. She told me they weren't ready to let Max go, but didn't want another male dog named Max so when he moved on to the great beyond they got a female Rottweiler. Oma laughed when she told me they named her Maxine. Although her laugher warmed me, it was painful to hear about Max's death, which brought me to tears and sorrow for a few days.

I also shed tears when I found out my father had died. Three years after I left Germany, he returned home due to a debilitating heart attack. From what my mother told me and how she expressed herself, I knew she showed great compassion in caring for him, but then that was no surprise for my mother deeply loved my father. I knew her capacity to love, unconditionally, was why she accepted what I had done in leaving Germany. She didn't like it, but accepted it, never casting me out like Gertrude's parents. I feel fortunate I was raised in a loving family for were it not for that bond that sustained us throughout the horrible years when Germany fell to dictatorship, I don't know where I would be today. I imagine it would certainly not contain the fullness of a loving heart.

My father's heart finally gave out, and when I speak with my mother these days she tells me she thinks it was God's kindness that took him peacefully in his sleep next to her for if he made it through to the war's end, he would have most likely been imprisoned for his role in the designing of concentration camps. She often says a big part of my father died when Jürgen died and he was forced to comply with orders to protect the rest of us. My mother felt his heart gave out because the atrocities caught up with him, and he was unable to sustain the pressure. What good heart could? Oma understood and concurred.

Oma, how sad I felt over not being there with her since she had a stroke and was wheelchair bound, but had recovered enough to get out of bed and walk to her chair. Apparently the stroke had no impact on her personality for she forbid me to travel in my state. My state compared to hers, I laughed, but when she threatened to lock herself in her room and ignore me if I came, I ceased resisting her stubbornness, promising once the baby was born, we'd all be on a plane. I laughed even harder when she responded the heavy metal birds, what she called airplanes since the days of the Wright brothers, didn't belong in the sky.

Every time I think of that conversation with Oma, it reminds me of all the changes that have occurred since the Wright brothers' flying machine. Yes, there have been a lot of changes in that time span and I feel grateful to be alive to look back. My gratitude is endless for everywhere I look these days, there is abundance. Things before Hitler became chancellor that I'd taken for granted like a warm cup of tea, enough food and shelter, I now wholeheartedly appreciate. I'm grateful I survived to see my thirty-second birthday, and more significantly I now live in a country with the highest standard of living in the world, where a G.I. Bill provides housing, education and monetary benefits for its veterans, where identical homes spring up in neighborhoods outside large cities, where many families own a car, and a rising birthrate enhances the economy for it gives young families the desire to purchase both needs and luxury items for their children.

As I sit here reflecting on my life, I feel my baby kick and I smile. My smile widens for I am a proud wife and mother. A United States citizen. My heart is full because I know how lucky I am.

I hear Paul come through the back door to our home to find me with my hand on the golden pendant on my neck. As if in a dream, he wraps his arms around me. "Your lucky necklace is back where it belongs." He gently kisses my forehead and lovingly asks, "The little guy napping?"

"Yes, my love."

He puts his hand on my rounded belly. "And how is our little missy Helga?" He chuckles, a smooth sounding satisfaction flowing from him. "Or our little Harald?"

A boy will take my father's name, a girl Oma's. I hesitated with the girl's name because Oma is still alive and I was sure she would be up in arms about it, threatening I was sending her to her grave prematurely. Nothing could have been more wrong for when I told her, she laughed and said that's what she wanted to name the new dog, but my mother overrode her saying it had to be Maxine.

I feel the life dancing inside of me, and I breathe easy. "The littlest one is very active today." I place my hand on Paul's, feeling his even pulse, the warmth of his skin, the warmth of his love filling me up.

As we share the beautiful moment, we bask in our appreciation. We have so much to look forward to.

POST NOTE

Years ago I was fortunate to have had a friendship with a woman who grew up in Germany in the 1930s and attended the BDM. During outings for coffee she told me her story and I took notes. From these meetings sprang the rough outline for the *Two Necklaces*. To fill in the missing timeline and flesh out the story, I did research on Germany in 1930s up to the start of World War II in 1939 to incorporate significant events into the storyline. At my friend's request to remain anonymous, her name and the names of her family and friends were changed. Whereas aspects of the *Two Necklaces* are based on facts told to me or discovered during researching other similar stories, this is a work of fiction.

ACKNOWLEDGMENTS

We sometimes think of an author as a lonely writer banging away on the keyboard, creating characters for readers to love and hate, forming the core of the story. Yet what brings them alive on the page is never a singular task.

Thank you to my remarkable editor Genevieve Montcombroux for your brilliant editing, the wealth of historical knowledge and attention to detail you give to your work, and for being an absolute pleasure to work with.

To my line editor Terrance Redpath, a heartfelt thank you for all your great work and feedback, for keeping my timelines straight, dates accurate and storyline consistent. You are a gem.

I love and thank my Ojai writing group for your helpful feedback and being the best support group any author could dream of. Katina Drennan, Terry Tallent, Nancy Decker and Sharon Hall you are the best.

To Reagan Rothe and the great Black Rose Writing team, thank you for taking a chance on me. Working with you has been a wonderful experience.

To my friends and family, a heartfelt thank you for all your loving support and positive feedback. In the long days of typing away on my laptop, when my hands were tired and back sore, you lifted my spirits and kept me going.

To Kashi and Jen for bringing El Rey into my life, my amazing dog friend. Now over the rainbow bridge and deeply missed, Max was based on him.

Lastly to my patient, kind and generous husband, Terry, for all the foot rubs and back rubs and meals and simply being the best partner a woman could ask for. None of this would be possible without you.

ABOUT THE AUTHOR

Paulette Mahurin, acclaimed author of *The Seven Year Dress*, is an international Amazon best-selling literary fiction and historical fiction novelist. She grew up in West Los Angeles and attended UCLA, where she received a Master's Degree in Science. She lives with her husband, Terry, and dog, Bella, in Ventura County, California, where she can be found tending to her natural habitat garden, exercising, doing volunteer work, attending the theater, and handing out dog treats to the neighborhood canines.

OTHER BOOKS BY
PAULETTE MAHURIN

THE PERSECUTION OF MILDRED DUNLAP

HIS NAME WAS BEN

THE SEVEN YEAR DRESS

TO LIVE OUT LOUD

THE DAY I SAW THE HUMMINGBIRD

A DIFFERENT KIND OF ANGEL

IRMA'S ENDGAME

THE OLD GILT CLOCK

WHERE IRISES NEVER GROW

OVER THE HEDGE

THE PEACEFUL VILLAGE

THE GIRL FROM HUIZEN

NOTE FROM
PAULETTE MAHURIN

Word-of-mouth is crucial for any author to succeed. If you enjoyed *Two Necklaces*, please leave a review online—anywhere you are able. Even if it's just a sentence or two. It would make all the difference and would be very much appreciated.

Thanks!
Paulette Mahurin

We hope you enjoyed reading this title from:

www.blackrosewriting.com

Subscribe to our mailing list – *The Rosevine* – and receive **FREE** books, daily deals, and stay current with news about upcoming releases and our hottest authors.
Scan the QR code below to sign up.

Already a subscriber? Please accept a sincere thank you for being a fan of Black Rose Writing authors.

View other Black Rose Writing titles at
www.blackrosewriting.com/books and use promo code
PRINT to receive a **20% discount** when purchasing.

Made in the USA
Las Vegas, NV
09 January 2025

16132878R10163